Whenever she shut her eyes, Sarah was tormented

Even in her dreams, she was haunted, either by Daniel Dubonet's sarcastic smile and insinuating questions, or by fragments of the past.

There was no going back, no changing the course of events. Everything she'd ever loved had been taken from her, and she wasn't willing to risk that pain again.

Though she couldn't change history, she could certainly control her emotions in the future. But would she ever be able to leave the shadow of the past?

Daniel troubled her *because* of the past. Something about him opened a lot of doors that Sarah had worked hard to nail shut. She reacted to him—and that was something she couldn't afford.

ABOUT THE AUTHOR

Caroline Burnes lives in Semmes, Alabama, with her three cats, four dogs and two horses. A member of numerous animal organizations, she urges pet owners to have their animals spayed and neutered in an effort to cut down on the many unwanted animals in this country.

Books by Caroline Burnes

HARLEQUIN INTRIGUE

* FEAR FAMILIAR Mysteries

Don't miss any of our special offers. Write to us at the following address for information on our newest releases.

Harlequin Reader Service
U.S.: 3010 Walden Ave., P.O. Box 1325, Buffalo, NY 14269
Canadian: P.O. Box 609, Fort Erie, Ont. L2A 5X3

Familiar Remedy
Caroline Burnes

Harlequin Books

TORONTO • NEW YORK • LONDON
AMSTERDAM • PARIS • SYDNEY • HAMBURG
STOCKHOLM • ATHENS • TOKYO • MILAN
MADRID • WARSAW • BUDAPEST • AUCKLAND

To E. A. Poe, Gumbo and Miss Vesta,
the cats in my life today.
And to Garp and all the cats who bring
such pleasure to the humans whom
they've adopted.

ISBN 0-373-22293-9

FAMILIAR REMEDY

Copyright © 1994 by Carolyn Haines

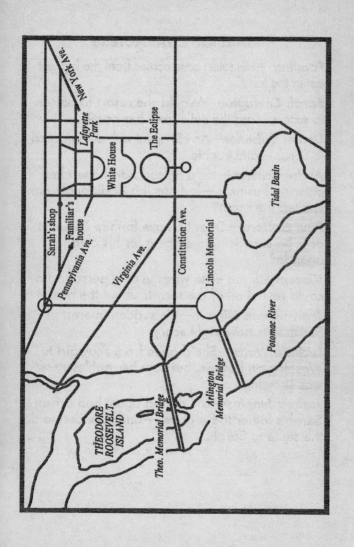

CAST OF CHARACTERS

Familiar—His latest case comes from the highest cat in the land.

Sarah Covington—Would she resort to poison to exterminate the evils from her past?

Daniel Dubonet—An FBI agent with an attraction to Sarah—and trouble.

André Croxier—He'd helped Sarah start her catering business—but has this additional cook spoiled the broth?

Paul Gottard—Does he have faith in Dubonet, or is he sacrificing the agent for his own agenda?

Vincent Minton—He was the only person who could reveal all of the secrets about the past.

Jean-Claude Minton—His sudden interest in Sarah was downright scary.

Lucinda Watts—She'd gone from showgirl to Washington hostess, but now her ruthlessness was showing.

Joshua Jenkins—The retired agent had driven Sarah's father to his grave—and intended to do the same to Sarah.

Chapter One

I never really knew my father. That's a sad fact of life for plenty of youngsters in this day and age. It's not that I actually feel sorry for myself, but hiding here, on the White House lawn, I can't help but wonder if maybe I could have been the First Cat if I'd had a dad. Well, there aren't any easy answers to that one. As it is, I haven't done so bad for myself. I am sitting on the White House lawn, even if it is to spy on a young chef. Well, spy is an exaggeration. Watch might be more accurate.

I have only Clotilde, my calico queen, to blame for this predicament. That and my own tender heart, and more than a smidgen of patriotic fever. After all, how many detectives get invited to help the First Cat?

That's right. I'm here by special request of Socks himself. One of his friends is being accused of a dastardly deed, and because of his prominent profile, he can't do much to help her.

Clotilde, who visits the White House regularly with her two humans, somehow convinced Socks that I was the feline he needed for this particular job. Clotilde is such a complete charmer, and she absolutely idolizes me, if I do say so myself. At any rate, Socks sent word that he would be more than grateful for a little help with this special prob-

lem. Naturally, I agreed to help. Who could refuse the First Cat?

I had only one request. An official title. Agent 009—for my nine lives, of course. Socks was very agreeable to the idea, though like all political creatures he wanted to argue whether I actually had nine whole lives left. I suppose I might be Agent 007½. Jeez.

Okay, there's my signal. Socks has moved to the second floor window. He's taking a seat. His tail is twitching twice! Yes! The game plan is on. The door to the kitchen has been left open so I can enter and snoop around. Imagine, looking into the president's refrigerator. I wonder if Socks gets his daily cream in a bowl bearing the presidential seal?

I see a bright future ahead of me on the talk shows. Oprah, you'd better practice up on your kitty talk.

Time to hustle these old bones across the lawn and slip in the door. It's midnight and I have to get home before the dame wakes up and finds me missing. Eleanor gets a little overprotective sometimes. Foolish woman. She forgets that I'm the superior being.

Well, at least the security system doesn't include those horrid, slobbering dogs. At least, not yet.

Wait a minute, buster! That big black limo almost ran me down. Nobody is supposed to be arriving here tonight. Socks gave the all clear. I'd better hide right here in this old bush and watch for a minute.

The limo's car tags are covered by red mud. Red mud? This is Washington, not the Deep South. And look, someone is coming along the walkway. A very slender someone wearing a long cloak and hood. I can't make out the features, but the way she walks and moves tells me it's a woman, and some kind of woman. Unconsciously sensual. A glimpse of blond hair, chef suit under the cloak. Yep, this is my quarry. No wonder Socks is fond of her. He's a cat with refined taste.

Sarah Covington, caterer to the White House.

Uh-oh, Socks, this don't look good for your girl. She arrives, and they blast out of here like they're on the shuttle schedule to Mars. And now she's preparing to enter the premises. Did she give them some sort of signal? If so, my Trained Observer eyes certainly didn't see it.

No time for further ruminations. I'd better get in that door before it swings shut on me.

White House, here I come!

SARAH COVINGTON put one weary foot in front of the other as she walked the short distance from her parking space to the front door of her catering business, A Taste of the South.

She glanced down at the confectionery cake that adorned the window and felt a sudden lurch in her midsection. The idea of anything sweet made her gag. She'd eaten enough chocolate and sugar during an afternoon of making ten dozen éclairs that if she didn't see chocolate or sugar again—for at least twenty-four hours—she wouldn't care.

Pulling her keys from her pocket, she opened the door of the catering shop and hurried inside. She groaned aloud, remembering the piles of pots and pans she'd left dirty in the sink when she'd gotten the summons for some emergency assistance to the White House's head chef. Instead of cleaning her own mess, she'd gone to make cream puffs with André. She owed a lot to Chef André. A whole lot.

Trudging up the stairs, she decided to skip the dirty pans and head straight for the bath. A hot soak and some classical guitar would be the perfect capper for a long day.

Her apartment above the shop was filled with dark greens and wicker. No matter where Sarah lived, she couldn't leave the color scheme of her Mississippi upbringing very far behind. She put the plug in the old-fashioned bathtub and turned the tap on full-blast. Every day she thanked her lucky stars that Uncle Vince had found her this quaint old building to lease.

Steam rose from the water as she watched it fill the big tub. Pinning her straight blond hair in a loose bun, she sank into the water up to her chin. Eyes closed, she listened to the music.

At the sound of a knock she thought she must be mistaken. It was midnight, or later. Who would be knocking at her business door? The pounding grew louder—and more demanding. Sarah sat up in the tub and listened harder. Who could it be? Had something happened to her mother? Or Uncle Vince?

She dried quickly and slipped into a ratty, gold terry-cloth robe that had been her father's more than twenty years before. It was reprehensible, worn and faded. But she loved it. Barefoot, she ran down the stairs to the front door.

Through the glass she could see that the man who stood waiting so impatiently was dressed in a suit. He was a very handsome man, and she felt her body tense. Men were trouble, especially good-looking ones. If she never allowed herself to get involved, she'd never have to suffer the consequences. She'd spent years perfecting her defenses, but she couldn't help the jolt of attraction she felt for this stranger. When he finally saw her, he flashed a gold badge up to the window.

Sarah opened the door the length of the chain. "What do you want?" At the sight of his badge, all thoughts of his good looks had vanished.

"Are you Sarah Covington?"

"What do you want?" she repeated. For no reason her heart started pounding. There was something about the man's tone of voice, as if he were accusing her of something. She'd had enough false accusations in the last day or two.

"I'm Daniel Dubonet, Federal Bureau of Investigation. I have some questions for you."

"Do you realize what time it is?" Sarah felt her temper ignite. What was an FBI agent doing knocking on her door at midnight?

"I realize the time, Ms. Covington. I would have questioned you at four, or five, or even six or seven. But you haven't been home. Now you are. I only have a few questions, and I've been ordered to get some answers."

"I'm not answering any questions. I'm going to bed." Sarah pushed the door to close it, but his hand suddenly blocked her.

"Three people were hospitalized yesterday because they ate something you cooked. Three people out of seventy-five. Three people who were all from the same state, the same city, and the same business. The defense business. Odds like that put it beyond mere coincidence. Would you like to explain that? You can do it now, or you can do it tomorrow when I have a warrant for your arrest."

"My arrest?" Sarah's bravado and anger fell flat. "But I didn't do anything."

"Then I suggest you let me in."

Unlocking the chain, Sarah moved back from the door. As Daniel Dubonet stepped inside the shop, she was acutely aware of his height and immaculate dress. The state of her bathrobe was painful. There were holes in the elbows and the collar was so badly frayed it could hardly be called a collar.

Dubonet was giving her the once-over with a professional eye that lingered a moment too long on the exposed flesh of her neck. "If you'll excuse me, I'll put on some clothes." Face flushed a becoming pink, she hurried up the stairs before he could approve or disapprove.

Daniel Dubonet pushed an unruly strand of hair out of his eyes. Damn, but she was a lovely woman. So becomingly disheveled in that old bathrobe. He was only a little ashamed of his strong-arm tactics in forcing his way into the shop. He'd been waiting for more than seven hours to talk with Sarah Covington. As an FBI agent, this wasn't even his turf. It was because of some kind of special favor to the Secret Service that he'd been sent to question Chef Covington. A special favor he'd drawn because he was in the doghouse with his superiors for his smart mouth. He wanted this interview over and done, even if he had to do it at midnight.

He could see the wet footprints Sarah had left on the floor. High instep, he noted automatically. She'd looked so frightened when he'd said arrest. And he'd exaggerated the charges a little. Well, a lot.

He heard her return and was caught by her lack of pretense as she came downstairs in deck shoes, jeans and a sweatshirt. She hadn't bothered to unpin her hair, but a lot of it was falling down her back. She had the bluest eyes he'd seen in a long while. The distant memory of his grandmother and a song she often sang about a girl with cornflower eyes made him smile. One day, when he got ready to settle down, he'd like to know a woman who looked like Sarah. Her voice interrupted his thoughts.

"I'm tired and I need some caffeine. Would you like some coffee? Or are you afraid I might poison you?" She was shocked at her own words, but she knew it was a reaction to her initial attraction to him. Now she was determined to be as cutting as possible.

"No, thanks." Dubonet looked around the shop. It was a small area with neat black-and-white tiles and a tidy display counter. Swinging doors hid what was obviously the kitchen. There were several books of color photographs showing Sarah's work in all types of food. Barbecues, formal dinners, teas. "How long have you been a chef?"

"I got my degree ten years ago." She twirled a strand of hair between her thumb and finger.

"And your license?"

"In Washington, two years ago."

"I imagine it's a very competitive business here."

It was a question without being a question. "Very. Lucky for me I have friends in high places." She disliked his implications, and her quick tongue formed the sarcastic reply before she could stop herself.

"High enough so that they would benefit from the serious illness or death of three businessmen from Mississippi? Three men heavily involved in defense contracts?"

"Not that high." She kept the anger out of her voice. "Whatever those men ate that put them in the hospital, it didn't come from my food. I served the same entrée to everyone. And I know, because I personally prepared the plates."

"But you didn't deliver them to the table, did you?"

"I did not, but the woman who did is my friend. If you think she did something to injure a client of mine, you're aiming at the moon. She's practically worked for free to help me make a go of this business."

Dubonet nodded. Her righteous defense of her employee made him want to smile. She was furious.

"I'd like a list of the ingredients you used and where you purchased them."

"Easy enough." Sarah motioned him to a desk behind the counter. "Have a seat, Mr. . . ."

"Dubonet," he supplied.

"Dubonet. I'll find a menu and make up a list of all ingredients. I can even tell you where I bought them. Has anyone determined exactly what made the three gentlemen sick?" She held her pencil aloft as she waited for his answer.

"Not exactly. It seems to be some type of chemical or something of that nature." He was not being deliberately vague. As sophisticated as the FBI lab was, they hadn't been able to pin it down exactly. This was a weak point in his case, and he knew it. All three men were staying at the same hotel. He'd been cautioned that whatever had sickened them might have been inhaled rather than eaten. His interview with Sarah was basically a matter of covering all possibilities. He just didn't want her to know that. Years of experience had taught him that it was best to keep as many people off balance as possible during an investigation.

Sarah saw his evasiveness as deliberate. So, there was some hesitation about making an outright accusation against her. It was the best news she'd had in the past twenty-four hours, ever since she'd learned that the three businessmen had been hospitalized shortly after the dinner she'd served.

"Let's see now. The menu is right here." She lifted a sheet of paper from a file. "Pork tenderloin." She started to rattle off the ingredients, making notes of them as she talked. "Sweet potato soufflé." She ran rapid-speed down the list.

Daniel checked his watch. There were a million ingredients, and judging by the sound of it, she shopped all over the city. This was going to take the rest of the night.

"Now for the desserts. I served three. There was banana pudding, pound cake with fresh peaches, and cherry cream cheese tarts. The ingredients are..."

He sighed softly to himself. Funny, but just listening to her talk, he was beginning to feel the definite stirrings of an appetite. And it wasn't for food. He could almost taste her lips. He looked at Sarah as she mumbled the ingredients more to herself than to him and made her careful list. How did she remember all of those things? She was describing the peaches she'd used in the recipe, completely unaware of how closely her complexion resembled that of a peach. A perfect peach.

He snatched his attention away from such thoughts and focused once again on the list. It was now two pages long.

"That's it." She handed it over to him. "Is there anything else?"

"Did you know any of the businessmen?"

"No."

"How did you get hired as a caterer to the White House?"

"What exactly is that supposed to mean?" She felt her temper kindle. She'd worked her butt off, and no one was going to imply otherwise. She could bite off her own tongue for that earlier comment about friends in high places.

"I mean, Washington is a very political city. Jobs like this one are usually given because of a friend." He watched the blank look settle over her face as she fought to control her temper. "You know perfectly well what I'm saying." He felt his own temper rise. She was acting deliberately obtuse.

"I have no political connections, Mr. Dubonet. I'm a good cook, and I do a good job. That's how I got work at the White House. Call Chef André. He'll vouch for my abilities."

"You may be an excellent chef, but you also have to have some kind of pull." Daniel wasn't about to back down.

"The suggestion that I've used some underhanded—"

"Whoa!" Daniel held up both hands in an act of surrender. The sudden brightness of tears in her eyes made him realize how personally she'd taken his question. "I did not imply you did anything underhanded. This is a town where pull is part of the natural order of things. Most people here are proud of whatever pull they have."

"I'm a very good chef. That's what I'm proud of, Mr. Dubonet. I was lucky to get an opportunity, but it was my skill that got me work as a caterer. Not anything else." Her voice softened as she finished.

No matter how she denied it, he was still certain that someone had spoken to someone about her. That was simply the way it worked in Washington, but he didn't have to press it with her. At least not now. "I have the ingredients—" he lifted the list, staggered again by the sheer volume of it "—so I'd better be going."

"Those men did not get sick because of something I prepared." Sarah rose as he did. "If there was any foul play with my food, I would have known it."

He evaluated that statement as he tucked the list into the pocket of his jacket. "I believe that." She babbled on about recipes, but she was nobody's fool. Intelligence shimmered in her eyes, as visible as the tears had been earlier.

"Where were you so late tonight?" He asked the question almost as an afterthought.

"It really isn't any of your business, but I'll tell you. And, yes, Chef André can corroborate my statement." She didn't try to hide the sting of sarcasm. "I was at the White House finishing up chocolate éclairs for a dinner tomorrow."

"Do you often work in the White House kitchens?"

"It depends. Many times I cater events which are only a peripheral part of some White House function."

"Like the businessmen's dinner?"

"Right. But there are times when Chef André is making something special, something that he knows I've done before."

"Like cream puffs."

"Exactly." She drew a breath and hesitated. "I've been thinking about what you said about pull, and I guess you're right."

He waited. Damned if she wasn't acting as if she was confessing to the Lindbergh kidnapping.

"Chef André is from New Orleans. As you probably know, if you've done your homework, I grew up not very far from the Louisiana line. My parents or an old family friend often took me to New Orleans for lunch or dinner." She took another breath and continued staring at some spot on the floor near Daniel's feet. "I met Chef André when I was a little girl, and even then I wanted to be a chef. He let me play in the kitchen in his restaurant. He encouraged me, and through the years he's continued to be supportive." She looked up. "When I decided to move to Washington, he didn't say he would throw some White House work my way, but I know he must have done something. As you say, there are plenty of talented chefs in this city."

The long, unwilling confession made him want to reach out and touch her peachy soft cheek. She was refreshingly sincere. "It isn't a crime to have people recognize your talent and recommend you." He spoke before he even thought of what he was saying.

"The way you said it made it sound... dirty."

Daniel Dubonet was a man who believed in hunches, and one struck him hard. Something in Sarah Covington's past made her sensitive to any accusations of wrongdoing. Overly sensitive. In some people that was a sign of guilt. In others, it was a sign of low self-esteem. Which was it in Sarah Covington's case?

"If I have any questions, I'll be back." He walked to the door.

"In that case, I hope I won't be seeing you again." Sarah unlocked the door and held it open. It had been a long night, and the conversation with Daniel Dubonet had taken the last bit of energy from her. She wanted him gone.

"Sorry to disturb you." He walked out into the chill Washington night.

Sarah locked the door behind him and watched him walk under the streetlight. Why was it that handsome men only came to her door to start trouble or to eat? She sighed as she flipped off the lights and started up to bed. The pots could wait until morning.

For a woman who cooks all day like a fiend, Sarah Covington keeps an active nightlife. Who is that man in the expensive suit and fine leather shoes leaving her business? Even more important, what is Agent 009 doing standing on a cold street corner in front of a catering shop? I'll bet there are some delicacies in that joint that would tempt even the most finicky kitty palate.

It's been a long but interesting evening. My first trip to the White House, and I discover nothing except puff pastries, rich cream and chocolate to die for. Whatever Sarah was up to with the limo, it didn't prevent her from finishing her cream puff duties. And then she left for home. I had to leave, too. Socks warned me that the security forces keep a close eye on the kitchen because of the high traffic there. A stray cat could be in big trouble, and we're not talking a lecture. We're talking kitty incarceration and deportation. So I skedaddled when Sarah did. Poor thing, she was so tired she didn't even notice me.

I, Trained Observer that I am, got to take some meticulous notes on her, though. She's a doll. China-blue eyes, blond hair that begs to be stroked, and legs that go on forever. When she came down those stairs in that repugnant bathrobe, I forgot all about her lack of taste in clothes when I saw those legs. If she ever decides to give up the oven, she should go to the stage. She could be an honorary Rockette, even if she can't dance.

Ah, humans are not always smart, but the female of the species has some admirable qualities. That's not to say that any gam on the biped species could compare to the tiniest toe of my Clotilde, but as a cat of the world, I can appreciate form and beauty. Besides, this dolly can cook. I think I'm going to enjoy this assignment, once I figure out how to get an invitation to A Taste of the South.

That's my chore for tomorrow. Now I have to rush back to Pennsylvania Avenue and the digs Eleanor and Peter are renting for the fall. Ever since someone bombed their home, they've been moving around a bit. And Peter's not sure how long we'll be in the city this time. That means fast action and foolproof results. I suppose I'm going to have to take up jogging again.

My pads are toughening up on the pavement again, so the walk isn't too bad. Burn a few calories so I can have a snack. But, wait a minute... That car parked down the street from A Taste of the South. It's been there ever since Sarah got home. Maybe I'll just take a stroll by it, a slight detour. I wouldn't have noticed except it's in a no-parking zone and, let me tell you, the meter maids in this town come with a tow truck instead of a ticket pad.

Dark sedan, nothing too conspicuous. That in itself is something to note. License plates coated in red mud. A flick of my paw and what do I see? My, my, a government car. I do believe that Dolly is under surveillance by someone beside Super Cat.

The question is, who? And what do they intend to do to her?

Chapter Two

Sarah closed the blinds in her bedroom in a futile attempt to block out the midmorning sun. She was exhausted. She had a million things she needed to do, but a slight headache pounded at her temples. Flopping back in the bed, she pulled the sheet over her head. All attempts to sleep the night before had been a waste of time. Whenever she shut her eyes, she was tormented, either by Daniel Dubonet's sarcastic smile and insinuating questions or by fragments of the past.

Dubonet troubled her *because* of the past. Something about him opened a lot of doors that Sarah had worked hard to nail shut. She'd reacted to him—and that was something she couldn't afford. Everything she'd ever loved had been taken from her, and she wasn't willing to risk that pain. Not ever again.

There was no going back, no changing the course of events that had led to her father's death. She couldn't control the past, but she could certainly control her emotions in the future. Would she ever be able to leave the shadow of the past?

The thought prompted the action of throwing off the sheet and reaching for the telephone. "My guilt synthesizer is working overtime," she said aloud as she stared at the beige receiver. She hadn't called her mother in several weeks.

Mora Covington *never* called her daughter. She wasn't "the kind of mother who constantly interfered in my grown daughter's life."

No, Mora didn't interfere. She just laid on a guilt trip that was a zillion times worse than interfering.

With a sigh, Sarah dialed the Biloxi, Mississippi, phone number and began to count the rings. Seven, eight, nine. Just as expected, the phone was answered on the ninth ring.

"Hello, Mother." Sarah felt a rush of feeling that was hard to untangle. She loved her mother, but Mora had always held herself so distant, had always been so easily bruised.

"Sarah, how kind of you to call."

Sarah sighed. It wasn't kind of her to call. It should be a delight for both of them. Why did her mother put everything in terms of obligation?

Forcing a bright note into her voice, Sarah chatted for a few moments about her upcoming jobs.

"I have a big party at the Bingington house. I have to go over this afternoon and make sure everything is in order." As she talked, Sarah felt her lethargy lift. No matter what dark shadows from her past troubled her, she still had her mother. "I just wanted to make sure you're okay."

"The strangest thing happened yesterday...." Mora hesitated.

"What?" Sarah was trained in patience. Mora found a lot of strange things in her life. It seemed that when Cal Covington died, all of Mora's nerve for living had departed, too.

"This man came by the house asking after you."

"What man?" Sarah couldn't help the suspicion that began to form in her mind. She'd been away from home far too long for someone to be trying to find her in Biloxi with Mora.

"He said he was with the Federal Bureau of Investigation." Mora's voice thickened with tears. "It was just like with Cal. It was just the same. He started out nice, and then he got so insistent.''

"What did he want?" Sarah swung her legs to the floor and sat up. The headache was fiercer than ever, but she no longer acknowledged it.

"He was asking where you were and where you'd gotten your training as a chef. He acted as if you'd done something wrong.''

Mora sounded so pitiful that Sarah felt her anger at whoever was meddling in her life begin a fast climb.

"I told him you were a good girl and that you'd never do anything wrong.''

"What exactly did he say?"

"Well, not really anything. It was just the way he showed up and wouldn't leave, and how he asked those questions. You remember how those agent people are, the same question again and again, with the words put in a different order." She took a trembly breath, but her voice grew stronger. "It was so much like the days when Cal was under investigation. I just went all to pieces.''

"It's okay, Mom." Sarah paced the length of the phone cord and back. "Don't let anyone in the house again. Do you hear?''

"Yes. What's wrong, Sarah?" There was real alarm in Mora's voice. "Is anything the matter up there? I do wish you'd come home. With the new gambling casinos along here, there's plenty of work for a good chef. Plenty of work and good pay.''

"I can't come home." Sarah was tired of repeating the phrase. There was nothing for her in Mississippi. Nothing except the past and a lot of painful memories. "Just don't let anyone in the house again. I'm going to call Uncle Vince and see if he can find out what's going on. That man may not even have been with the FBI or anyone else.''

"He had a badge, like they do on television.''

"Do you remember his name?"

"No." There was another hesitation. "He gave me a card, but I threw it away. I just didn't want it in the house."

"It doesn't matter." Sarah tugged her fingers through her thick hair, trying to pull some order into it. She wanted a cup of coffee and a hot shower—one without interruptions. And then she wanted a chance to talk with Vincent Minton, her adopted uncle and the only person she had ever really been able to rely on. Once her father had died and her mother had turned into a shadow of her former self, Sarah had sought out "Uncle" Vince as the only source of real strength. He was a mover and shaker in Washington. He had no official capacity, but he had plenty of reliable sources. "I'm going to get Uncle Vince to check into this guy."

"The man was very nice." Mora tried to catch hold of the situation. "I overreacted a little bit, I'm afraid. Really, Sarah, he wasn't mean at all. Not like that Joshua Jenkins."

Even the name brought back a surge of pain and anger. Joshua Jenkins had been the FBI agent in charge of investigating her father. Jenkins was a relentless man who'd decided that he was judge, jury and prosecution for Sheriff Cal Covington. And he'd succeeded in ruining Cal's life.

"Jenkins is retired, Mom," Sarah reminded her.

"Well, he should be dead."

The words were a shock to Sarah. Mora Covington literally could not bring herself to step on a cockroach. But Joshua Jenkins was another matter altogether. Mora might have turned into a wisp of a person, but where Jenkins was concerned, she still had plenty of passion. Passionate hatred.

"Listen, Mom, that man didn't threaten you, did he?"

"No, he was asking about you."

"Well, things are fine here. Don't worry about any of it. Uncle Vince will take care of it."

"Yes, dear, Vince can do that. God bless him, he's always there when we need him."

"Love you, Mom." Sarah replaced the receiver. Her own eyes were filled with moisture, but it was from anger. No one had the right to go around terrorizing her mother. No one. Not even the FBI!

Before she talked to her uncle, she decided to shower, eat, and try to calm down. It was an irritating fact, but whenever she got extremely angry, she found herself crying. The one thing she didn't want to do was cry on Uncle Vince this afternoon. She wanted to be professional, to show that all of his trust and effort on her behalf had been well spent.

Blinking away the unshed tears, Sarah showered and got dressed.

It was past noon, and she discovered that her sleepless night and angry morning had made her ravenous. From the depths of her refrigerators she pulled out the ingredients for a crabmeat omelet and set to work. It was hard, but she managed to ignore the mountain of dishes until she'd had two cups of coffee and something to eat.

Feeling slightly less volatile, she placed the call to Vince, only to discover that he was away for several hours. He was almost always at the specialty shop he ran in one of the touristy parts of the city. Though he was the head of Minton Limited, a corporation with real estate and banking interests, he seemed to prefer tinkering with his gift merchandise more than anything else. That, and attending social events. She left her name and asked that he return her call, and then she tackled her dirty kitchen.

While she loaded the dishwasher, she ran through the menu she was preparing for the luncheon at the Bingington house. As she'd learned through the busy Washington gossip circuit, Clyde Bingington was a very influential man. He ran a chain of newspapers in the South that exerted tremendous control over regional politics, and he was hosting a dinner for Southern governors.

At Chef André's recommendation, Sarah had been hired to prepare the extensive meal. It was going to be a gala affair with a Deep South theme that dated back to the days when cotton reigned. "Days of Economic Prosperity" was the way the evening was going to be billed. So that called for a menu with no holds barred. She could be as decadent as she liked, and that was great fun. Then she could sit back and watch the fireworks that any Southern theme generated in Washington. There had been a party only a few months back when a cake baked and decorated like a Confederate flag had almost created a national furor. The chef who had concocted the confection had gotten into a peck of trouble, even though his intentions were innocent.

Sarah glanced at the kitchen telephone, willing Uncle Vince to call her back. She checked the time. Almost four o'clock. She wanted to get to the Bingington house before much later. The family was out of town on vacation and she had her own key, but she didn't like the idea of wandering around someone else's house at night. Someone might mistake her for a burglar.

With the kitchen spick-and-span, she sat down at the table and started planning her menu. It would be a group of fifty. Clyde Bingington was hosting governors from ten Southern states and their guests, along with some businessmen and the Beltway politicos who hovered at every event that held the least promise of money or a deal.

Chicken and pork were the traditional banquet meats for Southern fare. She bit the soft wood of her pencil, concentrating. Since it was a meal primarily for men, a heavier menu would not be out of order. Baked honey-glazed ham or possibly even fried chicken . . . She considered for a moment before she wrote stuffed okra on her list. Okra filled with cream cheese and hot peppers, dipped in egg, battered in cornmeal and baked in the oven was something that never failed to please her guests.

She gently chewed the pencil, a bad habit that she'd never been able to break. Her mind didn't seem to want to cooperate. Somehow, the menu wouldn't come together.

When the phone finally rang, she almost jumped out of her chair. She hurried across the room and picked up the portable unit. Relief flooded her as she heard Uncle Vince's voice, and she quickly filled him in on what had happened.

"Daniel Dubonet," Vincent said in his big-city accent. Even though he'd grown up in a poor section of New Orleans, he was the most sophisticated man she'd ever met. "I can't imagine why the FBI would question you, Sarah, but I have some friends there. I'll explain some things to them and make sure Mr. Dubonet understands that he isn't to frighten you again."

"Thanks." Sarah felt a twinge of regret. She didn't really want to get the agent in trouble, but he had some kind of nerve showing up at her door at midnight to get a list of ingredients. If he got a reprimand now, it might save him from a bullet later in his career.

"These young agents." Uncle Vince sighed. "You know, I've been a successful businessman for nearly fifty years. There was a time when common courtesy was the code of conduct for all people. Now there's no consideration for the simple niceties of life. The young man could have conducted this business during proper working hours. He would not have upset you or startled you and none of this would have been necessary."

"You're right."

"And tell Mora not to worry. I'll check into the situation down on the coast, too. I suspect it's one of those cases where a couple of young agents are trying a little too hard."

"Thanks, Uncle Vince." Sarah replaced the receiver and looked at the pencil she still held in her hand. The numerous teeth marks indicated how nervous she'd been. With a tsk of disgust at herself, she threw it in the trash.

It was nearly five o'clock, and the early dusk of late fall was beginning to settle over the city. She ran upstairs to get her coat, her keys and the map to the Bingington house. With a little luck with the traffic, she could manage to get there before total darkness fell.

She threw open the door of the shop and stopped. A large black cat was stretched full-length in her doorway. Something about the cat's position warned her that he was injured. His pose was unnatural, and his breathing was shallow and rapid.

"Kitty, kitty." She eased toward him, not wanting to startle him into running out into the busy traffic. Her precautions were unnecessary. The cat was unconscious.

She hated to see anything sick or injured. There were so many animals starving to death in Washington, and in every other city and rural area in the country.

"Kitty, kitty." She offered a soothing sound as she settled down on her knees to examine the cat. His coat was healthy, and he was very well fed. She reached out a tentative hand to stroke him. He was sleek and warm. Perhaps he'd been caught by a glancing blow from a car and was merely stunned. There was no blood anywhere.

But where had he come from? No one with good sense would allow such a handsome cat to run around one of the busiest intersections in Washington.

Glancing up and down the street, Sarah honestly expected to see his worried owner hunting frantically for the cat.

A feeble meow drew her attention back to the patient.

"Kitty." She stroked him very gently, afraid that if he suffered internal injuries she might only make him worse. As she started to withdraw her hand, he lifted a feeble paw and caught her with the barest tips of his claws.

"You don't want me to leave you, do you?" All thoughts of the Bingington house disappeared. Very gently, she scooped the cat into her arms and took him up the stairs to her bedroom. With the tenderest possible touch, she placed him in the center of her bed.

"Meow." He rewarded her with a feeble sound.

"I'll get you some milk with an egg beaten into it," she said. "That's what my grandmother always said to give an animal that didn't feel well. Cream and egg." It was undoubtedly an old wives' recipe for sickness, but it had certainly piqued the appetites of her grandmother's kittens and puppies. She took the stairs two at a time and disappeared into the kitchen.

I LOVE A LADY with a tender heart. Now that I've gotten an up-close look at Dolly, I'm more positive than ever that the First Cat has excellent taste—for food and the female species of Homo sapiens. I'm telling you, that Socks wasn't born in a tuxedo for just any reason. That's one classy cat.

Now that I've managed to get into Dolly's lair, what am I going to do? She was on her way to run an errand, so that will give me plenty of time to check out the kitchen and prove that she's clean. I mean, she'd have to have a five-pound sack of poison to bring some of those politicians down. Talk about pork barrel politics. Some of those guys look like they've been eating at the public trough twenty-four hours a day, seven days a week.

Oops, I'm not supposed to be political. It might affect my judgment on this case. But I must say that if cats had the vote, this country would be a very different place.

Now I need a bit of time alone in the pad here to check out the resources. Luckily, my last adventures in Scotland taught me my way around a big kitchen. If there's a dangerous substance, I'll ferret it out. Which brings up one of my pet peeves. Humans have gotten into the habit—and me along with them—of using animals as verbs. Ferret. What kind of action verb is that? And though I'm not one to take up for the canine species, how about "I'm going to dog you till the day you die"? How unflattering, even for those

slobbering beasts. And "catting around." Really, how in-
appropriate. I think I'll coin a phrase. How about "human
environment"? That would describe a polluted beach or a
landfill.

Well, enough semantics. Here comes Dolly with my cream
and egg. I prefer my egg slightly poached with a side of
salmon, but she'll learn. Humans are slow, but they always
learn.

"POOR KITTY. Can you drink this?" Sarah eased the bowl
to the floor and helped a feeble Familiar to stand. He wob-
bled pathetically before he took several laps of the milk.

With amazing speed, he began to recover. His balance
grew steady, and he started looking around the room.

"That must be a miracle cure," Sarah said. "Now what
am I going to do with you?"

"Meow." Familiar rubbed against her leg and then
hopped in the middle of her bed. With great care, he walked
a circle and finally curled up, tucking his nose over his front
paws, his great green eyes closed shut.

"You need some rest, and I have an errand to run." She
went to the bed and sat down, taking a moment to stroke his
fur. "Maybe you should go to the vet."

Familiar rolled over and displayed his stomach in a most
inviting manner. When Sarah gently rubbed it, he purred
outrageously.

"I don't think you were injured at all," she said, suddenly suspicious. "I think you're a con man in a cat suit."

"Meow." Familiar's green eyes opened, and then he gave
her a solemn wink.

"Why, you are a con man!" Sarah couldn't help but
laugh at the cat. He acted as if he understood every word she
said. "You can stay tonight, but you can't stay any longer,"
she warned him—and herself. "I'm not the type of person
who can own a cat. I have to be gone for several days at a
time." She heard her own voice running out of steam. How

nice it would be to have a kitty to come home to. How long
had it been since she'd been greeted at the door by someone
who was really glad to see her?

"Now you behave while I'm gone." She had to get over
to the Bingingtons' before it got any later. Shaking her head,
she hurried down the stairs and out the front door.

It took her thirty minutes to drive to the Bingingtons', and
although the house was well lighted, she still felt awkward
about going into someone else's home. She slid the key into
the lock and walked in.

Switching on lights as she moved through the rooms, she
was immediately absorbed in checking the arrangement of
tables, flowers, and decor. As a caterer she sometimes
worked with florists and other accessorizers to create a
complete theme. This one was her baby. She was responsible for everything, from the magnolia blossoms to the bales
of cotton she was having brought in. The house was perfect, though. The dining room would easily seat fifty, and
double parlors fed off the west end of the dining room. It
would be easy to set up the hors d'oeuvre tables and a second wet bar. She nodded with satisfaction as she snapped
off the lights and moved on to the kitchen.

Sarah was halfway across the room, searching for the light
switch, when a noise outside the back door made her freeze.
It was the chink of something against the glass, followed by
a scraping sound.

Her mind went blank at the possibility of what the noise
could be, but her brain registered that it was a sound that
should not have been there. Moving as swiftly and silently
as possible, she found a doorknob in the dark and pulled it
open. Stepping inside, she pulled the door closed and felt for
a lock. There wasn't one.

Fumbling backward she stepped on an object and
grabbed into the darkness, catching it before it could fall. A
broom. Careful now, she reached into the darkness. Mops,
pails, brooms, the vacuum cleaner. She'd stumbled into the

cleaning supply pantry. Taking care not to make a sound, she burrowed into the pitch blackness and prayed that whoever was outside would not open the door.

"We're in."

She heard the voice and knew she was in terrible danger. Someone was robbing the Bingington house. If they found her in the pantry, they would more than likely kill her.

"Yeah, we're in. What a joint. It seems a pity to break in and break out without taking anything."

The second voice was just as unpolished as the first. Both were male and both young. Sarah could determine nothing else—her heart was pounding so hard she thought she might burst.

"Keep your paws off everything. We're here for the pepper. That's it."

Sarah swallowed. "Pepper?" Surely she'd misunderstood. Unless—! She felt a surge of adrenaline that mingled the fear. What if she'd stepped on someone's toes with her White House catering business? If someone else had been pushed aside to make room for her, they might well resort to putting something in her food. Not enough to injure anyone. But a few dinners where guests mysteriously got sick—no one wanted to risk that kind of fiasco at a political event. It would ruin a chef forever in this town.

Her churning thoughts stopped cold as the first man spoke again.

"This is what they call ironic." His laugh was short and there was the sound of cabinets opening and shutting.

"What?" The second man sounded hostile, as if he knew he was the butt of a joke.

"This cook's old man was a sheriff in Mississippi. He wanted a piece of the gambling action from the big boys, then got cold feet. He went back on his word, though, and he had to die. Now his kid is cooking up her own trouble."

The other man laughed, also a sharp sound. "Yeah, that's ironic."

A cabinet shut and silence fell outside the pantry where Sarah hid.

Gripping the edge of a shelf, Sarah listened until she thought she'd gone blind and deaf in the blackness of the pantry, until she felt as if all of the oxygen was being rapidly sucked from the room.

This was no professional prank or attempt to ruin her business. This was something else, something that went back to her childhood and the father she'd idolized. What gambling action? If her father had known about any gambling ring, he would have put the people in jail. Gambling was illegal in Mississippi at the time Cal Covington was sheriff of Hancock County. Who were those men, and what were they talking about?

A long suppressed fear rose up and nearly choked her. Was her father's death not really an accident? Dizziness made her grasp the wall behind her. That was unthinkable. It was the one nightmare that she'd had to bury just to survive.

She had to see their faces. She had to know who they were and how they knew so much about her business and her past.

Pushing away from the stabilizing shelf, she eased open the door and slipped into the kitchen. Once she found the light switch with her fingers, she hesitated. What if they had guns?

She wanted the light, but she wanted to be cautious even more. Slipping along the wall of the kitchen, she made her way to the dining room and listened.

The old house was silent, as if no one had been there in a hundred years.

They were gone.

Sarah knew it, but she didn't want to believe it. While she'd been cowering in the pantry, they'd slipped out again. Now she'd never know who they were and how they'd come to know anything about her father.

She thought of calling the police, but the reference to her father held her back. All of those dirty accusations came rushing back at her—that he was dishonest; that he had abused the power of his office; that he had consorted with criminals; that he had betrayed the public trust.

Those were the charges her father had faced, and they were responsible for his death. Nothing was ever proven against the lawman, but he'd gotten careless from worry and stress. When he was shot trying to stop a robbery, plenty of folks said he deliberately stepped in front of the bullet.

Sarah switched on the kitchen light. In the pantry, she found canisters of pepper—ground pepper, peppercorns, green peppercorns, white pepper, red pepper, cayenne pepper. She found a used grocery sack and dumped them all into that, careful not to touch the flat surfaces of the cans and jars.

If there was any hanky-panky going on with the pepper in the Bingington house, she was going to find out about it. And then she was going to find those two men who'd been in the kitchen. She was going to find them and make them tell her what they'd meant about her father.

She grabbed the bag of pepper and hurried to the front door. There had been times when she'd suspected there was more to Cal's untimely death and her mother's sudden collapse—and some of the people responsible for all of the tragedy had been not five feet away from her this very evening.

It was a terrifying thought, but one Sarah was determined to prove, no matter what she learned about the past.

Chapter Three

Daniel Dubonet watched the expression on the other man's face. There was no clue to his emotions.

"Check her out thoroughly. I have it from a very good source that this young woman could be serious trouble."

"What source?" Daniel knew he was pushing his luck to question his superior in such a manner, but the veil of secrecy that had suddenly surrounded a seemingly innocent young cook had piqued his curiosity. What gave with Sarah Covington? The first request from the Secret Service for FBI assistance was odd enough. Now the continued investigation was even more peculiar.

"That's an inappropriate question." Paul Gottard turned cold brown eyes on his employee. Daniel Dubonet was an agent with a lot of potential. But asking such stupid questions could end his career in a hurry.

"There are no inappropriate questions. Not in an investigation."

Gottard eyed the younger agent. Dubonet was impulsive and brash. Qualities that could be good or bad, depending on when and how they were used. He was also an agent who stood out—a fact that could make him a hero, or a scapegoat.

"Put your trainee's manual away, Dubonet. You want to know why we're so interested in Sarah Covington, I'll tell you. Miss Covington has a very interesting past."

Daniel started to make a retort, but he bit it back. He'd already pushed his luck with his boss. He could plainly see that by the lines of tension around Paul Gottard's eyes.

"Sarah is the daughter of a sheriff down in Mississippi. I should say, he was the sheriff. He's dead now. Died under suspicious circumstances. After a lengthy investigation by our agents."

Daniel was immediately alert. Corruption of local law enforcement officers was an area that particularly interested him. Lawmen, like ministers, were supposed to conduct themselves impeccably, Daniel believed. Men or women who took oaths to protect and defend citizens and then behaved illegally, were worse than other criminals.

"Tell me the background." He leaned forward in his chair.

"Cal Covington was serving his second term as sheriff of Hancock County. Seems he was doing a pretty good job, at least, according to his records. Looked like he could have been elected every four years for the rest of his life." Paul reached for a file on his desk. "Then there were rumors he was involved in an illegal gambling interest. Those coastal counties have always been wide open for gambling, prostitution and all the other vices. Been going on for years and no one seemed to mind all that much."

"So what happened?"

"That's the strange part. Covington was a real Wyatt Earp. Young girl was killed and he sent more folks up to the state pen than any other sheriff in the history of the county. Then we got a tip that he wasn't on the up-and-up. He made some enemies—" Paul dropped the file on his desk. "And then he walked into a bullet in a penny-ante robbery."

"Suicide?"

Paul shrugged. "We'd been investigating him for months. We could never find anything. Not really."

"How about the money?"

"We could never prove that he accepted it."

"Never?"

"Never." Paul tapped his fingers on the desktop. "Joshua Jenkins was in charge of the case. He was positive Covington was guilty."

"Old Man Jenkins?" Daniel couldn't help the impertinence of the question. Jenkins was a legend in the FBI, an agent more tenacious than athlete's foot. He never disappeared, and he never gave up. Not until he had the evidence necessary to bring his man to justice.

"Yeah. Jenkins." Paul's frown was the first emotion he'd shown. "Jenkins stayed after him. Month after month. He came up with *nada*. Zip. The big zero. But he always believed he could find the evidence. Then Covington was killed, and it became a moot issue."

"Jenkins thought it was gambling money?"

"That's what he thought. Lots of those syndicate big shots used to summer down along the coast. They'd come in from Chicago and New York and run all kinds of illegal games. As I said, the Mississippi Gulf Coast was not an area where people pointed the finger at high rollers."

"And Covington made it a little easier for them?"

"Not really." Paul rubbed his chin, the second display of unease. "Nothing was ever proven, but now his daughter shows up in Washington and some very powerful people get sick. It's not just coincidence that the three men who were stricken at her last dinner all have connections to Hancock County."

"You think Sarah Covington is in town for revenge?"

"Revenge, or to finish the job her father started. If Jenkins was right, Covington had sold out to the syndicate and then didn't follow through on his end of the deal. In essence, he betrayed his office *and* the criminals who paid him. And Jenkins believed they paid him handsomely. There should be a lot of money stashed away somewhere. If Covington was involved in something illegal, his girl may be trying to pick up where he left off, or she may be trying to get even with someone.''

''Money, power and revenge. Three powerful motives.''

''Right. We want to keep her under very close surveillance.''

''I'm afraid I may have blown my chances of any type of casual observation.'' Daniel remembered how he'd burst in on her at midnight. He wanted to kick himself. If he'd acted with some patience and a little maturity... But he'd thought the case was a nuisance—a punishment, actually. Would he never learn?

''We had a complaint about you.'' The expressionless mask had dropped back over Gottard's face.

''I know. It was too late when I knocked on her door. But I'd had her staked out, and I'd wanted to get the list of ingredients and get it over with.''

''Did you find anything on the list?''

''Nothing. They all checked out, and the stores she listed all knew her as a good client, a chef who is particular about her ingredients.'' He shrugged.

''Don't make any more midnight calls.'' Gottard tried to smile but his face simply wasn't used to moving in that direction. ''No point antagonizing her any more.''

''Right.''

''But you will watch her. Follow her wherever she goes. Find out what her assignments are, and we'll see that you get there in some capacity. She already knows you're an agent. Someone has to run protection for those events.''

''Yeah.'' Daniel repressed a sigh. Of all the assignments he hated, attending government functions as a dark-suited bodyguard was the worst. He wanted to solve crimes and apprehend criminals, not stand around at cocktail parties with a microphone in his ear.

"Then you'd better book yourself into the gym for a couple of extra hours each week."

The remark was so unexpected, Daniel looked up, unable to frame a reply.

"All of that eating and drinking. I'm sure you'll pack on a few pounds. Can't get out of training trim, you know." Gottard's smile was a little more relaxed. "I understand she's a wonderful cook."

"I'll bring you some take-out," Daniel remarked as he stood and prepared to leave. "Aren't you from the North?"

"Pennsylvania. And we had our share of delicious dishes. It's just that fried chicken and those vegetables." He sighed. "I attended a dinner several months ago that Sarah Covington catered. It was some of the best food I've eaten."

"Maybe if we convict her of something, we can get her sentenced to cook for the FBI." Daniel's face was innocent as he watched Paul Gottard. Old Stone Face had a real hankering for Sarah's cooking. He actually looked hopeful for a split second.

"You're in the wrong line of work to be a comedian," Gottard said quickly. "Now, find some way to get yourself invited to that Southern governors conference at the Bingington place. Maybe valet parking." He grinned. "I'll make the arrangements."

Daniel was about to object, but he knew it would do no good. He'd tweaked and poked at his boss too much for one session. Now he was going to have to pay the cost. Parking duties. He almost groaned as he left the warren of government offices. His big mouth was going to be his downfall yet.

So, Dolly has gone to work and left the big bad cat alone in her humble abode. I'd give anything for a prehensile tail and the strength to open that giant refrigerator door down in the kitchen. I only caught a whiff of possibilities, but I'll bet there's crabmeat, shrimp, cheeses, butter, milk, all the things a recuperating kitty needs.

Now where would I hide if I was something secret? Not a lot to discover up here in the living quarters. Dolly doesn't strike me as the type of girl who would have a safe in her wall. And she's not much of a housekeeper. She needs to get the dust bunnies out of the corners of her closet, and her desk is a mess. Books, papers, an address book, bills, all left out on top of the desk. This is all personal stuff. The catering bills will be downstairs. Seems to have an excellent method of keeping records. That should make her accountant happy. Not to mention the agents of the IRS. Well, it's not the tax men who are after little Dolly. It's another branch of the feds altogether. And I'd better get my sleek black butt to work or I won't have a thing to report to the White House.

Now for the interesting part. The kitchen. Bubble, bubble, toil and trouble. If there's ill deeds to be done by a chef, then it's the kitchen where the tools will be found.

And goodness gracious, there's plenty of stuff to poke around in. As I suspected, the refrigerator door will not yield to my paw. But what a lucky cat I am. There's a pedal-operated opener. What will they think of next to make the hardworking cook's life a little easier? If I jump up and down on this thing... Eureka! The door swings open, revealing a garden of kitty delights.

Lots of luscious goodies, but no time now to graze my way through them. Careful now, there are some of those tacky candid snapshots on the refrigerator door held in place by those gauche fruit magnets. What an ugly mug that guy has. Hope he's not a relative. No accounting for human tastes, that's for sure.

I want to check the spices. There's the usual assortment of fresh green stuff here. Nothing out of the ordinary. Now for the little bottles and cans. Everything is neat, orderly and scrubbed to a fare-thee-well.

And I do believe I hear the jingle of keys in the door. Best to scoot up the stairs fast and crawl back into my sickbed. Somehow, I've got to make an escape tonight and get back to Eleanor. She's going away for a few days next week, and I'll have more free time. For the moment, though, I don't want to worry one hair on her beautiful dark head.

SARAH'S HAND was shaking so badly that she dropped her keys three times before she could fit them in the door. The pepper was tucked in her coat, a lump at her hipbone that mashed into her uncomfortably as she held her groceries in one arm and tried to unlock the door.

Once inside, she eased her groceries to the floor and turned all of her attention to relocking her door. No one had followed her from the Bingington house. She'd made certain of that by taking a roundabout way and turning sharp corners unexpectedly. There had been plenty of traffic, but no single car had followed her intricate pattern.

The men who'd entered the Bingington house were gone. She was safely home, evidence in hand. And her heart was about to beat out of her chest.

"Kitty, kitty." She called up the stairs, afraid to go up for fear someone might be lurking about, waiting to get her. But she had to check on the cat. What if he'd taken a turn for the worse?

"Meow!"

His reply was much perkier. The milk and egg must have made him feel better. Sarah felt relief as she hurried upstairs and found him just as she'd left him. He was a handsome creature and seemed to understand that she only wanted to help him. And if the truth was admitted, she needed him, too. It was nice to come home to something alive.

"Hey, kitty." She went to the bed and stroked his back. He was curled into a sleepy ball, as if he'd never moved.

"I got you some food. Hungry?"

His golden green eyes seemed to brighten.

"Well, come on downstairs." She was surprised when he sat up and stretched, ready to follow her. For a stray, he was certainly a well-mannered cat. If no one else claimed him, maybe she could keep him for her own pet. As she watched him stretch, his rear poked up in the air, she smiled. He was one hundred percent cat.

Together they strolled down the stairs, and Sarah picked up the groceries and the sack of pepper. She took them all to the kitchen and put everything except the pepper away. What was she going to do with all of the Bingingtons' pepper now that she'd stolen it? In the bright light of her kitchen, it seemed like a stupid thing to have done. What would she tell the Bingingtons tomorrow when she saw them? "Excuse me, I stole all of your pepper canisters because I heard someone break in, and I was afraid they were going to try to poison some of your guests."

Great! That would do the trick. She'd be labeled a crazy and no one in town would ever hire her again, no matter what magic Uncle Vince and Chef André were able to pull off.

She couldn't call the police. The reference to her father stopped her cold. Cal Covington had suffered tremendously in his last days. The accusations and rumors had killed him as surely as the bullet. Until Sarah could discover what door to her father's past had suddenly been reopened, she had no intention of involving the authorities. After all, she'd seen exactly how the FBI and other law officials worked. Her father had been guilty until proven innocent. And if someone had killed him, the FBI could very well have been involved!

But what to do about the pepper?

She would replace all of the canisters with brand new ones. Unopened. Untampered with. She lifted the lid of her trash can to throw the others away. The green eyes of the cat watching her every move made her stop. It was almost as if he willed her not to throw the pepper away.

What if someone was trying to kill the Bingingtons or their guests? If she didn't report what she'd heard, would she be an accessory to murder?

She closed the garbage can, the sack of pepper still in her hand. Putting her burden on the counter, she got out a handful of gourmet coffee beans and set about to brew herself a cup of coffee. Caffeine would clarify her brain. She was still a little shaken up by what had happened that night.

When she sat down at the big kitchen counter, the cat leapt into her lap and purred a kiss under her chin.

"What a fine cat you are," she murmured, stroking the sleek fur. He belonged to someone. She was going to have to put an ad in the paper. It wasn't fair to keep someone else's pet. Someone was probably looking for him, worried that he was injured or worse.

The black cat rubbed his whiskers along her jawline, tickling her neck with his whiskers.

"You won't let me feel sorry for myself, will you?"

"Meow." He put his paw on her wristwatch.

"It's nearly ten." She answered him before she blushed. She was actually answering the cat, as if he'd asked her the time. She needed a shrink, not a pet.

The black cat patted her wrist again, then hopped to the telephone. When she didn't move, he leapt onto her counter and knocked the pepper sack onto the floor. The metal canisters clanked and rattled while the glass clattered ominously.

"Get off that counter this instant." Sarah clapped her hands and the cat leapt down to the floor. In a moment he had one of the pepper bottles out and was batting it around. She'd never seen an animal make such a rapid change in personality. He'd been sweet, loving, docile. Now he was a hellcat, hopping and leaping on every flat surface and knocking things around the floor. He was acting like a kitten, and he was very much a full-grown cat.

"You act as if you're very familiar with my home, Mr. Cat."

At the sound of the word "familiar," he looked up and cried.

She said it again. "Familiar."

"Meow!" He stopped all of his frantic activity.

"Familiar."

"Meow, meow." He nodded his head once.

"Okay, I'll call you Familiar. You act like the best friend of a witch. But you have to stop tearing my kitchen apart."

Familiar batted a pepper bottle so hard it rolled into her feet. Then he jumped back to the telephone and lifted the receiver with his paw.

"You want me to call someone?" She felt stupid asking the question out loud. The cat was beginning to give her the creeps. He'd named himself and now he was demanding her action.

"Meow, meow." Familiar punched a few of the buttons.

"You're a pushy thing." She retrieved the pepper from beneath her feet. "I suppose I should call that arrogant agent." A smile crept over her face and she looked at her watch. It was going on ten. That wasn't exactly tit for tat, but it was close enough. He'd rushed into her house at midnight. Maybe it wouldn't be such a bad idea to give him a call late at night.

He'd given her a card, along with the stale admonition to "Call if anything develops." Like she was expecting developments. But the pepper was something . . . and it would solve a host of problems. She could report the break-in, have the pepper tested, and absolve herself of any responsibility for future events. And she didn't have to tell him anything about the bit of conversation she'd overheard. That could be her secret.

Before she could change her mind, she lifted the big telephone directory by the binding and shook. A dozen business cards fell to the floor, Daniel Dubonet's on top, face-up.

She picked it up and dialed his home number, her satisfaction and hesitation growing as she counted the rings.

"Hello?" Daniel had just fallen asleep. The day had been a bad one, and his mood was not improved by the ringing telephone.

"Mr. Dubonet. This is Sarah Covington. You asked me to call if anything developed. Well, it has."

Daniel sat up in his bed, realizing he'd fallen asleep with the light on and a book beside him. "Sarah Covington?" He was having a hard time adjusting to reality. He'd been dreaming about the blond chef. She'd been standing beside his bed with a tray of delectable desserts, ready to serve him. Except that he wasn't interested in any of the tempting pastries she was offering. He was tantalized by the sweep of her hair against her cheek and the display of long, long legs that showed beneath the imaginative white chef suit she wore. He swallowed.

"Mr. Dubonet? This is Sarah Covington, the chef." Sarah felt a moment's annoyance. He'd spoken with her the night before. Had he forgotten her so quickly? She certainly hadn't forgotten him. In fact, he'd deviled her thoughts constantly.

"Of course. I know who you are." He was irritated at his sudden desire for a woman he barely knew. The sound of her voice was enough to trigger the urge to see her. "I was asleep."

"I'm so sorry."

He could tell by her tone that she was not one bit sorry, and he smiled. She was not only lovely, but bright and spunky, too. He had that one coming. "What can I do for you at this hour of the night, Miss Covington?"

She heard the teasing note in his voice, and she couldn't suppress her own smile. He did have a sense of humor, after all. Maybe he wasn't quite as arrogant as she'd first thought.

"I ran into some difficulties tonight." She couldn't help the tremble in her voice. Even talking about the two men made her frightened.

Daniel heard the change in her tone. "Why don't I come over, and you can tell me about this?" He'd been given a direct order to work with her. His luck couldn't get any better.

"It's late. I can tell you over the phone. I have some things, some spices, that I'd like to have tested for..."

"For what?" Daniel felt a tingle along his spine, suddenly wondering if this call was good luck or not. Was she trying to set him up?

"Pepper canisters. Someone broke into the Bington house tonight while I was checking it for the dinner tomorrow. I think they might have put something in the pepper containers."

It sounded crazy. How did she know this, and why would she suspect the pepper canisters? Unless she knew a lot more than she was telling.

"I'd better come over and talk with you in person." Was it official duty that prompted that remark or human desire? Daniel had a hunch he already knew the answer.

"No, it's late." Sarah felt a pinch of guilt. She'd meant to wake him up but not to drag him from his bed in the middle of the night. Besides, seeing him only confused her.

"I insist."

"I'm really fine. We can talk about this tomorrow. I was wondering if I should keep the pepper containers. I was going to throw them away—"

"Don't! Don't throw anything away. I'll be there in less than half an hour." Before she could disagree, Daniel replaced the receiver. As he reached for his clothes, he was already thinking ahead. If Sarah intended to do any damage tomorrow at the dinner, the perfect alibi would be to call and say someone had broken into the house and tampered with the spices. Even more perfect would be to call the FBI.

If someone were poisoned, Sarah would be sitting pretty. She would have done everything in her power to prevent a calamity.

She was one smart woman. Smart and dangerous. He checked the clip in his automatic as he slid it into the pocket of his coat.

Chapter Four

Daniel tugged at the starched white collar of his shirt and tried not to show his restlessness. Shoes shined to perfection, he was standing under the front portico of the Bingington house waiting for the last guest to arrive. Waiting to make sure that nothing unexpected happened. Although everything, so far, had gone as smooth as glass, there was still the feeling that warned of danger. He'd never made a claim to be psychic, but there were times when he *sensed* danger. And that extra edge of alertness had saved his life at least twice. Sarah and her pepper troubled him—enough to have him send the pepper to be tested.

As he nonchalantly adjusted the weapon in his shoulder holster, he could feel the gaze of the other valet resting on his back. As far as he knew, the valet was a regular guy who picked up extra bucks parking cars at a few posh parties. He had the look—trim, handsome, good manners. Daniel dropped his hands to his sides and slowly turned around to face the young man, a smile at the ready. "Hot today, isn't it? I think I'll get a glass of water." Without waiting for a response, he made his way around the house to the kitchen entrance. It was time for a check of the premises, and a look in on Sarah Covington.

At the large windows that gave a view of the enormous kitchen in the Bingington house, he paused. Sarah, her blond hair tucked neatly in a French twist, was bending over the oven. She wore white chef pants, but even in the baggy uniform, he could detect the outline of her firm posterior. She was a very attractive woman.

His perusal of Sarah was interrupted by another sensory assault—the most heavenly aroma wafted out to him. He identified it immediately as honey-baked ham. He could almost taste it when Sarah and a helper lifted the last huge ham, spiked with pineapples and cloves, from the oven.

There were four helpers in the kitchen with Sarah, and the place was a beehive of activity. Even though the room was large, every inch of space was in use. Checking his watch, he saw that the luncheon was due to officially begin in another fifteen minutes.

All of the expected guests had arrived except Governor Lester Peebles of Virginia. He'd been detained by some personal business—several members of his staff had quit in a tiff with his impossibly demanding wife—but he was coming. There had been no unexpected guests, no deliveries of any kind. Nothing had occurred that would indicate that any foul play was afoot.

Had Sarah been lying about the pepper?

The lab report would be complete later that afternoon. Until then, he was on the alert for any tiny detail that might warn of danger to the dignitaries attending the event.

The swinging door into the kitchen pushed open and a uniformed maid quickly refilled a tray of colorful hors d'oeuvres and went back out. It was rather amazing to watch the kitchen staff work so efficiently. He grinned at the thought that he could never manage to cook a steak, potato and peas and get everything done at the same time.

A tall, slender blonde he recognized as Ashley Bingington entered the kitchen and spoke to Sarah with a big smile. All appeared fine in the kitchen, and he continued around the house. As he checked the back entrance and found nothing, he couldn't help but remember his boyhood dreams of becoming an FBI agent. Like all kids, he'd pictured it as a life of sirens, guns and high drama. He'd wanted to chase down the bad guys and win the day. The reality wasn't quite as exciting. More often than not, he spent a great deal of his time reading reports and profiles, sitting in parked cars and standing in the hot sun on the alert. There had been moments of excitement, but those times always came with a price. Oftentimes, innocent people were the victims.

He made his way around the perimeter of the estate, then doubled back to the front. The valet on duty with him shot him a curious look just as a long, black Towncar arrived. Governor Peebles, looking harried, climbed out of the driver's seat. His chauffeur was obviously one of the staff members who'd departed.

"I'll take care of it," Daniel said agreeably to his coworker. "Why don't you take a break? There's some great food in the kitchen."

"Hey, man, thanks." The valet gave a small salute as he left.

Daniel drove the car down the drive to the tree-shaded area that had been designated for guest parking. The Bingtons had thought of everything when they'd laid out the grounds for their home. He eased the car into a parking space. He had about two hours to kill before it would be time to begin the process of returning the cars to their owners. In that time, now that he had keys to all of the cars, he intended to do a little unauthorized checking.

If Sarah was being set up, then it was possible that one of the governors, or one of their guests, was involved. It was highly unlikely, but at least his search would help him pass the time. There was also the possibility that Sarah was working *with* one of the governors. With the economy on the downswing, each state was getting more and more competitive to attract new business.

He got out of the Towncar and went around to the back. As he popped the trunk open, he didn't hear the stealthy footstep in the grass. He never saw the flashlight that swung in a high arc and caught him just above the right temple. He never felt the gritty trunk of the car as he fell into it.

"That's what happens when a person sticks his nose into other people's business."

With a quick surge of energy, two strong arms lifted Daniel into the trunk and slammed it shut on him.

SARAH BLOTTED the faint glow of perspiration from her brow and wiped over the counters one final time. Around her the Bingington house echoed with welcome silence. All of the guests were gone and the Bingingtons had retired upstairs. Sarah had dismissed the kitchen staff. Only the cleanup crew remained.

"Everything is spotless," Charmine, one of the crew, assured her. "Go on home. You're about to drop." She grinned. "But don't worry about those leftovers. I'll take care of them."

"Mrs. Bingington said we were to take everything." Sarah grinned back. The menu had been a smashing success. Though she had prepared abundant supplies of everything, most of it had been eaten as the governors asked for second helpings.

"I do believe you'll get some new clients," Charmine teased. "You'd better watch out, though. All of your clients are going to weigh two hundred pounds. You're going to become known as the Calorie Killer."

Sarah winced at the unintentional reminder of her earlier problems. Then she laughed, fatigue making her slightly slaphappy. "I certainly hope not. Now I'm going straight home. I've got another luncheon next week. You want the cleanup detail? I'll be glad to recommend you."

"You bet." Charmine winked. "Get some rest, hon, you look beat."

Sarah had parked her compact at the rear of the kitchen. All of her pans were already loaded. As she walked out the door, she wondered what had happened to Daniel Dubonet. She'd expected him to show up in the kitchen to eat. The other valet had taken a break for a quick lunch. She shrugged. Maybe Daniel had gotten a more urgent FBI call.

She drove straight home, barely noticing the flow of traffic or the familiar sights of the city. When she'd first come to Washington she'd been intimidated by the traffic and the sweep of humans who seemed to be in constant motion. Now, she hardly noticed it at all.

She did, however, notice the silver Mercedes parked at the entrance to her shop. A large smile spread over her face. As soon as she parked in the tiny slot behind her building, she ran to the car and tapped on the window. The door swung open and a tall, thin man in an expensive suit swept her into his arms.

"Chérie," he said, hugging her tightly. "You look exhausted. You are working too hard."

"Uncle Vince." She hugged him. "What are you doing here?"

"I came to check on my girl." He held her away from him. "You look tired. How about a vacation? I'm going to New York tomorrow. Come along with me."

She grinned. It would be a great trip, but she had business. "I'd love to, but I can't."

"How is Mora?"

She motioned him inside as she unlocked the door. They went directly to her large kitchen. Sarah was always delighted whenever she heard Uncle Vince's special knock at her door. They'd spent many pleasant hours at her kitchen table and now, without asking, she put on a pot of strong coffee. "Mother's okay. You know how easily she becomes upset. We're perfectly fine." The temptation to tell Vincent Minton about the strange occurrence in the Bingington house was almost irresistible. But Sarah had given her word to Daniel that she would say nothing until the tests on the pepper were complete.

"Is something wrong?" Vincent asked. His dark brows, threaded with silver, drew together. "Is that agent still bothering you? Was there trouble at your job? Lucinda Watts was at the party, and she said everything went fine."

"No." She couldn't help but smile. "Nothing is bothering me. I've had a wonderful day, in fact. And I owe all of it to you." She kissed his cheek before she went to the cupboard for coffee cups. "I think my catering business is really getting off the ground." She started telling him about the Bingington event as she poured coffee for them both.

"You have talent, and you work very hard," Vincent said as he leaned back in his chair. His dark eyes followed her every move. "My son is accompanying me to New York. I would love for you to come along. You haven't seen Jean-Claude since you were children."

Sarah swallowed the hot coffee. "Yes, it has been a long time." But not nearly long enough, she thought. She had a vivid memory of a thin little boy with scabs on his knees and a mean streak a mile wide.

"Jean-Claude has grown up, Sarah. He is a handsome man. Very refined. With good manners." He laughed. "I know that's hard for you to believe. You knew him when he was a little monster. But all boys must be civilized. It was a long, hard, and in Jean-Claude's case, very expensive process."

Sarah laughed warmly, delighting in the twinkle in Vincent's eyes. Ever since Sarah and Jean-Claude were children, Uncle Vince had insisted that one day they would marry. Sarah had never given the idea more than a horrified thought. Even though Jean-Claude wasn't her blood cousin, she had no desire to even *think* about him romantically. But lately, Uncle Vince had mentioned it more than once. And now this trip...

"Jean-Claude has been working in the Schelbet vineyards for three years. He started out with the vines, learning everything from the very bottom. It has been good for him." Vincent reached across the kitchen table and picked up Sarah's hand. "He is very handsome."

"Like his father?"

"Ah, you are a flirt." He laughed. "I am glad to see that your heart has not turned into a lump of dough. I worry that you don't go out and have fun. You're only young once, *chérie.*"

"I meet more eligible men than any other woman in Washington," Sarah declared. "And if a man struck my fancy, I'd do something about it." Daniel Dubonet's face popped into her mind. He was the most attractive man she'd met in a long, long time. And he constantly made her remind herself of her desire to stay clear of men and relationships. "You and I both know my career comes first," she added, evading her own feelings.

"Think about New York."

"I can't." She shook her head. "I would go if I could, but I do have obligations. Maybe next time, but you have to give me a little more notice."

"Agreed," he said, putting his cup in the saucer. "Now, I must be off, and you need to finish up your work so you can relax."

"As soon as I finish my work, I'm going to take a long, relaxing walk, rent a movie and climb into bed," she promised him as she stood to give him a hug. "Thanks for everything you've done for me. And Mom."

"Thanks aren't necessary." He kissed her cheek.

Sarah walked him to the front door. She wanted to put the Closed sign up and make sure the locks were in place before she went upstairs to bed. She also wanted to check her messages on the answering machine. Maybe Daniel had called. He said he'd have the test results, and the day was drawing to a close.

She was slipping the latch into place when she remembered the handsome black cat. She hadn't heard a peep out of him since she'd returned.

"Kitty, kitty," she called up the stairs. Disappointment touched her heart. He was gone. He'd left as strangely as he'd arrived. With a heavy step she went up the stairs and searched her living quarters. Familiar was gone. Sarah consoled herself with the thought that such a well-kept cat belonged to someone and that he'd simply gone back to his home. Cats were notorious for their wanderlust.

But just to be on the safe side, she decided to check the street. If he'd gotten out of the building while she was hauling food in and out, he might be lurking around somewhere.

"Kitty, kitty," she called as she stepped into the street. "Here, kitty, kitty." She walked halfway down the block, noticing that all of the chairs in the beauty salon were filled with women holding magazines. On the way back to her door, she saw the car. It was dark navy or black. In the late afternoon shadows cast by the taller buildings on her street, she couldn't be certain. A man sat at the wheel, his face turned away from her. Nothing unusual—except that she could have sworn the same car had been there the day before. And possibly the day before that.

She stared at the man, who immediately lifted a newspaper, blocking her view of his face. He was too far away for her to be able to get a really good look, anyway. But why was he sitting in the car reading the newspaper?

"Maybe he's waiting for someone in the hair salon." She spoke aloud, trying to rationalize the situation. It wasn't impossible that it was some husband waiting for his wife. The Proud Peacock Salon was a popular place with a large clientele of middle-aged and older women. Often they were driven to their hair appointments by their husbands.

But something about the car bothered her. As soon as she got inside her door, she put the Closed sign in the window and drew the blinds for good measure. That was something she rarely did because she liked for people walking along the streets to look into her shop and see the menus and displays. One never knew where the next order would come from.

Just as she started for the stairs, she heard a sharp knock on her door.

"Sorry, I just closed." She needed business, but she needed sleep more.

"Ms. Covington, please open the door."

She'd come to recognize the difference between a request and an order. This was an order.

"I'm sorry, I'm closed." Every sensor in her brain was warning of trouble.

"Ms. Covington, I'm a friend of Daniel Dubonet's. I'm afraid there's been some trouble."

Sarah walked back to the door and peeked through the blind. The man standing at her door was a carbon copy of the typical agent. Dark suit, white shirt, conservative tie. "Let me see your identification."

He held the gold badge up to the glass. Agent Glen Henderson, FBI.

"Okay." She opened the door, but just wide enough so that she could speak with him. This was exactly what she deserved for involving Daniel in her problems. Now she had agents all over the place. Still, the thought that Daniel was in trouble made her heart race. The depth of her concern frightened her. Her feelings for Daniel weren't completely clear—and she fought them every inch of the way. But what if he had gotten injured because of her? What if he'd...? No, he was perfectly fine. She'd seen him not more than six hours before, and he was his normal, tall-in-the-saddle, FBI self.

The man glanced up and down the street. "This is important. May I step inside for a moment?"

Reluctantly, Sarah opened the door and he stepped inside. He closed it behind him.

"Have you seen Agent Dubonet this afternoon?"

"He was at the Bingingtons'."

"When was the last time you saw him?"

Sarah thought. He'd come back to the kitchen at about eleven o'clock. She'd spoken with him briefly about the guest list, checking to make sure they both expected the same people. And that had been it.

She told the agent, watching the slight frown that drew his forehead together.

"After the luncheon, you didn't speak with him?"

"No. It was odd, too. I expected to see him. He just disappeared." Now she felt a twinge of real concern. "Nothing has happened, has it?"

"We're not certain. He didn't complete his assignment. In fact, the valet working with him said he just disappeared right before lunch. The young man went to the kitchen for a break, and when he returned to his post at the portico, Dubonet was gone."

Sarah picked up a strand of hair that had fallen from her twist. She tugged it gently without even being aware of what she was doing. "Daniel doesn't strike me as the kind of person who disappears in the middle of a job."

Agent Henderson sighed. "Daniel and I went through training together. He *isn't* the kind of person who walks out in the middle of something."

She saw the genuine worry in the agent's face. "Where could he have gone?"

"Nowhere, voluntarily."

"You think he was abducted?"

Agent Henderson tightened his lips. "I wouldn't be surprised. Mind if I use your phone?"

Sarah showed him to the phone on her desk, and then retreated into the kitchen to give him privacy. As she cleaned up the coffee cups from Uncle Vince's visit, she couldn't help the growing worry she felt. When the agent tapped lightly at the kitchen door, Sarah turned anxious blue eyes on him.

"Any word?"

He shook his head. "Nothing at the agency. I have some other locations to check." His frown deepened considerably.

"What can I do?"

"Nothing, for the moment." He started to speak, then hesitated.

"What is it?" Sarah could see that something was troubling him.

"If you hear anything from Daniel, would you call me immediately?" He handed her a card with only a number written on it. "This is my private line. There's a machine to answer the call if I'm not there. Daniel could be in serious trouble with the agency. Unless he has a very good excuse for leaving his post today... well, it could be the end of his career, especially since he got that harassment complaint."

Sarah tugged her hair more violently. What had Uncle Vince said?

"Daniel and I are old friends. Good friends. I'll do what I can to protect him, and I'm certain that whatever happened, he has a good excuse. Just don't call anyone but me. Okay?"

The guilt Sarah felt almost made her sick. She hadn't intended to cause that much trouble for the agent. "Of course." She took the card in fingers that were not completely steady.

"Remember, call me before you do anything." Agent Henderson gave her a tight smile. "Daniel and I have been in some bad spots. Don't worry."

As she saw him out the front door, she glanced across the street. The dark car was gone. She shook her head as she turned the dead bolt into place. Whatever had happened to Daniel, it wasn't her fault. She had to believe that or she'd spend the rest of her life like her mother, terrified of any decision, of any action, of any desire to live her life. Daniel was a grown man. Whatever he'd done, he was responsible, not her.

From such a perfect beginning, the day had taken a definite downhill slide. First the cat was missing, and now Daniel.

She was halfway up the stairs when the telephone began to ring. Increasing her pace, she ran up the stairs and picked up the extension in her bedroom before the answering machine was activated.

"Sarah?"

She felt a rush of fear at the familiar voice that sounded so distant and faded. "Yes."

"This is Daniel Dubonet. I need your help."

"Where are you, Daniel? Everyone is looking for you—"

"Don't tell anyone about this call. Can you meet me in Falls Church?"

"Virginia?" Sarah couldn't believe it.

"Right. Just off the interstate on Compton Road. At the Waffle House."

"You want me to meet you at a Waffle House in Virginia?" Sarah wanted to pinch herself. Surely she was dreaming.

"Listen to me. Something happened at the Bingingtons'."

"You'd better call in. An Agent Glen Henderson was here not ten minutes ago looking for you. He sort of said that you were in serious trouble."

There was a long silence. "Glen Henderson?"

"Right. He said he went through training with you."

"Did he show you a badge?"

"Just like yours. Why?" A creepy feeling was beginning in the pit of her stomach.

"I didn't train with any Agent Henderson."

"Why would—?"

"Sarah, can you pick me up? I don't have any identification or money. I'm stuck out here in a tuxedo. I had to borrow a quarter from one of the waitresses here to use the phone. I'm afraid if I don't order something they're going to throw me out, or worse, call the authorities on me.''

"Okay, I'll come get you. What happened, though?''

"I promise, I'll tell you everything as soon as I see you.''

An odd note in his voice made her pulse quicken. "Are you okay? You sound...funny.''

"I have a terrible headache, but other than that, I'm fine. Just hurry.''

"I'm on my way.'' She replaced the receiver and picked up her keys off the counter. She'd been exhausted, but now she was pumped full of adrenaline. She checked the clock and noted that it was nearly five. It would take an hour or better in rush-hour traffic to get to Falls Church. Sighing, she picked up her purse and hurried out the back door to her car.

Darkness had fallen over the city in the short time she'd been on the phone. As she stepped into the alley, she drew herself up short. A big man hung above her on the telephone pole.

"Sorry to startle you, ma'am. We had some trouble reported on the line and wanted to get it repaired.''

Sarah took a deep breath. The man had scared the fool out of her. She glanced around, but saw no truck.

"What kind of trouble?''

"That beauty shop. Static, broken connections. Have you had any difficulties?''

"No.'' She couldn't distinguish his features. "Isn't it a little late to be climbing around on poles?''

He laughed. "Yes, ma'am, it is, but it's my shift, and we try to keep repair crews going twenty-four hours a day. In a city like this, communication is more important than water.'' He smiled. "Don't worry, we'll take care of whatever's wrong.''

Chapter Five

Sarah could smell the bacon cooking in the Waffle House as she got out of her car. Lights glowed brightly through the plate-glass windows and inside waitresses in orange uniforms and white aprons filled coffee cups as they took care of their customers. Sarah, who'd spent summers waiting tables, knew exactly how hard and tiring the job could be.

She spotted Daniel instantly even though he was doing his best to disappear into a booth in the far corner of the restaurant. Contrasted with the truck drivers and tourists who frequented the all-night restaurant, Daniel and his tuxedo were a bit of a sore thumb.

Pushing the glass door open, she walked over to his table. She felt all the eyes in the restaurant directed at her, but her only concern was for Daniel. His face was pale, and an enormous goose egg distorted one side of his head.

"What happened?"

"I know, it's a costume party, right?" A burly guy at the counter stared at her.

Sarah looked down at herself, realizing too late that she was still in her food-smeared chef's uniform. When she looked back at Daniel, she was relieved to see his grin.

"If you'll pay for my coffee, we can leave," he said.

"My pleasure." Sarah couldn't help teasing him. Even though he looked terrible, she was relieved that he was okay.

Too relieved. She was on the verge of serious emotional trouble, but she didn't know how to stop it now. Her feelings for Daniel had grown against her wishes. "On the condition that as soon as we get to the car, you tell me what happened."

"It's a deal." He stood and took the money Sarah offered him to the counter.

"Where's the party?" the burly guy asked, grinning.

"Not far," Daniel answered.

"Looks like you got started early." The man laughed. "Better watch out. They'll put you in jail for drinking and driving, these days."

"We'll be careful," Sarah assured him. She waited at the door while Daniel paid up. Once in the parking lot, she saw he was weaker than she'd thought. His step was slightly woozy, as if he *had* been drinking.

"Maybe we should stop at a hospital and get your head checked," she said carefully.

"No. I need a telephone."

She pointed to the pay phone across the parking lot.

"No, let's get back to D.C. I need to check in with the agency and let them know what happened. I want you to tell me about this Henderson guy."

Sarah started the car and eased into the flow of traffic. She recounted the meeting with Henderson, word for word as closely as she could remember. Daniel did not interrupt her until she was finished.

"What did he look like?"

"Handsome, very athletic and trim. Neatly dressed and groomed. A lot like you," she said.

"Meaning, all agents look alike?"

She could hear the tiniest edge of sarcasm in his voice. "Same clothes, same shoes, same manner. But he was blond." She grinned.

"Well, I don't know a blond Agent Henderson and I never went through training with anyone like him."

"Then who was he?"

"I wish I knew the answer to that question."

A long stream of oncoming headlights took all of Sarah's concentration, and she waited for Daniel to continue. "Did anything happen at the Bingingtons'?" he finally asked.

"Everything went like clockwork. No troubles at all. I didn't know you were gone until that Henderson fellow came by. What did happen to you, Daniel?"

"Someone knocked me out and put me in Governor Peebles's trunk. I came to and knew we were on the road. When the governor pulled into that service station for gas, I clipped the lock from the inside and got out and slipped over to the Waffle House."

"Didn't you tell him?"

He gave her a look. "He might have been involved. I wanted to get away."

"And why did you call me?" This was something that had troubled her all during the drive to Falls Church. Why hadn't he called someone from the agency to help him?

"This is going to sound very strange." He looked out the window and then back at her. "This entire assignment has been ... unusual. The FBI was invited to join the investigation by the Secret Service. That's unusual. Then I get the job—to investigate a chef." He shook his head. "It just didn't ring true."

"And ... ?" she prompted.

"I called you because I didn't want to call anyone at the agency. I may have been set up."

"I could have set you up," she observed.

"That's true. But if that was the case, you never would have shown up." He looked at her in the dim lighting of the car's dashboard. "Someone else would have, and I probably wouldn't be alive."

Sarah tightened her grip on the wheel. "What's going on here?"

"I don't know, Sarah, but I promise you one thing, I'm going to find out." He straightened his shoulders. "Would you mind taking me to my apartment? I want to pick up a few things." His hand traced his left side where his weapon should have been.

"No problem," Sarah said. What was she going to do, let him off at a street corner? "What about keys?"

"I have those." He pulled them from his pocket. "They took my gun and my identification."

Sarah didn't comment. When her father was sheriff, a lawman who lost his weapon lost face, if nothing else. She could see that Daniel was smarting over the situation, and there wasn't anything she could say that would make it any easier. She felt a growing knot of guilt. Daniel would never have been at the Bingington house if she hadn't called him about the pepper. She had some responsibility for what had befallen him.

"What about the pepper report?" she asked, hoping for a topic that would take his mind off his own troubles.

"Needless to say, I haven't gotten the report, but I will, as soon as I get home. I can call the lab and see what they turned up."

"Daniel, everything at the luncheon went perfectly." The impulse to twist a strand of hair was strong, but she kept both hands on the wheel. "Maybe there won't be anything in the pepper."

"Maybe there won't. But once we have the report, at least we'll know for certain."

"Those men who broke into the Bingingtons'..." She took the exit that he directed. "Well, there was something I didn't tell you." She didn't see what possible difference it could make, the conversation about her father, but after everything that had happened to Daniel, she felt she owed it to him to be completely honest.

Tension knotted his shoulders. Sarah had lied to him—and that lie could have cost him his life. "What exactly didn't you tell me?"

The harsh tone in his voice made her wish she'd never started this. "It's personal."

"How personal?"

"Gee, you won't give me a break, will you?" Her temper flared. She was trying to do the right thing, and he was acting like he had her in an interrogation room for bank robbery.

He heard the concern in her voice, and the pain. His head throbbed and his body felt as if he'd been beaten with a bat, but he forced himself to relax, just a little. He'd gotten off on the wrong foot with Sarah because of his impatience. Now she was trying to help. "I'm sorry. Tell me what you left out." That was as non-accusatory as he knew how to phrase it.

"They said something about my father." The sting of shame made Sarah stop. Even after all these years, she couldn't discuss what had happened to her father without reliving all of the horrible lies.

"Your father?" Daniel waited. Nothing was clear yet, but it had been Cal Covington's past that had interested Paul Gottard, his boss, in Sarah in the first place.

"I don't remember exactly what was said now." Sarah had to force herself to continue. She felt the tears welling in her eyes and knew them for what they were—a sign of deep-seated anger at what had happened to her family. But she couldn't allow herself to cry.

"Try to remember. Just do the best you can. This may be important."

Sarah took a ragged breath. "They said something about how my father had messed up the job where the gambling was concerned." She had to bite her bottom lip for a moment to halt the tears. "And then they said that it was ironic that I was involved in what my father had started."

"What could that mean?"

"I don't know." Sarah's grip on the wheel loosened slightly as she made another right-hand turn at Daniel's direction. "I will tell you, though, that my father was an honest man. He was never involved in anything illegal."

"That's not the way the FBI saw it."

Daniel's words were gentle, but it was more than Sarah could take, especially from him. She slammed on the brakes, pulling the car over to the side of the road. "Get out!" She reached across him and opened the door. "Get out and get home the best way you can."

"Sarah, I was only trying—"

"You're like all the others. You decide a man is guilty and then you set out to prove it. The FBI ruined my father's life. And my mother's. And now you're trying to ruin mine. I must have been crazy to talk to you. How many times do I have to learn a hard lesson?" She pushed at his shoulder. "Get out of my car or I'll drive to the police station and file charges against you."

Daniel slowly unbuckled his seat belt. His own anger had been caught off guard and he had no defenses for the raw pain he heard in Sarah's voice and saw in her face. "I didn't mean—"

"Get out." She panted with anger and with the effort to control her tears.

He eased out of the seat. Traffic whizzed by them, but he knew he was actually within walking distance of his apartment. He was going to be fine, but it was Sarah he was concerned about. He'd not only struck a nerve, he'd trounced up and down on it.

"Sarah, please let me explain—"

"Tell it to your superiors. Put it in my file. Stick it—" She pressed hard on the gas, and the car screeched back into the flow of traffic, the passenger door closing under the force of the takeoff.

Standing on the side of the road, Daniel watched her tail-lights blend into the steady flow of traffic. He'd learned a couple of valuable lessons in the past twelve hours. First of all, he should have checked the parking lot before he bent over that trunk. Second, where Sarah's father was concerned, she harbored a lot of anger and pain. The question that danced in his mind was whether it was out of guilt or frustration.

The tuxedo was little protection from the chill wind, but Daniel set his body to the task of walking and his mind on what he was going to do next. He was in something of a jam, but it was his own doing. He had been poking into Governor Peebles's trunk without a warrant and without any probable cause. He'd merely been killing time and fishing. Now he'd been knocked unconscious, transported across a state line, and worst of all, his badge and gun had been taken. He could forget the headache and the uncomfortable ride—in fact, he was too humiliated to mention it—but the gun presented a problem. He had to report the theft, and he wasn't the kind of agent who lied to make things look better for himself. The whole sordid tale was going to have to come out, and Paul Gottard was going to have his head.

On top of the fact that he'd disappeared from his assigned post. That was another black mark. Daniel sighed as he deftly climbed the chain-link fence on the interstate and started to cut through a bad neighborhood. A car approached him, radio blaring the sounds of raucous music. Great. All he needed now was an encounter with a bunch of macho teenagers. But the car passed without stopping, and Daniel ducked into a narrow street where table lamps burned as families gathered around the television.

He'd grown up in a neighborhood where everyone ate dinner as soon as the news was over. His father had come home from work at the same time every evening, and his mother had put their meal on the table, bowls of vegetables, steaming hot. It had been a comfortable childhood, complete with neighborhood pals and bicycles and dogs. There had been plenty of games of cops and robbers, and Daniel had always been a cop. It seemed he'd never dreamed of anything else.

His pace increased as the thin jacket seemed to grow even thinner against the wind. Good thing Sarah hadn't put him out forty minutes earlier. Then he would have really been in a pickle.

In fifteen minutes he was in his own neighborhood. The streets were wider, more brightly lit, with nicer cars parked along the curbs. The old quadruplex that he rented was fronted with a screened porch and enormous sycamore trees. He loved the porch in the spring and fall, when he could sit and listen to the sounds of kids down the block playing. Lately, though, he'd had very little time to enjoy his home or anything else.

Trotting up the steps, he stopped with his hand on the screen door. He knew before he saw the tear in the screen that someone had been in his apartment. He knew it and knew that danger might still lurk in the darkness.

Backing off the porch, he eased around the apartment to the garage where he kept his car. All four tires were flat, the car resting on its hubs. He kept his anger tightly checked as he moved back to the front of the apartment.

Very quietly, he eased the screen open. He knew every creaky board on the porch and avoided them all as he moved silently to the front door. As he expected, the knob turned uselessly in his hand. Someone had popped the lock completely out of the door.

He eased his hand inside and hit the light switch. The sight that greeted him made him groan out loud. Every piece of furniture he owned was either gutted or broken. Whoever had been in his apartment had meant to destroy it, not simply search it.

As he stepped into the room, his foot scrunched on shards of glass, and he picked up the broken frame of his parents' wedding anniversary picture. The anger was delayed in coming, but the sight of the ruined picture brought it on hard.

Aware that he was weaponless, Daniel moved through the rest of the house, making sure that it was empty. The more destruction he saw, the angrier he became.

He was in the front bedroom when he saw the sweep of headlights in his driveway. Dropping to the floor, he crawled into the living room and waited for the footsteps on the porch. The two creaky boards both gave a low screech as he counted the steps coming toward his door.

Before the intruder could knock, Daniel launched himself at the door. He pulled it open, then barreled through it and caught the intruder in a bone-crushing grip. Together they collapsed on the hard boards.

"He-l-p!"

As he pushed the intruder to the porch floor, he realized that it was a she, and that she was slender. Even before he looked, he knew it was Sarah Covington. He eased his shoulder out of her diaphragm.

"Help! Get off me!" Sarah's voice was surprisingly strong.

As he clamped a hand over her mouth he also realized she had surprisingly strong teeth.

"Damn!" He shook his hand. "Sarah, shut up."

"Shut up, yourself!" She drew in a deep breath and tried to roll out from under him. "Get off me, you oaf."

He clamped down harder, putting his bitten hand on her shoulder and pinning her to the floor. "Will you listen to me?" His tone dared her to say no.

"Get off me or I'll—I'll boil you in a big pot until your flesh separates from your bones!"

Daniel felt the chuckle easing up his throat. It was the last thing he expected to feel, but he couldn't help it. Sarah's threat was so ridiculous. He laughed out loud, a soft but completely amused chuckle.

"Let me up," she warned him, not amused at all. "I came over here to apologize, and you tried to kill me. If you hadn't already lost your badge, I'd see that it was taken away from you."

He laughed harder, but he was smart enough not to relieve any of the pressure that held her down. Once he let her up, it was going to be more of a rodeo than he cared to think about. It was hang on or get gored.

"Daniel Dubonet, take your body off mine this instant." She wiggled beneath him, then stopped, suddenly aware of the hardness of his body pressed against her.

Daniel looked down into Sarah's big blue eyes. The streetlight gave him a good view of her features, and he could see that her anger had changed to something else. Her breasts were pressing into his chest, soft mounds that only served to accentuate the firmness of her torso and the long, lean length of her legs beneath his. In that moment he knew he had to let her up.

"Sarah?" He heard the huskiness in his voice and tried to clear his throat. Damn, but he was aware of her. Of every inch of her beneath him, and he realized he was no longer cold at all.

He gave up trying to explain and slid to the side, rolling onto his knees as he did so. Without waiting for her response, he grabbed her shoulders and pulled her to a sitting position.

"I thought you were trying to break in."

"Yeah, that's my second profession. I cook by day and burgle by night." Sarah hid her confusion behind bluster. She could still feel her heart racing from the feel of him above her, but she would rather die than have him realize her reaction to him.

"Someone trashed my apartment."

His simple statement shook her out of herself. "Daniel! How bad is it?"

"Wrecked. They destroyed everything." He rocked back on his heels and stood. With a fluid motion, he gave her his hand and pulled her to her feet. "When you came creeping across the porch, I thought it was whoever did it, coming back."

"I wasn't certain I remembered your address correctly. I was going to come up to the porch, peek around and see if anyone was home." She shook her head. "I was worried about leaving you on the interstate. That was a stupid thing to do. I went back to look for you, but you were gone."

Daniel signaled her into the house. At the doorway, Sarah stopped. The destruction was complete, as Daniel had said. Even his books had been torn apart, the pages ripped and thrown around the room. "Whoever did this deliberately meant to hurt you."

"That was my exact thought. All I have to do is figure out who did it—and why."

"What are you going to do?"

"Check my answering machine and then call in for a fingerprint team. At least this will give my story of being abducted a little substance."

"Can I help?" Stepping over the rubble, she followed him into what had once been a bright and cheerful kitchen.

Daniel gave her a long look that ended in a smile. "Dare I ask again for a ride to a hotel? I don't want to disturb any of the evidence here. There might be a set of prints or some clue that the forensic people can pick up. But I do have money now, and I can call a cab if you're going to put me out on the interstate again."

Sarah gave him an answering smile. "I promise to give you a ride to your chosen destination if you promise not to... to involve yourself in my past."

The stiffness of her shoulders told him that this wasn't a request he could deny. "The past is off limits. For now."

Sarah didn't like the last sentence, but she didn't argue. After all, she was the one who'd brought up her father and the past. "Let's go."

Daniel pressed the buttons on his answering machine and then swore loudly. "Why did I think they wouldn't destroy this, too?" He nudged it back against the counter.

"I may not be an FBI agent, but I do know a little about electrical devices." Sarah walked over to the counter and plugged the machine in.

In a few seconds it had rewound and Daniel began playing back his only message.

"Dubonet, this is Cody at the lab. We have an affirmative on the pepper. Stop by and talk to me."

Daniel's eyes sparkled with energy as he met Sarah's questioning gaze. "There *was* something in the pepper!"

"I heard." She couldn't help her own excitement. "Do you think he identified the substance?"

"Cody couldn't say that over the phone. Bad form. But he'll have a full report. Let's go."

Sarah reached out a hand and touched Daniel's arm. "Wait a minute."

"What?" Her slender fingers touched his arm with the softest pressure, yet he could feel it all the way to the bone.

"The people who did this to your apartment. Do you think they heard the message?"

Daniel looked at the machine. Since it had been unplugged, there was no way to tell. "I don't know." He didn't have to add that the idea worried him. It was evident in his voice.

"Maybe we should check on Cody right now." Sarah didn't want to say it, but based on the chain of events that had already occurred, she or Daniel, or both of them, were bad luck for whoever tried to help them.

"Good idea." Daniel picked up the phone and dialed. The longer he held the receiver to his ear, the more worried his frown became. "The lab man is not supposed to leave the office."

"Maybe he went to the bathroom."

"Maybe." Daniel put the receiver down. "And maybe we'd better get over there."

"Right." Sarah pulled her keys from her pocket. "Let's just hurry."

Chapter Six

Daniel remained lost in silent thought for most of the drive to the FBI laboratory where Cody Pruett worked. Sarah cast covert glances at the agent as they sped along the black asphalt, turning finally among a nest of government buildings with blank edifices and plenty of parking.

As she pulled into a space, she kept the motor running. The night had gone from chill to downright cold.

Daniel's gaze swept the parking lot, indicating one of the cars. "That's Cody's. He should have answered the phone."

Sara's heart trip-hammered. Had something happened to the lab tech because of her? The sensation of guilt was so familiar that she immediately thought of her father. Even as a child she'd always wondered if, somehow, she was to blame for the tragedy of her father's death. If she'd been a better daughter. If she'd been more helpful, more aware of the devils that tormented her father. If she'd listened more closely. If... If she'd done anything other than what she'd done, maybe things would have gone differently.

"Sarah?" Daniel's voice registered concern. "Are you okay?"

"Of course." She killed the motor, wondering how long she'd been sitting, staring at the steering wheel. She glanced over at him, catching the intensity of his look at her. Their eyes held for a split second, and Sarah felt her perception of the world tilt. She glanced out the window.

With the heater off, the car began to grow cold. Unwilling to risk another look at Daniel, she snuggled deeper into her seat. She was still wearing her ridiculous chef's suit. But Daniel looked like a maître'd who'd been in a barroom brawl. She realized she'd etched into memory the way his lapel was torn and the smudge of grease on the front of his white shirt.

The play of emotions across Sarah's face was kaleidoscopic. Anguish, guilt, discomfort, awareness, Daniel saw them all, and he was frankly caught in the web of her emotions. She was completely guileless—or else the best damn actress he'd ever seen.

That thought sobered him. "Let's go," he whispered.

The touch of his hand, light though it was, galvanized Sarah. She nodded, not trusting her voice, and got out of the car, taking care to ease the door shut. Without a word, she followed Daniel to the front door.

With a few expert touches on an electronic pad, Daniel coded the door and it swung open soundlessly. A long hall, pale green with institutional carpeting, stretched before them. Heavy doors opened off the corridor, but there was no sign of any living person.

Daniel motioned for Sarah to stay behind him and to keep quiet. She had no intention of making any noise at all. Moving swiftly and without a sound, they slipped along the hallway to an unmarked door. With his shoulder braced against it, Daniel pushed it open.

Peering over Daniel's shoulder, Sarah saw the lean body slumped over the desk, tousled blond curls touching the blotter. She felt Daniel tense. Then he burst into the room, dropping to the floor as he signaled her to get down. He rolled across the room until he was at the lab tech's side. In a second he had his hand on Cody's neck, feeling for a pulse.

"Cody?" Daniel's voice was strained with worry.

"What?" The startled lab tech jumped up, almost knocking Daniel in the chin with his head. "What is it?"

Sarah rose to her feet and slipped into the room, quickly closing the door. At first glance, she'd thought the lab tech was dead, stretched across the desk. But she realized he'd been asleep—a fact that was dawning on Daniel as he clasped his friend's shoulder.

"You scared me to death," Daniel said, his voice registering relief and chastisement.

"You didn't do a lot for me, either." Cody shrugged his arms, straightening his shirt. "And you look like hell." He caught sight of Sarah in her white chef's suit. "Who are you supposed to be, Julia Child and Jeeves the butler after a food fight?"

"It's a long story, and it's been a long night. What about those test results?"

"I was wondering if you were going to collect the data." Cody rolled his chair briskly across the room to a file cabinet. "I had to put it on record, but I made a copy of the report for you." He pulled a legal page from the folder and rode the chair back to his desk. With a flourish, he handed it to Daniel. "Pretty hot stuff, if I can manage a little pun."

Daniel groaned as he took the page and studied it quickly. "What is this substance? Ipecac? It isn't any poison I've ever heard of."

"It's a very common substance, available without a prescription, also known as emetine." Cody lifted his eyebrows, assuming a professorial stance. "It's used to induce vomiting. Used to be sort of a home cure for alcoholism." Cody was over his scare and was eager to talk about his favorite topic, poisons.

"Oh, great." Sarah suddenly visualized the luncheon with every dignitary in the Southern states grasping their stomachs and running for the bathrooms. It would have ruined her career.

Cody picked up the thread of his conversation with enthusiasm. "The bottom line, though, is that with the limited use of ipecac in the pepper, no one would have been injured. Worst case scenario, two or three very sick people. More likely a tableful of slightly queasy folks." Cody tapped the paper in Daniel's hands. "Looks to me like someone was planning a prank."

"Did you check the pepper for other poisons?" Daniel wasn't willing to let it rest. Men didn't break into a highly protected home in a ritzy neighborhood to play a prank.

"Everything under the sun. There was nothing else there that we could detect. The ipecac was in the black peppercorns, the most commonly used pepper. My guess is that the intention was a broad-based assault. Almost everyone uses a little pepper, so theoretically, almost everyone would have been affected. But," he emphasized, "no one would have been seriously affected."

"How did they do it?" Sarah asked.

"Ipecac is made from the *Cephaelis ipecacuanha,* a plant common throughout Europe and the Americas. The berries *and* the juice are toxic." His face grew stern. "This can be a very dangerous substance if taken in concentrated doses. It can easily kill."

"Not sprinkled on food like pepper, though," Daniel said.

"Right. My guess is that whoever did this soaked the peppercorns in a mildly concentrated solution of ipecac liquid, then dried the peppercorns, and repeated the process a couple of times. They were heavily saturated."

"Wouldn't someone have tasted it?" Sarah asked.

"Doubtful. And keep in mind that many people put pepper on almost all of their food. It would have blended with the different courses."

"Would it have shown up in later tests?"

Cody grinned. "Doubtful. And who would test for it in food? As I said, this is an old-time remedy. People used to

put it in liquor to induce heavy vomiting. The theory was
that a person wouldn't drink if he thought the alcohol would
make him deathly sick. Wrong assumption, I'm afraid."

"And where could a person get this substance?" Daniel
folded the lab report and put it into his pocket.

"Anywhere. It's certainly easy enough to find. But keep
in mind, if the poisoner had wanted deadly results, then he
would have used something else, or administered this differently. By the way, ipecac can be used over a long term, a
slow poisoning that is lethal."

"Thanks, Cody." He hesitated. "I called earlier and there
was no answer."

Cody looked down at his desk. "I stepped outside to
smoke a cigarette."

"I thought you'd quit." Daniel's frown was back in place.
"Nicotine is a poison, too. You don't need me to tell you
that."

"Soon. I promise." Cody leaned back in his chair and
looked at Sarah. "Well, Ms. Covington, I'm sorry we had
to meet under these circumstances. Now, tell me about those
outfits you're wearing."

"We were working the Bingington luncheon, and we
simply haven't had a chance to change clothes." She gave a
crooked smile. She hadn't completely absorbed all the information, and implications, of what Cody had told her, but
she understood he'd done a very thorough job on her behalf.

"Looks like the two of you had a rough day." Cody's
glance lingered on Sarah's slim figure and long legs.

Daniel caught the glint of interest in Cody's eyes. "It's
time for us to go," he said, walking over and taking Sarah's
arm. "Thanks, Cody. And could you send a team over to
my apartment? Someone trashed the place and I'd like to
have it swept for fingerprints."

Cody whistled, his casual pose disappearing as he stood. "You've gotten hold of something nasty. Or it's gotten hold of you."

"And we'll see who comes out on top." Daniel's words were a vow.

"I'd hate to get between you and whatever you wanted," Cody said without rancor. He looked at Sarah. "Once this guy has his mind made up, you'd better step back and get out of the way. I've known him since we were in college together."

Daniel's jaw tightened. "Speaking of old friends, do you recall a Glen Henderson from the academy?"

Cody took his glasses off and cleaned them on his shirt. "That name doesn't strike a bell. But maybe if I saw his picture."

"Doesn't strike a bell with me, either. I'll let you know." He moved toward the door, still holding Sarah's elbow gently in his hand. "Thanks, Cody."

"I'll call for the fingerprint guys. Daniel—" he waited until his friend looked at him "—be careful. You're a good agent, but don't put yourself in a place where a mistake can be too costly."

Daniel stared at his friend for two seconds. "I hear you, Cody. I hear you." He nodded once and then assisted Sarah out to the front door. As they started to exit, he repeated the same procedure with an interior electronic pad.

"I can understand safety precautions getting *in* the building," Sarah said, "but going *out?* That seems a little odd."

"If someone broke in here and got into our files, he might not be able to figure the code to get out. It's just a little extra precaution."

"I see." But Sarah was too tired to worry about precautions. She wanted to go home.

Daniel gently took the keys from her hand and maneuvered her around the car to the passenger door. When he finally pulled up into the alley behind her business, Sarah was sound asleep.

In the light cast by a mercury vapor bulb, he studied her sleeping face. Her skin was as clear and perfect as alabaster, set off by eyebrows several shades darker than her hair. Dark lashes curved against her cheek. She looked barely out of her teens as she slept, face turned toward him on the headrest of the seat.

"Sarah." He spoke gently.

A furrow touched her forehead. "No," she murmured.

"Sarah." He brushed her hair off her cheek, noting the heavy weight of it.

"Doesn't know," she whispered, and her eyebrows drew together. "No." She shifted, turning slightly. "No, I won't do it."

"Wake up, Sarah." Daniel grasped her shoulder, shaking very lightly.

Her eyes opened, unfocused, and she stared at him a moment as she adjusted to where she was.

"What did I say?" she asked slowly.

"Sounded like a bad dream to me." Daniel felt a vague worry begin to gnaw at him. Was it a dream? Or was it a guilty conscience? "What were you dreaming about?"

Guilt filled Sarah's eyes before she turned to gather her purse from the floor. "My sordid past, Daniel." She blinked several times before she looked up at him. "Thanks for driving me home. You're welcome to stay on the sofa. I mean, most of the night is gone and..." She didn't want to be alone. But she wasn't going to come right out and say it. Daniel Dubonet didn't owe her a single minute of playing bodyguard.

"It might be better if I stayed." He felt a confusion of emotions. Was he staying to protect her—or to spy on her? To shut off his own uncertainties, he got out and went around the car to help her.

From the corner of the building, a black shadow darted toward the car, landing on the hood with a thud.

"Familiar!" Sarah felt a surge of happiness at the sight of the black feline. "Where have you been?"

I COULD ASK the very same question of you, Dolly. I've been hanging around this alley freezing my elegant black tail off, and finally you come home, with an escort in tow. A federal agent, no less. Well, it could be worse. It could have been that creep in the dark blue car who's been sitting out in front of the beauty shop on and off for the past three days. I can only hope this fellow is at least of average human intelligence. The longer I live, the more I wonder how humans became the dominant species.

Take for instance that old harridan who runs the beauty shop. She threw a glass of cold water at me. She has no inkling that I'm in the service of the First Cat! It takes a mighty mean person to try to douse a cat with cold water simply because he's walking down the street.

I'd better get my quota of pets and cuddles. I detect a certain light in this gentleman's eyes that tells me he has some hopes pinned on future strokes and kisses himself. Ah, the budding of a new love, perhaps. All well and good—if he meets Socks' and my approval!

"I DIDN'T KNOW you had a cat." Daniel eyed the black feline with some doubt. He'd always had dogs as a boy. Dogs and bicycles were a natural duo, in his opinion. Cats were an unknown—with sharp teeth, sharp claws and an arrogant attitude.

"I don't, really." Sarah bundled the cat to her chest. "He's freezing, though. I found him the other night, lying outside my door. I thought maybe he'd been hit by a car. But he seemed to be okay, and then he disappeared." She stroked his head. "I thought he'd gone back to his home."

"He looks fine to me." There was something about the cat that made the agent wonder. Daniel could have sworn the big black rascal winked at him.

The three of them entered the shop, and Familiar hopped lightly to the floor. He paused, as if sniffing the place, and then trotted to the kitchen, pushing open the swinging door.

"He's made himself at home," Daniel remarked.

"I think he might be extremely intelligent," Sarah said. "He gives me that impression." Sarah looked longingly up the stairs. "Would you care for anything to eat?"

"Just a blanket, a pillow and that sofa you offered," Daniel said.

Sarah nodded. She went to the kitchen door and called Familiar, but the black cat ignored her. Working with quick efficiency, she put out a saucer of milk and a small serving of poached salmon, then headed upstairs with Daniel right behind her.

When she was certain that the agent was comfortable on the sofa, Sarah crawled into her own bed. Daniel was not ten feet away, a fact that made sleep difficult to find even though she was exhausted. Every time she closed her eyes, she was tormented by thoughts of him, close enough to touch. And so forbidden. It was a strange mixture of emotions that made her toss from side to side. In spite of her attraction to him, Daniel's presence outside her door gave a sense of security she hadn't known since she was a child.

She remembered how safe she'd felt with her daddy, a sheriff, in the house. He was a lawman, like Matt Dillon on "Gunsmoke." And no harm was ever supposed to come to those he loved.

Sleep finally claimed her, and she dreamed that she awoke to the smell of coffee. Yawning, she kept her eyes closed and burrowed deeper into the pillow. It was a nice fantasy, a cup of hot coffee waiting on her bedside table.

"Sarah?"

"Yes," she answered the sexy male voice in her dream.

"I brought you some coffee."

"Wonderful." She relished the dream.

"Sarah?"

The note of worry in the voice struck her as wrong, and she opened her eyes. Daniel Dubonet, face darkened by a growth of stubble, was staring at her with very worried eyes.

"What are you doing here?" She clutched at the sheet and pulled it to her neck. A long black paw shot out of the blanket and grabbed her wrist. Familiar didn't want to be disturbed.

"I made some coffee and realized you weren't going to get up unless I forced the issue. Sorry, but I didn't want to leave without saying something."

"Well, I can drive you..." She looked around. What time was it? Morning still, the sun was slanting into the room from the east.

"I've called a cab. I'm going over to Cody's to clean up. He'll take me to my apartment. They're certainly through with the investigation, and I can get my clothes and things. If anything is left."

Sarah reached for the mug of hot coffee that enticed her on the bedside table. She felt completely disoriented, and Daniel wasn't exactly at ease. He kept sneaking peeks at her with sideways glances.

She sipped the coffee and tried to get her thoughts in order. "Why don't you let me run you over there? It won't take but a minute for me to get ready."

Daniel couldn't take his eyes off her. Her blond hair was tousled from sleep, and she was completely unaware of how appealing she looked. "I've already called a cab. Thanks for letting me stay here."

"Thanks for staying. And for checking the pepper. It makes me feel like I'm not a complete fool."

That was the thing that had been troubling him. "Sarah, what are you going to do now?"

She knew what he meant, but she didn't want to confront the issue. "Take a shower, and—"

"Sarah." His voice was half command, half request.

"I don't know." She shrugged and drank more coffee.

"I've been giving this some thought." And what he'd come up with was a big zero. Why would someone want to ruin Sarah's career? What good would that accomplish? "Do you have any rivals who might want to run you out of business? Or someone who wants to get even?"

Sarah thought. "Everyone has enemies, but I don't know of anyone who would do such a thing. I mean, it's one thing to wish someone out of business and another to make an entire roomful of people sick."

Daniel nodded. That's what he expected. There was the chance that she was lying—that she'd doctored the peppers herself. There had been no evidence of a break-in at the Bingington house. None. Sarah could have made it up.

But the evidence pointing in her behalf was his own abduction.

"What is it, Daniel?"

"I'm just trying to put the pieces together. Listen, I'll call you later this morning. About ten. Let me get cleaned up and go to the office. There's some stuff I need to take care of. What are your next assignments?"

"Let's see." She'd hardly given it a thought. "I have a birthday party for the daughter of Georgia's Senator Banks. That's tomorrow." At the thought, she felt the need to jump from bed and get ready. It was a cowboy theme, and she had to bake a bucking bronco cake and tend to the rest of the party. Children's birthdays were a real pain, but it often brought in a lot of business. Every little tyke present had parents who gave serious Washington gatherings.

Daniel stifled a groan. Paul Gottard would delight in assigning him to some backyard fete.

Sarah could almost read his thoughts. "They're going to have real ponies. Maybe you could be a wrangler?"

"No! No way am I going to lead those brats around on ponies."

Sarah couldn't suppress her grin. "Just kidding. But it isn't a bad idea."

"I have to go, but I'll call no later than ten. Just stay here until then, can you?"

She heard the concern in his voice and nodded.

He hurried out of the room and took the stairs in rapid succession. Then there was the sound of the front door closing.

"I'd better go lock it," she whispered to Familiar. She didn't like the idea of being up in her apartment when the downstairs door wasn't secured.

She pulled on a robe and hurried down, her legs chilled by the morning. Peering through the blinds, she saw Daniel duck into the back of a cab. They pulled away from the curb with more force than necessary.

SARAH HAD JUST begun to mix the cake batter when the telephone rang. "A Taste of the South," she answered.

"Sarah, I've heard wonderful reports about yesterday."

"Thanks, Uncle Vince." Sarah had given up trying to figure out Vincent's grapevine.

"I found out that pesky agent had been assigned to the party. I wanted to apologize. I was given a promise that he wouldn't trouble you again." Vincent sighed. "There are no manners anymore, *chérie*. A man's word means nothing any longer. I am sorry."

"Don't worry about it. Daniel Dubonet didn't bother me at all," Sarah said. She was grinning. It would be too difficult to explain to Uncle Vince that the agent in question had spent last night at her apartment. Had left only an hour before.

"Then nothing marred your wonderful day yesterday?"

"Not a single thing."

"That's what I love to hear, my darling. Now, since you won't go to New York with me and my son, what if I make arrangements for dinner one night when we return?"

"I could cook some—"

"Absolutely not!" He laughed. "You are the best cook I know, but I believe I can throw some steaks on the grill and make do with potatoes and a salad. How does that sound?"

"Perfect." Everything except Jean-Claude. But based on past actions, Jean-Claude was liable to jet-set over to Paris for an evening with his friends.

"Then I'll count on it."

"Perfect." Sarah glanced at the kitchen clock. If she put the cake in now, it would be out at ten-fifteen. She slid it on the rack and shut the oven door.

"Sarah?" There was hesitation in her uncle's voice.

"What?"

"I hear that Dubonet fellow may be in trouble with his superiors. He's something of a renegade. You know, doesn't follow orders, goes off on his own. If he bothers you again, it's very important that you let me know."

"Of course." Her answer was automatic. The first taste of doubt was very bitter.

"My sources in the FBI say he had been pulled from a big case and reassigned when he visited you so late that evening. Just keep that in mind. As you well know, just because a man is a federal agent doesn't mean you can trust him. Remember your father. They hounded him."

"I remember." Sarah's voice sounded as empty as she felt. "I'll never forget that, Uncle Vince. You don't have to worry."

Chapter Seven

Daniel forced his body to relax in the backseat of the cab. He was on an adrenaline high as he tried to decide the best course of action. Cody was at home, waiting for him to arrive. But Daniel wanted a few minutes with Joshua Jenkins, retired FBI agent and the man who had been assigned to Cal Covington's case. If Sarah was involved in something from her father's past, Joshua Jenkins would know the details of it.

He knew his boss would disapprove of any disruption of Jenkins' personal life. The word was out in the Bureau that Jenkins was an irascible old curmudgeon who was like gum on the shoe when he got started. Daniel knew he was opening a can of worms, but he didn't care. He gave the cabbie Jenkins's home address. Everyone in the Bureau knew it—they'd all driven him home at one time or another after he'd been to the Bureau to deliver some tirade about how ineffective the "new agency" had become, about how "soft" the new agents were, and about how he'd been such a dogged investigator that some men simply turned themselves in to get rid of him.

Right.

Daniel was so busy with his thoughts that he didn't see the quizzical look the cabbie threw at him as he moved into the flow of Washington traffic.

It was rush hour, and the streets were dangerously clogged. Daniel half watched the blocks pass. Time ticked along, and he grew more and more nervous as the cab slowly made its way to Jenkins's house.

"Wait for me," Daniel directed as he finally got out in front of the neat brick house with its postage-stamp yard. Flowers bloomed in profusion in window boxes. A divorced man, Jenkins had turned his considerable energies to horticulture.

Daniel jabbed the bell once hard, and then again. He knew he was acting impatient. At last he heard the slow shuffle of someone at the door—someone who was practicing precautions. Daniel could almost feel the eye staring at him though the peephole in the front door.

"What do you want?" Jenkins called.

"I'm Daniel Dubonet with the FBI. I'd like to talk to you."

"ID."

Daniel shook his head. "I was abducted yesterday. Someone took my badge. And my gun." He pulled his jacket back to reveal the lack of a weapon. "It's about Cal Covington. The sheriff—"

"Down in Mississippi." Jenkins's voice had attained an interested edge. "What about him?"

"I'm working on a case where his past may prove to be significant. I need some background."

"Did Gottard send you?"

Daniel hesitated. If he said no, Jenkins probably wouldn't talk to him. If he said yes, it would be an outright lie and easily checked. "No. He doesn't know I'm here."

Jenkins's laugh was more of a cackle. "You're a rogue, aren't you, Dubonet? You're working on your own." He laughed again. "I'm glad to see someone at that agency has enough backbone to use his brain. That's what they're producing now—clones. Little dark-suited agents who do everything they're told. They never think. They never put two and two together. They follow the rules.''

"Please, Mr. Jenkins. I've got a cab waiting and I desperately want to change out of this monkey suit."

The door opened suddenly and a blue-veined hand reached out to pull Daniel into the house. "Don't stand on the street and advertise what you're about. Get in here."

Daniel sighed and didn't bother to argue with Jenkins. He felt suddenly that his idea to visit the retired agent was flawed. The old goat would probably complain and moan for twenty minutes and tell him absolutely nothing. Then Jenkins would call up the Bureau as soon as he left and report the incident. Gottard would be furious.

"Quit dragging your feet and get in here," Jenkins ordered. "Now sit and tell me what you want." He pointed to an old, well-worn leather chair. With a groan, he dropped into a chair across from it.

Daniel sat on the edge of his seat. He studied Jenkins's face a moment in the lamplight. The room was dark, paneled, and filled ceiling-to-floor with bookshelves. There must have been a couple of thousand titles neatly arranged on what appeared to be fiction and nonfiction shelves, as best as Daniel could determine.

"Well, are you going to investigate the room or talk?" Jenkins pulled off his thick glasses and cleaned them.

Without the lenses, Jenkins's eyes looked red and runny. Daniel noticed they looked strained, too, as if he'd been up half the night reading.

"It's about Covington. I want to know why you thought he was guilty of..."

"Of what?" Jenkins leaned forward eagerly. "What did I think he was guilty of?"

"There was an alleged connection with the mob. Gambling." Daniel was pulling it out of his memory. "As I recall, there was some concern that Covington was using his

office as sheriff to allow illegal gambling into the Mississippi coast."

"Right. So far." Jenkins was like a big dog teasing a
smaller dog with a bone. "What else?"

"I haven't read the file." Daniel could feel his patience
slipping away. He wasn't there to be interrogated. Who did
Jenkins think he was, anyway?

"Why not? Why did you come here half prepared? That's
my problem with the 'new FBI.'" He spat the last words.
"When I was an agent, we were prepared before we went to
question a suspect."

"Perhaps that's the difference." Daniel's voice had developed a deadly coldness.

"What?"

"You aren't a suspect, Mr. Jenkins. I came here to talk to
you as a fellow agent."

"I see." He cleared his throat. "I see. So, what can I help
you with?"

"Covington?" Daniel watched Jenkins's expression. He
was acting like an old fool, but there was a sharp intelligence in the red-rimmed old eyes.

"Sheriff. Hancock County. I spent better than a year on
the case. Then he was killed in a robbery. No one ever
proved that he stepped in front of the bullet deliberately, but
that was the talk."

"Do you believe it?"

"Hell, yes. The man was guilty, and he knew I was going
to find him out. He couldn't walk out of his house without
seeing me. He couldn't take his daughter for an ice-cream
cone that he didn't know I was on to him. He got the money,
I'm sure of that, but he never had a chance to spend it. He
was never convicted, but he never got to enjoy his ill-gotten
gains."

Satisfaction dripped from Jenkins's voice. Daniel felt a
twinge of anger. What if Covington had been innocent? His

life would have been a real hell. He put that aside and focused on the questions Jenkins needed to answer.

"How much money? Why do you think there was a payoff?"

"I got a tip." Jenkins shrugged. "It's old now, so I don't
suppose I'm exposing my source to any danger."

Daniel forced himself to lean back in the chair. Time was
tick-ticking away, and he was going to have to hear the
whole story, from front to back. He wondered how long the
cabbie would wait—a long time, because he hadn't been
paid.

"My informer was a member of Covington's staff. He
said he was positive beyond a doubt that the sheriff accepted a payoff from a prominent member of the New Orleans mafia. Covington was to look the other way when they
established high-stakes games in some of the beachfront
hotels. There were roulette wheels, craps, blackjack, the
works. Mini-casinos, with a special guest list. And there
were women. Prostitutes trained in New Orleans in some of
the finest houses. But that was just the beginning. They were
looking for a permanent home, not a floating joint."

Daniel found it all a little hard to believe. Gambling was
legal in Mississippi now. And prostitution was a crime that
had never been heavily punished. The Mississippi Gulf
Coast, like New Orleans, seemed more tolerant of human
frailties. Jenkins was making it sound as if Cal Covington
had single-handedly brought the Gulf Coast to moral corruption.

"You don't know how it was back then," Jenkins said,
reading the doubt on the younger agent's face. "The coast
was hammered down. Most of the people didn't want organized crime and that violent element on the water. They
had penny-ante crime, like every place else. It was a quiet
community then. Decent folks who didn't care about a
poker game, but they didn't want the big guys from New
Orleans coming over with their gang-style killings and the

entire corrupt mess. That's what I was involved in—fighting corruption."

"And Cal Covington brought in organized crime?"

Jenkins snorted. "You make me sound like a fool. He didn't bring them in. He just didn't slam the door hard enough." He stood with sudden vigor and paced the room. "Covington was guilty. My source said the payoff was positively delivered."

"How much money?"

"A suitcaseful. He never could find out how much. They knocked him out and locked him in a jail cell while they made the exchange. Then Covington pretended that he'd just arrived. You know the old story. But my man wasn't out cold. He was conscious. And he could see through a crack in the door. He saw the suitcase. He saw the money. And he saw Covington. Then he called the FBI."

"But you could never get the cold evidence?" That point troubled Daniel. "After a year, you never got enough to convict him."

"He never touched that damn money." Jenkins pounded a fist into the open palm of his hand. "How many men could go a year without spending a dime? He never bought his daughter a new bicycle. Never bought his wife a ring. Never bought a car. He hoarded that money, hoping I would give up. But I didn't."

"Why didn't you?" Daniel saw a passion in the old man that was surprising. Talking about the Covington case had rejuvenated him. He acted twenty years younger. "Your source might have been lying."

"He was telling the truth. Covington was the worst of the worst. He was a lawman, and he sold his people out for a suitcaseful of cash. I couldn't prove it, but I was determined not to let him enjoy a penny of it. And he didn't. He might have had the money, but neither he nor his widow have ever been able to spend a dime."

"Or his daughter?"

"Or her. She's a cook. She went to school, but it was on scholarship. Don't think I didn't keep an eye on that. I was called back here, but I never forgot them. I always remembered to look. But I'm old now. They know once I'm gone, no one else will care. That's when the money will come out. You'll see." He sank back into his chair, suddenly tired. "They'll win in the long run."

An awkward silence touched the room. Daniel felt a pity he'd never expected for Joshua Jenkins. He'd devoted his life to a single case, and he'd lost. Time had beat him, at least in his opinion.

"Why are you so certain Cal Covington took that money? Maybe your source was lying."

Jenkins's head snapped up and his brown eyes blazed. "I know he wasn't lying. I know it for a fact."

"Why?" Daniel tried to put a soft touch on the word, to make the question gentler, less aggressive. He could see that Jenkins was on edge about his unnamed friend.

"He was a young man and he worshiped Cal Covington—until he saw him dirty. That's what made me determined to bring Covington to justice. He was a great lawman and he sold out. What Covington did, selling out like that, is the worst any lawman can do. My own father was a sheriff. In Tennessee. Last time I saw him he was in the state penitentiary with the very men he'd arrested. Dad decided that moonshining was more profitable than sheriffing. He deserved what he got."

"I'm sorry." Daniel could see what it had cost Jenkins.

"It was a long time ago. Why are you so interested in ancient Covington history?" Jenkins sat straight in his chair.

"I know Covington's daughter. It was a matter of personal interest."

Jenkins's face hardened. "Don't trust her. I was an agent for a long time, and I found that corruption is often in the blood. It runs in families. That's why I've fought it so hard. My blood was tainted. But I never gave in to it."

Daniel was taken aback by the harshness of Jenkins's tone. The old man believed what he was saying. "I've discovered that often circumstance is the corrupting force."

"Ha! That's what all these mumbo-jumbo psychologists would have you believe. They want to blame society for all the ills of mankind. They want us to think that somehow we're all to blame for the street gangs and the dope smugglers. Ha! It's weakness in those people. They want easy money and they don't care who they hurt to get it. And weakness is bred in the bone, young man. Don't ever forget it, or it could cost you your life."

Daniel sat forward and eased to his feet. "Thank you for talking with me."

"And you'd just as soon that I didn't mention this little visit with Paul Gottard, right?" Jenkins kept staring straight in front of him.

"It wouldn't hurt if we kept this between ourselves."

"Consider it done, then."

"Thank you." Daniel wanted to go, but he hated to leave the old man staring into space. "I have an appointment."

"Close the door after you. It locks itself."

After a moment, Daniel moved to the door and let himself out. The cabbie was smoking a cigarette and staring into traffic. Daniel checked his watch. He was really late now, and he had to have a shower at Cody's.

"Let's go," he said to the cabbie. "Twenty-two West Elm."

"Your wish is my command," the cabbie said sarcastically, throwing the stub of his cigarette onto the manicured lawn. He got behind the wheel and revved the engine. Slowly he turned around. "You said, 22 West Elm?"

"Right." Daniel looked up into the bore of an automatic. His gut clenched.

"I don't think you really want to go there." The cabbie grinned.

"What do you want?"

"You're interfering in some unfinished business. I want you to stop."

Daniel knew he was in big trouble. The cabbie had made no effort to conceal his identity. He was on a public street in a security guarded neighborhood with a weapon that looked as big as a cannon.

"I don't pick my assignments."

"There's a lot at stake here. Leave the woman alone. I don't know how to make this any clearer to you." His grin widened. "But then, maybe I do."

Before Daniel could react, the gun swung through the air and clipped him under the jaw with so much force that his head snapped to the side and into the window frame. Daniel fought against the blackness that swept over him. He knew he was losing consciousness, and he tried to fight. Sarah. Her face was in front of him in all the vulnerability of sleep. But before he was lost to the darkness, he saw her open her eyes, and there was a cold, calculating look on her face.

THE HANDS OF THE CLOCK seemed to hang at ten forty-five. Sarah tested the bucking bronco birthday cake and found it cool enough to ice. The sugary sweet icing had been dyed fantastic colors of red and blue for the cowboy's clothes, and a golden dun for the bucking pony. It was going to be a great cake, but Sarah could take no satisfaction in it. She kept looking from the clock to the telephone. She didn't know Daniel Dubonet very well, but she believed he was a punctual man. Why hadn't he called?

The telephone rang and she nearly dropped the decorating tube she was using to fill in the cowboy's bandanna. She left daubs of icing on the phone as she grabbed it. "Hello?"

"Miss Covington?"

"Yes."

"This is a friend of Daniel Dubonet's. Could you tell us where he is?" The voice was cold and sinister.

"I might. Who is this?" Sarah could feel her heart thumping.

"I work with Mr. Dubonet. He's failed to show up now for almost twenty-four hours. If he's nearby, please put him on the phone." The voice was all cold reason.

"Who is this?" Sarah demanded.

"I'm calling in his best interest."

"Then tell me your name. My father told me never to talk to anyone who wouldn't give a name."

"Look, he's in serious trouble. The agency doesn't like a renegade. Put Dubonet on the phone." The voice was angry now.

"Dream on." Sarah slammed the phone down, and when it rang again, she refused to answer it. Her hands were trembling to the point that she couldn't continue to work on the cake. It would simply be a mess. She cleaned her hands and picked up the phone book. Cody Pruett was listed, and he lived on West Elm. It wasn't that far away. She could drive over there and give Daniel his message.

When she opened the door to leave, Familiar darted between her feet. He gave her a halfhearted meow as he trotted toward the alley and disappeared. "Well, come back when you can stay longer," she called after him. He was one strange cat, but she had other worries now.

She climbed into her car and headed for the West Elm address of the lab tech. If Daniel wasn't there, he might have gone on to his own apartment. With all the damage, the telephone had probably been ripped out. There was a logical reason for his behavior. Just because he hadn't called didn't mean anything bad had happened.

But even as Sarah tried to calm herself, she knew better. Something bad *had* happened. She could feel it, and she'd had plenty of experience in that department. The night her father was killed, she had been a young girl, but she knew before anyone told her. She knew before there was the first reason to suspect anything had gone wrong. It had just been a feeling, like something trapped inside her. Something big and anxious and determined to get out. And that was exactly what she was feeling now.

She sped, hoping that this one time she might attract the attention of a traffic cop. She'd gladly pay a ticket for some backup.

When she turned onto West Elm, she was struck by the old beauty of the neighborhood. The small houses were neatly maintained, several yards filled with the sounds of children playing. She was in a safe place, a place where bad things didn't happen. She tried to believe it, but her foot pressed too hard on the accelerator and she continued to speed down the tree-lined street.

At Cody's address, she parked on the street and got out. There was a red car in the driveway. Cody was home.

Walking up to the front door, she pressed the bell twice. When no one answered the door, she pressed it again, and then again.

"Cody!" She called his name through the curtained glass. "Cody, it's me, Sarah Covington."

There wasn't a sound inside the house.

Sarah twisted the knob and the door opened easily. She stepped inside, taking in the neatness of the modern furniture. There wasn't a magazine out of place. Everything was dusted; it looked as if the maid had just left.

"Cody?"

A faint moan drifted down the hallway.

"Oh, no." Sarah whispered the words as she slid along the wall toward the hallway. "Cody, is that you?" She kept her voice down. What if someone was with him, waiting for her to open a door?

She thought of the telephone, but the moan came again, this time as if the person was in great pain. She hesitated, then moved down the hall to one of the back bedrooms. What if she was making a terrible mistake? What if Cody was with a girlfriend?

"Cody?" She called a bit louder this time.

"Hemmmp!"

The answer came back muffled, but obviously distressed.

"Oh, hell." She threw open the door to an empty bedroom, her heart pounding. The sound came again, accompanied by a pounding noise. She rushed to the next door and threw it open. For a second the sight of Daniel tied hand and foot on the floor didn't register. There was a gag in his mouth, and he was just getting ready to pound the floor with his tied feet again.

"Daniel." She rushed to him and pulled the gag away.

After a few gulps of air, Daniel shifted so that she could loosen the knots on his hands.

"What happened?" Sarah asked. "Where's Cody?"

"Two good questions." As soon as the knots were loosened, Daniel wiggled free. He was up on his feet with a large flashlight in his hand for a weapon. "Wait here," he ordered Sarah.

Sarah decided instantly that staying with Daniel would be the best route. She moved behind him, ignoring the angry glance he sent her.

Together they made their way to the last bedroom. Daniel pushed open the door and then turned to block Sarah's view.

"Don't look," he ordered.

But it was too late. Sarah would never forget the sight of Cody Pruett lying in his bed, blood soaked through the white sheets and puddled on the floor.

Chapter Eight

Sarah sat in the passenger seat of her car and allowed the numbness to take over her body and her mind as Daniel drove her away from Cody's house. She wanted to look at Daniel, but she couldn't. She knew that she was afraid of what she would see. Pain, certainly. But also guilt. Daniel held himself responsible for his friend's death. And there was a good chance Cody Pruett would be alive if he'd never run those tests for Daniel. And for her.

"We should report this," she said for the third time. "We can't pretend this didn't happen and that we weren't there. They'll find evidence. You of all people should know that."

"Maybe. Maybe not." Daniel's eyes were red and nearly squinted shut with tension and fatigue.

"Why won't you report it?"

"Because I don't know who to trust anymore." He looked at her a long moment while they were stopped at a red light. "I don't trust you. I don't trust myself."

Sarah didn't say anything, but she understood exactly what he was saying. She didn't trust him completely, yet the odd chain of events had undoubtedly bound them together.

They were both accessories to a crime—an unreported crime. For all she knew, they could be held accountable after the fact. But Daniel was rocklike in his decision not to call the FBI, or any law agency.

"Cody was one of my best friends," he finally said. Beneath the anger, grief was beginning to seep through. "He's dead because he helped me."

"That's ridiculous, Daniel. He was doing his job."

"That's right. And as soon as I get some clothes, I'm going to check his files and make sure that the tests he ran for me are in there. You heard him say he had to make a formal report and the sheet he gave me was a copy."

"That's right." Sarah hadn't thought about such a possibility. "You think they're gone, that someone tampered with the files?"

"I'd be willing to bet my life on it." Daniel's jaw hardened. "And that means someone inside the Bureau is responsible. That's why I can't call. They'll be looking for a way to pin this on me. If that's what's going on, I'm the target." He looked over at her, his eyes narrowed. "And you."

"Me?" Sarah's fingers clutched her seat belt as he swung wide on a curve. "Why me? I don't know anything about the FBI."

"That's what I keep asking myself. All of this started with you, Sarah. Why do you suppose that is?"

Color rose to her cheeks. "I resent the implications of what you're saying. What can I tell you? The first time I saw you, you were pounding on my door. I didn't call you up and start this."

"But you did call. And then I asked Cody to check those peppers for you."

"Right. Like I knew this would happen." She tried to front her pain with bravado, but her voice trembled.

Daniel blinked, then pulled the car into a side street. He found a place to stop and pulled over. "I'm sorry, Sarah." He reached over and picked up her hand. The fingers were cold and lifeless, and he wrapped his own around them. "I don't know..."

Sarah saw the shimmer in his eyes. She squeezed his fingers. "It's okay. Cody was a friend. I'm sorry, too."

Daniel leaned his head back, his breathing slow and deep. "I can't believe this has happened. I don't know what to do."

"I do." Sarah pressed his hand, feeling the callused palm and the long fingers, the potential for strength. "I have a good friend. He knows what to do in the most unusual circumstances."

"We can't tell anyone about this." Daniel's head was up and his eyes alert.

"Uncle Vince would help us. He has contacts all over the city. All over the world."

Daniel shook his head. "Sarah, this is my career. I left my friend dead and didn't report the crime. I have to think this through. Both of our lives could be at stake."

Sarah recalled the telephone call she'd received earlier. As Daniel drove back to the shop, she told him what had happened.

"You didn't recognize the voice?"

"No."

"You have that party, right?"

"Good grief." Sarah slapped her forehead lightly. She'd completely forgotten.

"I want to go with you." He sighed as he put the car back in the flow of traffic. "I never thought I'd volunteer to be a pony wrangler at a seven-year-old's party, but I guess there's always a first."

"What about the Bureau?"

"I'll take care of that," Daniel assured her. "Can I use the car? I'll be back in time to help you load up for the party."

"Sure." Sarah saw the furrow pull his brow down. He was up to something. Probably something dangerous. She felt a shiver of fear. "Just be careful, okay?"

"You bet."

"Where are you going?"

"To a department store to get some clothes. Then to Cody's lab. I have to check his records before I do anything else. I'll call in to the office, so don't worry."

"I can't make that promise." Sarah opened the car door as he pulled up to the front curb. She glanced over to the shady side of the street. The dark sedan wasn't there. Caution made her check farther down the street. There was no sign of it. She waved Daniel off and was pulling her keys out of her pocket when she heard rapid footsteps approaching.

"Does that black cat belong to you?"

Sarah turned around to face the angry scowl of Sandra Fowler, owner of the Proud Peacock Salon. "What?"

"That scroungy black cat that's been lurking around here. Is he yours?"

"Yes." Sarah didn't know what prompted her to lie.

"Well, keep him inside or I'll have him picked up by the animal people. He's terrifying my customers and he attacked the telephone man." Sandra shook her fist in the air. "Cats are awful creatures. Nasty. Just keep him away from my shop, or he'll find himself at the pound."

Sarah stepped inside her front door and slammed it in Sandra's face. The old witch! She opened the door again. "Listen, Mrs. Fowler, if you want to start trouble, you can. Just remember, your clients block my alley. I've never made a fuss, but I will. I can have their cars towed away." She slammed the door again.

The truth of the matter was that the street was dangerous for the cat, but he seemed to have a mind of his own. As if he'd conjured him up out of thin air, Familiar turned the corner from the alley and stepped up to the door. He put both front paws on the glass, asking to be let in.

Opening the door, Sarah checked down the street. There was no sign of Sandra Fowler or the black car. "Get in here, you little troublemaker. Between you and Daniel..." She stopped. It was true. Ever since she'd met the black cat and the FBI agent, her life had been topsy-turvy.

HANG ON TO YOUR SOCKS, Dolly. You aren't the only one who's been hit by the flat hand of fate. Eleanor is ticked at me for staying out all night, and I've been put on a diet. What cruel and inhuman punishment. She thinks I'm eating out on the street. Little does she know that I've spent a major part of the day performing feats no mere human could accomplish. And I have some brilliant deductions.

Chef André at the White House is one busy, busy man. The black car with the muddy license plate has been hanging around the White House kitchen, and I've seen Chef André step outside for a few words with the driver. I wasn't close enough to hear, but it was not a friendly exchange. Could it be that the master chef is in trouble and Sarah has been set up to pay the price? This is what Socks was so concerned about—that someone was trying to use Sarah. And the First Cat may be on the right track.

I've also been watching the clients who come in and out of the Peacock henhouse. Not a single one of them shows any interest in the spy car that's been parked down the street. That's what it is, too. That man behind the unobtrusive newspaper has been spying on Sarah. But who does he work for? I might have found out if that old harridan hadn't come at me again. She's been after me for several days now. First it was water, and then earlier today she got after me with a broom. Can you imagine? I was thinking she might hop on it and ride around.

There's been some strange activity in the alley. I may not be able to win the College Bowl in trigonometry, but I can count. There have been two meter readers back in the alley in the last two days. Not to mention the phony phone man working after five o'clock. Give me a break! Those guys work late—after a storm or during an emergency. They're great then, but this guy was just hanging around on the pole doodling with the hookups. I'll have to figure it out. I can't expect too much help from the humanoids. Not even the FBI agent. E.A. Poe would be quite put out by the lack of reasoning abilities in the modern branch of law enforcement.

Ah, that's why Socks hired me. Agent 009, the feline with a strange and brilliant mind.

"YOU LOOK MIGHTY self-satisfied." Sarah picked up the cat and hurried into the kitchen. "I have to finish this cake, the cupcakes, and about a million other things. Now you can have a little snack and help me."

Familiar gave her a purr and put his paw on her chest. "Meow."

"Good. I like a cooperative cat."

Sarah set to work, keeping one eye on the clock. She had to stop by the party store for a few extras, but she'd make it in plenty of time. Along with the cake and homemade peach ice cream, made, of course, from only the finest of Georgia's peach crop, she'd decided to serve peach fizz punch and a series of crunchy snacks. The little urchins would be on a sugar high so intense by the time they got home—

She heard the bell to her shop ring, and she was ready to pick up the broom, just in case Sarah Fowler had decided to strut back over and fan her tail, when she recognized her uncle's special knock.

"Sarah!" Vincent Minton's voice held surprise. "Do you always arm yourself with a broom when a customer comes inside?"

Sarah couldn't prevent the chuckle that rose to her lips. Just seeing Uncle Vince made her feel much, much better. "No. I thought that old witch from the beauty salon next door was coming to complain about my cat." The events of the morning seemed to rise up in her throat, and more than anything she wanted to tell him about them. But she couldn't. "How about some coffee?"

"No, thanks." Vincent's eyes finally settled on the sleek black tom. "An elegant creature, to be sure. Should he be in the kitchen where you're preparing food?"

"He doesn't eat cake and icing, Uncle Vince." Relieved to have her thoughts focused on something other than the horror of the morning, Sarah almost laughed at the expression on his face. He was clearly not a cat lover. In fact, she'd never known him to have a pet of any kind. And just as well with Jean-Claude in the house. He would probably have tormented an animal to distraction.

"Cats are happier out of doors." He looked at the back door.

"Not in Washington, D.C., where the chances of surviving the traffic are about one in a hundred."

"That's a point." He took a seat on the opposite side of the table. As if to prove a point, Familiar jumped up into the chair across from him. The cat began to thoroughly clean himself, extending one back leg in a long line.

"He is cute," Vincent said with some hesitation. "I think it's a good thing you have a companion."

"Well, he's sort of a come-and-go type of buddy. He shows up when he's hungry, and he takes off when he's ready to go. I'm not sure he doesn't belong to someone else."

"Take a picture and post it," Vincent suggested. "If he lives around here, the owner will claim him. He looks well cared for."

"I might." Sarah was reluctant to pursue the topic. If she did find his rightful owner, she'd have to give him up.

"So, where have you been this morning?" He eased his elbows on the table and relaxed as she picked up the icing tube and proceeded to finish the cake.

"I ran an errand with Daniel." She found that her voice was higher when she lied—or didn't tell the complete truth. But she'd promised Daniel she wouldn't say anything about the day's events. When she looked up, Vincent was watching her closely.

"Is something wrong, Sarah? I thought that agent was going to leave you alone." She saw the set of his jaw and knew he was angry.

"It's okay. He left something here, and when he came to get it... well, it's a long story. But he didn't bother me."

"He should not speak with you." His hands clenched on the table. "No one can understand what you and Mora went through. No one except me, because I was there to watch it. A loving family was destroyed by the FBI. This young man is not good for you, Sarah. Stay away from him."

Sarah slowly put the icing tube down. "I've never seen you so adamant about who I see or don't see. Is there something you haven't told me?" She could feel her heartbeat increase with anticipation.

"Did he tell you he was visiting Joshua Jenkins earlier this morning?" He nodded. "No, I can tell by your expression that he did not. He is not a truthful man, and someone is going to be hurt by his lies and deceptions. I don't want it to be you."

"Someone already has." Sarah sank into the chair beside Familiar.

"What are you saying?"

She looked across at the tall man who had always shown her such kindness. More than anything, she wanted to tell him what had happened, to ask his advice on what she should do. She could. Daniel would never know. And if what Uncle Vince said was true, she didn't owe Daniel any allegiance whatsoever.

"Sarah, who has been hurt?" Vincent leaned across the table and took her hand.

"It's, uh, no one." No matter how much she wanted to, she could not break her word. As soon as she saw Daniel again she would confront him with what she'd learned and then let him know that she was calling the police. Better late than never.

"Sarah, what in the world is wrong with you, *chérie*? You're very pale. Your hands are trembling."

"I, uh, need some breakfast, I think." She hurried to the refrigerator and got out a slice of homemade raisin bread. "Would you like some raisin toast?"

"No, I must be going. I just wanted to stop and make sure you were okay." He got up and walked over to her. "You are not. I'm going to insist that you take a vacation."

"I can't. I have too much work—"

"The party this afternoon. When it's over, I'll send one of the men to get you. Since you won't come to New York with me at noon, then you can stay at the Idlewild house for a couple of days. It'll give you a chance to rest." He looked over at the cat. "And bring your friend, if you must. I know that's going to be your next excuse."

Sarah put her arms around Vincent's neck. "Thank you," she whispered. "I think getting away for a few days will be the very best thing in the world for me. But don't send any of your employees. I'll drive myself. I prefer to have my car."

"Excellent. You work too hard, *chérie*," he said, kissing the top of her head. "I have never regretted helping you because you work so hard to make things happen." A frown touched his face, "Jean-Claude takes so much for granted. But you take nothing. You push and work and struggle. You will succeed. You could be a good influence on my son."

Sarah hugged him. "I don't think so. Jean-Claude will mature. He's just slower than I was. He had the luxury of taking it slowly."

Vincent gave her another squeeze. "And you're such a little diplomat, too. You will have the biggest catering business in D.C. Now, I'm off. If you speak with Mora, give her my love."

"I will," Sarah promised as she waved him through the front door. When she returned to the kitchen, she buttered her toast and finished the cake and cupcakes. Thirty minutes later, just as Daniel pulled up to the alley, she had everything ready.

"Thanks for the use of the car," Daniel said as he stepped in through the back door.

Sarah saw that he was wearing casual slacks and a pullover. "Where's the suit?" She'd decided to give him a chance to tell her about Jenkins.

"I'm officially suspended." He shrugged, but it didn't hide his worry. "I called in and Gottard said I was suspended for not reporting back from duty."

"Did you tell them you'd been kidnapped?"

Daniel shook his head. "I'm not sure how that fits into the puzzle, Sarah. I'm afraid to tell anyone anything."

"Are you afraid to tell me you've been talking to Joshua Jenkins?" She looked up at him, blue eyes sparking with an anger that was upon her suddenly.

"I didn't see any point in telling you that." Daniel knew she was enraged.

"Well, I don't see any point in lying for you anymore. I just wanted to tell you to your face. I'm calling the police and reporting Cody's death. I'm going to tell them everything."

"Sarah—"

"It won't do any good to try and talk me out of it. I hate liars, Daniel, and a lie of omission is just as damning as an outright lie in my book."

"I didn't tell you because I knew it would upset you."

"Great." She tossed a dish towel into the sink. "You lied to me to protect me from my own emotions. That's a good one. Isn't that sort of like the bank robber who took the money so the tellers wouldn't be tempted?"

"Sarah, it isn't like that. I asked Jenkins about your father."

"And that's the one area I asked you not to meddle in."
Sarah picked up the cake and strode past him to the car.
With great care, she placed it on the backseat. "I'm going
to the party, Daniel. Alone. I'm going to report this mess,
even if I have to take the coward's way out and report it an-
onymously."

"If you do this, there's a chance I could get in serious
trouble."

"Maybe you need to get in serious trouble. My uncle said
that you were a renegade, a troublemaker who broke the
rules to suit his own purposes. I didn't want to believe that."
Sarah felt the tears building. "So I ignored him. Now I'm
partially responsible for a man's death. *That's* what I get for
not listening to my uncle." She pushed past him and went
back into the kitchen, bringing out the trays of cupcakes.

"What uncle?" Daniel let the question slip before he
thought of the consequences.

"Oh, right. You know my background. I don't have any
blood uncles. But I do have an adopted one." She was even
angrier than before.

"Who is this man?"

"None of your damn business, Daniel. Now you'd better stay out of my way." Three trips later she had everything loaded. Daniel stood helplessly and watched. She
wouldn't allow him to assist her.

"Sarah, if you'll let me explain, I know I can make you
understand. I wasn't doing anything wrong."

"Maybe not in your books, but in mine you're nothing
but a convenient liar. Stay out of my life, Daniel. Every
shred of trust I had for you is gone." She finally looked at
him, taking in the handsome face and the big shoulders. She
had begun to develop feelings for him. Now she was going
to pay the price for allowing anyone inside her private
world. When would she learn that bitter lesson—she
couldn't be hurt if she didn't let anyone in.

"I'll call you this evening."

"You can call until the cows come home, Daniel. I won't be here to answer it."

"Where are you going?"

Sarah picked up the cat and put him in the car, along with a bag she'd packed earlier. "That's none of your business. I'm telling you, though, tonight I'm going to call the police. That will give you six or seven hours to do whatever you have to do."

Frustration, anger, and concern for Sarah were all mixed together as Daniel watched her drive away. Lucky for him he'd had his flats repaired and the car delivered to Sarah's shop. He waited until she'd turned left out of the alley, and then he ran for his car and followed her.

She might be mad at him now, but he was a trained agent. He could follow her without getting caught.

Two hours later he was hiding in a hedge on the lush lawn of the U.S. senator from Georgia. The party was a smashing success, and the bronco birthday cake had just been cut. Daniel toted up the cost of the party—at least a couple of grand, what with the trained ponies fitted out in silver saddles and the actors dressed as cowboys and cowgirls who were playing with the seven-year-olds.

There had been a staged gunfight and a roping exhibit. Not to mention the cowboy with the guitar who sang a few cowpoke songs and then "Happy Birthday." The entire extravagant affair had been wonderfully coordinated, and Sarah had taken care of all the food. Now the kids were stuffing their faces with ice cream, cake and a million other goodies.

Shrill laughter rang out as the children ate and played, but Daniel's gaze was focused on Sarah. She was packing up her things and putting them in the car. And that black cat was sitting on the passenger seat as if he knew what was happening.

After a few brief words with several of the grown-ups, Sarah got into her car. She was finished. Daniel made a dash for his car, pulling around to the service entrance so that he could wait for Sarah to come around. In less than a minute, she did, and he pulled into traffic after her, aware that she was headed due east, away from the city. And she was in a hurry.

When the dark sedan pulled in after her, Daniel didn't realize at first that the car was following Sarah. It was only after several turns that he knew she'd picked up an additional tail. He eased up as close as he dared to the car, feeling a sudden thud of acknowledgment as he realized it was the same car he'd seen parked on her street. He'd recognize the mud-covered car tag anywhere.

Chapter Nine

"What's wrong with you?" Sarah asked the black cat as they pulled into the shadow of Vincent Minton's beach house. It was a beautiful building, constructed of natural wood and glass, built on pilings against the chance of floods. In the rear of the house, stairs led to a wraparound porch, and the front of the house faced Chesapeake Bay with a view that increased the value of the property ten times over. Uncle Vince had inherited the house from his grandfather, who'd received the property from his own grandfather. Through the years, it had been improved and modernized, but it had never lost the rustic appeal that Sarah loved. She stared up at the darkened house, ignoring the cat as he continued to look out the rear window of the car, giving an occasional low growl.

"This isn't exactly the city, I know, but I think you can adjust to a little peace and quiet for a night or two. It'll do you good." Sarah stroked the cat's head. "It might even make you realize that you enjoy living with me. You might want to stay around a little more than you do."

"Meow." Familiar rubbed hard against her hand, then hopped to the ground and started up the stairs.

"Eager little rascal, aren't you?" Sarah was relieved to see the cat so adaptable. She'd had some concern about bringing him, but she couldn't leave him in the city with no one to look out for him. And to be honest, she wanted his company. She'd been so busy all afternoon that she kept Daniel's betrayal tamped down. Now, though, she was going to have to call in and report what she knew about Cody Pruett's death. And no matter how hard she tried, she hadn't been able to avoid thinking about that.

Strange, though, the more she thought about it, the more she realized she didn't know a lot. She wasn't even certain how Cody had died. Daniel had checked the body, but he'd forced her from the room before she'd seen any wound or indication of how Cody had met his death. When she called, what was she going to tell the police? The truth was, she wasn't even certain the lab tech was dead. She'd taken Daniel's word for it—and she'd discovered exactly how good Daniel's word was.

''Meow!''

Familiar was at the top of the stairs demanding entry into the house. He shifted from the door to a lookout position back down the long, winding drive. Normally Sarah loved the solitude that several heavily wooded acres gave the house, but this time she couldn't help the slight shiver that passed through her. It was a long driveway, and the trees and undergrowth had been left thick and unkempt. For privacy.

Sarah pulled the key from her purse and opened the door, tossing her overnight bag in behind Familiar. Just to be on the safe side, she scanned the driveway, then walked around the deck to check the boat dock. The motorboat that Uncle Vince used to explore the bay was hanging from the lift in the boathouse and there was no other boat in sight. She was completely alone.

So this is Unc's pad on the bay. Nice digs. Very private, very solitary, very expensive. I just wonder if the car that's been following us is one of Unc's hired protectors, the hard-headed Agent Dubonet, or the black sedan from the beauty salon. All I can say is that I'm glad Eleanor and Peter left this morning for a three-day trip to New York. They assumed, wrongly of course, that I would remain in the house. Magdelene, that dear, kindly woman, is supposed to look in on me. I hope I don't worry her too much, but I don't see how I can make it home tonight. All in all, it's been a rather hectic day.

I enjoyed the party. All those young bipeds shrieking and stumbling after the ponies. I'm telling you, those ponies deserve a tolerance award. Young humans have to be taught that animals feel pain, and let me tell you, some of those youngsters were pulling tails and poking those ponies. I'm afraid it would have been "To the moon, Alice" for a few of them if I had been a pony.

The only person of any real interest was Lucinda Watts. She must be in her fifties now, but she's a looker. Ever since I've lived in Washington, I've heard her name bandied about by those who want to appear to be part of the inner circle. Lucinda's parties are legendary, as is her past. Even Eleanor knows the gossip that Lucinda was once a stripper on the Gulf Coast and that she's closely linked with a former vice president. As in, romantically linked. Well, whatever exercise she does to keep her figure, it works. She looked great.

Now, let's explore this joint. Master bedroom and bath upstairs. Guest bedroom and bath, upstairs. Kitchen and den, complete with a cozy fireplace, downstairs. Sensible and easy. I like this. But what are we going to do for two days? We have a mystery to solve back in Washington. Maybe I can convince Dolly to pack up early. I'm not exactly the kind of cat to lounge around and watch television all evening. I need to be where the action is.

Uncle Vince's taste in magazines is interesting. Here's one on architecture, another on medical advances, one on interior design, and one on history. And, what's this? A family photo album. It might be interesting to see this Jean-Claude. Every time Unc mentions his name, Sarah cringes. He must

*have been a real pain in the old butt when they were grow-
ing up.*

*Here's Unc, with his arm around a handsome woman.
She looks French or Italian with that nose. Dark hair, dark
eyes, very striking woman. I wonder... I never hear any
reference to Auntie Minton. We know there was one, à la
Jean-Claude. But what happened to her? Divorce or death?
That's an interesting question.*

*Now here's the little tyke. A very handsome young boy.
The clothes are a little too much. He looks like a store window mannequin, but that's not enough to make Sarah dislike him. But there is something about the smile. Sort of
thin-lipped, if I do say so myself. Maybe I'm just looking
for a reason to dislike him, since Dolly is so against him.*

*Now who is this? A very tall man with... yes, that's a gun
on his hip. And I think the edge of a badge hidden by a little girl's head. Yep, it's Dolly, and that must be her father,
Cal Covington. I like the way he's holding her on his lap,
sort of looking at the top of her head and not at the cam-
era. And there's the mother, next page. Mora. She looks like
Marilyn Monroe. Now I know where Dolly gets her looks.
What a classic face! And that blond hair done up like Tippi
Hedron in* The Birds. *Very chic. She doesn't look so unhappy here. She's actually smiling. Life can certainly throw
a few hard curves.*

*Now here's Unc and Daddy. They're both tall, but Dad's
a little taller. They look like they've shared a lot together.
There's a warm friendship there. Oops, here comes Dolly.
Maybe I should put this away. Or maybe it would be more
interesting to see what she does.*

"OH, FAMILIAR." Sarah reached for the album and drew it
over to her lap. She stroked the cat. "That's my family." She
stared at the page, and then traced the outline of her father's face. "He was a good man, Familiar. He didn't do
anything wrong. No matter what anyone says."

The sound of footsteps on the stairs made Sarah slam the album shut. No one was expected. No one knew she was at Idlewild.

A key slid in the lock, and the door swung open. Sarah felt her stomach drop.

"Hello, Sarah." The tall man's dark eyes took in her unhappy expression. "I hate to intrude on your solitude, but Father made me promise that I'd check on you."

"Jean-Claude." Sarah stood. "It's been a long time."

"And I get the feeling you'd prefer that it was even longer." He waved away her denials. "I was horrible to you when we were youngsters. I know there's no way to make you believe I've grown up, except to show you. And I have grown up." He noticed the cat. "I didn't realize you'd brought a pet with you. I hope it doesn't have any fleas."

"Sorry." Sarah couldn't even make it sound convincing. "Uncle Vince said I could bring the cat." She took in the sight of her adoptive cousin. He was tall, a little too thin, but muscular, like a runner. With his dark hair and eyes and skin, handsome didn't begin to do him justice. But he also seemed ill-at-ease. He kept looking around the room as if he expected to see someone else.

"Yes, he could never deny you anything, could he?" Jean-Claude's dark eyes were impossible to read. "So, what were you planning for the evening? Perhaps we could go to dinner. There are some wonderful places nearby, and I know you must be sick and tired of cooking."

"Not really." Sarah saw her hopes to call the authorities slipping away. She couldn't possibly make the call with Jean-Claude there.

"Father tells me you've become quite the success. How did your party go? Was Lucinda there?"

"Yes, but I hardly had a chance to notice. She's been at the last several functions I've catered." Sarah had never thought about it, but Lucinda Watts had been present at all of the entertainments. In contrast to her reputation as a party girl, Lucinda had been quiet, reserved, and conservatively dressed. A big change from her youthful days when she'd been the hottest attraction along the Gulf Coast strip. She'd known Sarah's father—a friendship of sorts. Sarah had sometimes suspected that Lucinda was throwing some chef business her way.

"Lucinda is a fascinating woman," Jean-Claude said as he took a seat in a chair across the coffee table from Familiar. "It wasn't that long ago she was jumping out of birthday cakes at parties. Now she's one of *the* most significant hostesses in the city, or so Father says."

"Yes, so I've heard." Sarah found it difficult to talk with Jean-Claude. There was an edge to his voice at any mention of his father. Almost an anger.

"Father wanted to tell you, but..." His smile was genuine as he handed her a slip of paper from his inner coat pocket. "She's going to hire you for a big bash next week. She asked me to give you these instructions and dates." He handed her a slip of paper from his inner coat pocket.

"Did your father put this together?" Sarah was delighted.

Jean-Claude tensed. "Lucinda was enthralled with the cake and ice cream. So perfect for the senator. Subtle yet eclectic. I believe those were her words." Jean-Claude's accent was more foreign than his father's, a reflection of his recent years in Paris.

"I'm glad I impressed her." Sarah felt as if she were talking to a stranger. Not once had Jean-Claude mentioned his work or his interests or himself.

"Sarah, in all of the years we've known each other, our families have teased us, saying we would marry."

Sarah was at a loss. "I'm sure you find that as uncomfortable as I do."

Jean-Claude lifted his eyebrows. "To be honest, I don't. We have a common background. If Mother had lived, she would have viewed you as a daughter."

"But..."

"But what?" He leaned closer. There was a measure of desperation in his face.

"Just because our families know each other doesn't make this a match made in heaven." Jean-Claude was making her very uncomfortable. Paris had not smoothed the rough edges of his behavior.

"Your mother would be very relieved. She's worried about you. About your future, about the fact that you seem to prefer to live alone."

"And how do you know these things?" This time Sarah was definitely interested. She couldn't believe Mora was spilling her guts to Jean-Claude.

"Our parents are close, *chérie.*"

The endearment that sounded so natural on Uncle Vince's lips was much more intimate coming from Jean-Claude. Sarah inched closer to Familiar, who obligingly sprawled across her lap.

"Jean-Claude, you've been living in Paris and have traveled around the world. Surely you've met women you've felt some true affection for. You don't really know me. You just have a tiny shard of memory of a little girl."

He shrugged, a gesture as foreign as his accent. "One thing I've learned in my travels is that affection grows between two people who share the same goals. Besides, we have the past, *chérie.* And the future is treacherous." He must have realized how intense he had become, because he smiled and he leaned back. "As you say, I've been away. For most of my life I've been at boarding school or in Europe. Since I've come home, I've learned many things, especially about my father's business. You have no one to guide you since your father is dead." His expression was unreadable. "I would protect you."

"Do you remember my father? Do you remember how he spanked you for biting me?" Sarah felt the need to goad

Jean-Claude. His talk about marriage was positively givin
her the creeps.

"I remember Cal. He was a wonderful father. An hon
orable man who was destroyed by forces outside his con
trol." He sighed. "Let me get us some wine. I see by th
tears in your eyes that I have finally touched you. We hav
much together, even though it was long ago."

He disappeared into the kitchen, and Sarah got a grip o
her emotions. Jean-Claude had grown up. He seemed t
have developed a sense of himself and others that he'
lacked as a young boy. But there was something else goin,
on with him, too. Something she didn't understand at all.

Jean-Claude returned with two glasses of red wine. H
offered her one. "Your father's death was an unnecessar
tragedy. One I don't want to see repeated."

"What?" Sarah almost spilled her wine.

"Uncle Cal was not a fool, nor was he a careless man.
believe someone killed him."

"Jean-Claude." Sarah felt the blood rush to her face a
hearing her own worst fears spoken aloud. "This isn'
something I want to discuss. You were away at school i
New Orleans when this happened. We were both just chil
dren. You have no idea about the facts, and I'm not certai
I do, either. A lot of things were kept from me, to protec
me. I still haven't learned the truth. Mother isn't one to tal
about the past, you know."

"But if someone thought your father knew something, c
that he had something, they might have killed him and mad
it look like he was shot during a robbery. That way, no on
would ever think to look for the guilty party. Don't you see
It's perfect."

His reasoning was well ordered, but Sarah pushed it a
away. She didn't want to discuss it with him. More tha
anything, she needed time to think.

"I can see I've upset you." Jean-Claude put his wine
glass down. "I become too intense. Even as a child—" h

aughed with a light note of self-deprecation "—I was too ntense. But you know that, *chérie*." He walked around be-ind her and put his hands on her shoulders. "I will ask only ne thing."

"What is that?" She felt her back stiffen and couldn't top it.

"That you think about what I've said. All of it. I am oncerned for you, for reasons I cannot explain." His grip ightened. "And remember, for all of my shortcomings, I m my father's son."

Sarah nodded. "I will think about everything you've aid."

"Perhaps it would be better if we postponed our din-er."

"I think that *would* be best."

Familiar, who'd been relaxed in Sarah's lap, lifted a paw nd slapped Jean-Claude's hand with just enough claw that . startled him.

He withdrew his hand and examined the four tiny pin-ricks of blood. "I don't believe your cat cares for me. 'erhaps he's jealous."

Sarah eased the cat to the sofa and stood, effectively lipping out from under Jean-Claude's remaining hand. Perhaps he is."

"I'm going back to the city. If you pursue the matter of e past, I'd like to help you."

"I don't know. I have to think about it. There's Mother,)o."

"Yes, it would reopen wounds."

"Why are you suddenly so interested, Jean-Claude?" She ced him fully. "After all of these years, why now?"

"I have heard Father speak of you recently. I never lis-ned to a lot of things. Today I saw you at Senator Banks's arty. I knew I wanted to take care of you."

Sarah flushed, and she found no words to ease the ten-on that grew between them.

"I'll call you later and make a formal date. By the way, Father said that agent who was annoying you is in serious trouble. There's been a murder, another agent. They suspect Mr. Dubonet is involved."

"What did you hear?" Sarah knew she was too eager, and she saw Jean-Claude's surprise.

"Only that. Father probably knows more if you'd like to call him in New York."

"No." Sarah couldn't do that. Besides, she probably knew more than anyone, except Daniel and the murderer.

"Beware of that man. He's trouble. If he bothers you at all, call me or Father."

"Of course."

Familiar sat perched on the arm of the sofa as Sarah followed Jean-Claude to the door and locked it behind him. She turned back to face the cat, her face pale. "What can happen next?" she asked Familiar.

The knock at the door came so close to where she was standing that Sarah jumped forward, stifling a scream.

"Sarah? Are you okay?" Daniel's voice filtered through the heavy door.

"What are you doing here?" Sarah felt an odd mixture of relief and anger.

"We have to talk. Someone was following you from the senator's today."

"I know." Sarah put her hand on the door. She had a choice: she didn't have to let him in. "He was a friend of mine."

"He? He, who?"

"It's really none of your business, Daniel." Sarah's patient tone was laced with sarcasm. "It was someone who's interested in my well-being and safety. And they warned me to stay away from *you*."

"I have to talk to you."

"We are talking, Daniel, but not for long. You need to leave here. There's nothing we have to say to each other."

"Listen, Sarah, I'm in big trouble. They think I might have been involved in killing Cody."

She heard the worry in his voice, a worry she couldn't allow herself to believe. "I don't trust you, Daniel. Every time I let you into my life something awful happens."

"Sarah, please. I came all of this way to tell you something."

She looked at Familiar, shaking her head. Sighing, she unlocked the door. She didn't trust Daniel, but she wasn't afraid of him. "What?"

"I got into Cody's files. There was no record of the tests he did on the pepper. Someone had cleaned everything out. It's as if he never ran the tests."

She motioned him inside and closed the door. Logically, she had to understand that Daniel himself could have removed all the files. He had the opportunity.

"What about your apartment? Did they find any fingerprints?"

Daniel tugged at his eyebrow. "There was never a request to check. Cody never got around to filing it, or..." He looked at the two wineglasses sitting on the coffee table, both still full. "Or someone intercepted it."

"Someone in the Bureau?"

"Yes." His shoulders sagged. "I honestly don't know what to do. Cody was the one person I could trust. And I've checked on Glen Henderson. No one by that name ever attended the academy. That's a dead end."

Sarah stamped down hard on the sympathy she felt for Daniel. He looked so beaten—but he was the one who had dragged through her past with Joshua Jenkins. Maybe he was just getting what he deserved. "What are you going to do?"

He took a step toward her. "You're not going to like this, but whatever is going on involves your past."

"You can just take this line of bull and get out." Sarah pointed at the door. "Why is it that everyone is suddenly so interested in my past? No one wanted to probe into my father's death when he died. Now it seems everyone and their brother is interested in Daddy. Well, it's just another attempt by the FBI to ruin a good man's name. Get out!''

"Sarah—"

"Get out or I'll scream."

Daniel's grin was a mere ghost that flickered across his face. "To point out the obvious, no one would hear you."

"Daniel..." She felt her breath grow short. Was he threatening her?

"Don't scream, and don't call the police. I'm sure by now every law enforcement agency in the world is looking for me. I'll leave, but at least let me check the house and make sure it's secure. I wasn't lying about someone following you."

"I know that. As I said, it was a friend." Daniel's interest in her visitor went beyond concern for her safety. She looked down at her hands, unable to meet his questioning gaze. Why should it matter to her that he was jealous? But it did. Even at the thought, her heart beat faster. Daniel Dubonet was a man in whom she could have developed a real interest. Except that he was a liar and God knew what else.

Daniel saw that she wasn't going to give him any more information. He started at the windows, checking the locks. As he worked his way around the room, Familiar darted between his legs. "Hey." He looked down at the black cat who had swiftly untied his shoelaces. "What gives with the kitty?"

"Familiar is a peculiar cat." Sarah tugged at a strand of her hair. "It's as if he can understand everything I say to him. And the worst part is, I think he may be smarter than I am."

At Sarah's friendlier tone, Daniel felt a rush of gratitude to the cat. Bending over, he picked him up and carried him to the sofa. "Now I have to retie my shoes." As he sat down,

Familiar pushed the family album toward him. With a quick flick of a black cat paw, he revealed the page with the picture of Jean-Claude as a young boy. There were several snapshots, including one of Jean-Claude and Sarah playing together in a sandbox. Familiar slapped Jean-Claude's face with a soft paw.

"Meow."

"Meow, what?" Daniel pulled the book closer. The black paw came down on the young boy's face again.

"Who is this, Sarah? Familiar has an intense interest in him."

"That's my uncle Vince's son, Jean-Claude."

Daniel looked up, startled. "Your cousin?"

Sarah dropped her hair. "No, not really." But it *was* almost as if they were blood relatives. She felt awkward even thinking about Jean-Claude and his recent romantic interest in her. "Uncle Vince is my adopted uncle. There's no blood kinship, just a lot of affection."

"Meow!" Familiar slapped the picture and then ran to the front door.

Daniel didn't believe what he was seeing. "Was Jean-Claude the guy who was here?" He motioned to the wine-glasses.

"How did…?" Sarah looked at Familiar. "You little rat fink!"

"Meow!" Familiar's voice was indignant.

"Thanks." Daniel gave Familiar a long, approving look. "That's one hell of a cat."

"I should have known that you guys would stick together. I can't believe he—"

"Ratted on you?" Daniel laughed.

Familiar leapt across the room and swatted Daniel on the shin as if to say enough.

"Well, at least Familiar is on my side," Daniel gloated.

"And what side is that?" Sarah asked coldly.

"The side of truth, justice and the American way." Daniel's face grew serious. "And I'm hoping it's the side that will prove to you that I'm a good person, Sarah, because it's becoming more and more important to me that you believe that."

THERE THEY GO AGAIN, using animals as verbs—ratted. What a crude and ugly term. In my days of wandering the alleys of Washington, rodents gave me some of my better moments. They may be sneaky and steal food, but I've never known one to turn—forgive me, birdies—stool pigeon. Ah, well, that only goes to show what poor observers of animal nature human beings are. See, I've often discovered that people will inform on each other. How would it sound to say "You humaned on me"? Much, much more logical.

At any rate, Daniel and Sarah have acknowledged that little spark between them. That's a step in the right direction. I'm not certain that I have a true reading on Jean-Claude. He's very sophisticated, and I do believe that humans can grow up and change for the better. I've seen it happen.

That isn't my primary concern at the moment. Dolly and Bureau Boy may believe the coast is clear now, but I don't think so. It wasn't Jean-Claude who was following us. I'd be willing to stake one of my lives on it. He knows the way here. He didn't have to follow anyone. And if it wasn't him, it had to be someone else. And it wasn't Daniel, because even though he was tailing us, he saw someone else.

My kitty instincts tell me there's going to be some trouble tonight. If I have to figure out a way to trick Daniel, he's going to stay around. Dolly is pretty self-sufficient, but tonight she's going to need the brawn of a man and the brain of a cat.

Chapter Ten

"That sounds very noble, but I'm not buying into it. I think it would be best if you left." Sarah couldn't allow herself to believe what Daniel was saying. He'd tricked her before, had drawn her into something that could well cost her the career she'd worked so hard to establish. She didn't believe that Daniel was involved in killing anyone, much less Cody, but that still didn't make him an honorable man. And both honor and honesty were her basic requirements.

"I'll leave the house, but I'm staying outside in the car. I'm concerned for you, Sarah."

"I'm perfectly safe here. No one knows where I am. Besides, today went perfectly fine. There were no problems. You think this relates back to my past. Well, I've got a news flash for you. I think this is all something to do with you and your past. You're the one with make-believe agents coming back from training. You're the one who was abducted at gunpoint by a cabbie. You're the one whose apartment was destroyed and whose reports have gone missing. Not me. I'm only involved on the periphery of this, and I didn't have a trouble in the world until you showed up at my door at midnight."

Daniel nodded. "You're right in most of what you say. But I was at your place because three people got sick. And you called me back because of the pepper, remember?"

Sarah did. She couldn't deny those facts. As much as she wanted to blame Daniel, it seemed as if their fates had been thrown together by some outside force. She was definitely caught up in something beyond her control. Maybe he was, too.

She glanced at him and caught the hungry look in his eyes. Her body tensed in anticipation of both pleasure and pain. She'd never trusted herself to care about anyone. Not care in the sense that she was willing to give more than a small measure of herself. Until now. Daniel wasn't the best candidate for the position in her heart, but he was the one her heart had chosen. She hadn't wanted to admit that fact, not even to herself. But as she looked at him, she knew it was true.

"I did call you back," she admitted in a softer voice.

"You did that because you thought you could trust me."

She couldn't help a slight smile. "I did it to pay you back for coming to my house at midnight."

"And because you thought I would test those peppers. And I did. I didn't believe you completely, that's true. But I gave you the benefit of the doubt and asked Cody to run the tests."

Sarah scooped Familiar into her arms. "Why did you do that? You could have refused."

"I probably should have refused. I didn't know at the time why I did it, but I think I know now." He walked to her and gently reached out to stroke Familiar's head. "Sometimes your heart is smarter than your brain. When you saw this cat, you risked taking him into your home. You risked caring and losing because your heart made the decision. I think when I saw you, my heart made a decision, too. It recognized that you were the person I could become deeply involved with, and though my brain tried to throw up all the roadblocks of training and caution, my heart won out." His hand moved from the cat up to Sarah's chin. He lifted her face with the utmost gentleness until she was staring up at him.

"I don't know you well enough to say that I love you, but I believe that, given time, I will. If you give me the chance, I'll love you like you've never been loved before. And I believe you'll love me."

Sarah knew that a wise woman would back away from this. Here was a man employed by an agency she had every reason to despise. He'd lied to her, by omission. He was in danger of being labeled a murderer. Everywhere he went, troubled followed. Yet the touch of his hand on her face was the most reassuring thing she'd felt in years.

"I can't handle this now." She spoke the only defense she had left. Very slowly, she stepped away.

Daniel's hand lowered to his side. "You don't have to. All I'm asking is that you let me stay. Close enough to look out for you, but not close enough to crowd you. I've made a choice, Sarah. I've given up my career." He lifted his eyebrows. "Not exactly my choice. Circumstances played a big part in it. When I drove out here to follow you, I knew that I was making a decision that would cost me my job."

"You shouldn't have done that! I'm perfectly fine here." Sarah felt a moment's panic. She couldn't be responsible for this, not for Daniel's loss of career. It wasn't fair that he was going to try to pin that on her. Not with everything else.

Daniel smiled. "You might be part of the reason, but I made the decision. It was the decision I *wanted* to make. I guess you could say I've lost my confidence in the Bureau." His smile was bitter, and he held a finger to his lips to hush her protests so that he could continue. "That's wildly understated. It would be fair to say I think someone in the FBI is actively trying to injure me, defame me, and possibly kill me."

"Why?" Sarah knew he wasn't kidding.

"That's a good question. One we'll solve together, if you allow me to."

"This isn't up to me."

"Whether we work together is completely up to you. I have to resolve this. My good name is at stake. If I'm ever going to have a future in law enforcement, even outside the Bureau, I'm going to have to figure out what happened to Cody. I believe, and I think you do, too, that we're tied together. I don't know how or why, but we are linked."

Sarah nodded. What he was saying made sense. His honest assessment of his emotions had frightened her, but he wasn't going to push that issue. Why, suddenly, did she have two men vying for her when in the past twelve months she couldn't have scared up a date to save her life? Nothing made sense. Nothing at all.

"Let me stay tonight and make sure you're okay. We need to put all of our cards on the table and see if we can figure this out. My past, your past. No secrets."

She hesitated, then nodded. "Okay."

"Good." Daniel started to go to her, but he stopped. "No pressure, I promise. Tonight is strictly business. When all of this is behind us, we can think about the personal element of our relationship, agreed?"

"Let's cross that bridge when we get there," Sarah answered. Caution had always been her motto, and she wasn't about to jump off the cliff now. "I'll see what's in the cupboard and make some dinner for us." She glanced out the window. The bay had taken on a dark, dull cast that spoke of a storm brewing. "It looks like bad weather is about to set in."

"Why don't we call for pizza delivery? That'll save you from cooking, and we can sample that wine."

Sarah grinned. She was tired of cooking, and pizza sounded perfect.

An hour later she was lying on the floor, her head on a pillow, and a fire crackling in the fireplace. Familiar dozed in her arms, and Daniel had assumed a comfortable position on the sofa. To Sarah's surprise, she found herself talking about her childhood. She'd already told Daniel about her early love of cooking and the trips to New Orleans with her parents and Vincent Minton.

"He encouraged me, I suppose. And he introduced me to the finest chefs in New Orleans. They all took me seriously, even though I was so small I had to stand on a stool to stir a pot." She was smiling at the memories.

They'd avoided any talk of her father, but Sarah knew they were headed that way. She was of two emotions. Her first inclination was to resist, to protect herself and her family by remaining quiet. But there was also the impulse to tell Daniel, to set the record straight once and for all.

"Does your mother cook?" Daniel asked. He relaxed on the sofa and enjoyed the fact that Sarah was only a few feet from him. He studied her profile against the fire and wondered at the pale softness of her skin. It was almost more than he could bear not to reach out and touch it, just to feel the sensation of it beneath his fingertips. But he held himself in check.

For the first time since he'd met her, Sarah was actually relaxing. He'd never noticed how wound up she was most of the time, until now. With her head propped on a pillow and her third glass of an excellent merlot in her hand, she was mellowing into a woman who compelled him deeply. He wanted to touch her, to kiss her, to hold her, and to talk with her until there were no secrets left between them. The raw power of his emotions frightened him enough to keep him still.

He'd felt varying degrees of sexual attraction for many other women, and he'd wooed and won his fair share of them. Many of them he'd enjoyed in every sense of the word—as friends, lovers and comrades. But Sarah was something else. She stirred his blood in a slower, more enticing fashion.

He realized she was answering his question, talking about picnics and fried chicken and apple pies. She made it sound as if she'd lived the American dream of childhood. But he knew that wasn't the whole truth.

"And your father, was he a chef, also?"

"Daddy cooked great spaghetti. And he actually made better piecrust than anyone I've ever known. But he didn't cook often. Every time he got in the middle of something, he was called out, so he said it wasn't worth the effort. Mom agreed, because she had to clean up his mess, and she said it was amazing how a man could cook one dish and mess up every pot in the house."

They laughed together, and Daniel leaned down to refill her glass. He felt a twinge of deceit as he moved the questions along to where he wanted to go.

"You father loved his job, didn't he?"

"Until the last." Sarah felt her body begin to tense, and she willed herself to relax. Daniel was asking what he had to know. Once it was said, he'd believe what he wanted. But if she wouldn't tell him, then she couldn't really blame him for going to Jenkins for whatever lies that old agent had to tell. Daniel was a man trained to seek out facts, and he had to look wherever he found a clue.

"After the accusations were made, Daddy kept doing his job, but it was like he didn't walk as proud. He felt that everyone thought he was a crook. It ... diminished him."

The anger and bitterness in Sarah's last words made Daniel want to go to her. He reached down to grip her shoulder, one small gesture that showed he understood how tough that would be for a man of character. "I'm sorry," he said. How was it possible that Sarah saw her father one way and a trained FBI agent saw him another? He sat up, not knowing what to do with his sudden burst of anxious energy.

Sarah turned so that she was staring at the fire, and he saw the cat rise to lick a tear from her cheek. Lucky cat, he thought ruefully. But he had given his word he wouldn't pressure her, and if he had to go dunk himself in Chesapeake Bay to keep that word, he intended to do so.

"You're wondering how I could love my father so much, and yet how other people thought he was a crook, aren't you?"

"Yes." He tightened his fingers in his hair, tugging just enough to put pressure on the roots. He noticed that Sarah, too, had a strand of hair that she was twisting and pulling. They both had some of the same nervous habits.

"That man, Jenkins. The reason I got so upset when you went to talk to him is because he had a personal vendetta against Dad. Believe it or not, he did. He set out to prove Daddy was guilty of something, anything. And he didn't stop until my father was dead. I think he may be the only person in the world my mother wishes dead."

The cold starkness of her words reached Daniel. He believed her—and he understood. "Agents trained by the FBI aren't supposed to work on personal vendettas," he said softly, "but it's happened in the past, and it will happen again. A law enforcement agency is only as good as the men in it. Some men are corrupt, and so are some agents."

Sarah shifted so that she was looking up at him. "You believe me?"

"I believe it's possible. Jenkins was . . . *is* a highly respected man."

Her hopeful expression fell away, exposing deep sorrow.

"But even to me, his determination to nail your father seems obsessive." Daniel struggled to put his feelings and intuitions into careful words. He didn't want to raise Sarah's hopes that he was committed to her way of thinking. He wasn't. But he wasn't one hundred percent in line with the FBI's stand, either. His thoughts had taken some radical curves since Cody's death.

"Then you're willing to consider that my father was an innocent man?" Blood rushed through Sarah's heart, giving her a feeling of light-headedness. She put her wineglass on the hearth and eased into a sitting position. Familiar, dislodged, recurled himself against her thigh.

"Perfectly willing to *consider* that possibility."

"If he was innocent, then you might go one step further and think about the possibility that he was...murdered?"

Daniel had wondered if Sarah's thinking had ever gone along those lines. "If he was innocent and someone was going to that much trouble to frame him, then it is very possible it became cost-effective simply to kill him."

Spoken so factually, the words did not pierce Sarah as deeply as she'd expected. The same thought had been percolating in her head for some time. She'd always resisted, because with that line of thinking came a necessary line of action—revenge.

Daniel watched her jaw harden. He started to admonish her against the thoughts he knew she was having, but he knew he'd think exactly the same thing. Exactly.

"Tell me what you know," Sarah requested.

Her request was unexpected, but Daniel was glad to see her emotions hadn't overpowered her ability to reason. She was some kind of woman.

"Jenkins was certain your father took a payoff. He said he had an informant."

"An informant." Sarah repeated the words as she tried to think of who that might be. "Male or female?"

"A man, but he didn't say who. Only that it was someone he trusted implicitly. He implied it was someone who'd worked with your father." Daniel didn't want to tell Sarah too much. What if she went off half-cocked and got herself in trouble, or even worse, in a dangerous position?

Sarah rolled onto her knees and hobbled the few steps to the telephone.

"What are you doing?"

"I'm calling my mother," she said, as if he were asking the most foolish of all questions. "She'll remember every one who ever knew my father at that time. If there's an informant in the woodwork, we'll sniff him out."

Daniel pressed the switch hook down. It was well past midnight, and the fire they'd built in the fireplace was glowing embers. "Wait until morning. You'll have her up all night, fretting and worrying, and she won't be able to think a bit better."

Sarah hesitated. She wasn't used to having anyone second-guess her actions. It was an odd feeling, to listen to Daniel and accept that he was right, even in such a minor thing. "Okay."

His hand slipped over her fingers and curled them inside his. "You are one very together woman," he said. "I know how hard this is, and you're thinking, sorting, using your brain. Not just turning on the emotions."

The warmth of his hand on hers was doing something strange to her body, but Sarah didn't want to acknowledge that. "I've had a lot of years to think about things. There were always some loose ends, some questions without answers. My mother won't talk about this. Or she hasn't in the past. Now she's going to have to. After Dad died she became so... passive. If someone killed him, that would explain a lot of things. If, and I know it's a big if, my father was murdered, I want to find out who did it and make them pay."

"And we will."

Sarah felt the tickle of a smile at the corners of her mouth. We. Daniel was still with her. So far.

"Why are you doing this?" she asked.

"The way I look at things, I don't have any other choice. Not because I want to show you that I care for you, or to try to make you care for me, though I do want those things. Basically, this is the right thing to do. If a wrong was committed, then it should be righted. That's why I wanted to be an FBI agent. You know, one of the good guys." He smiled.

Sarah found herself fascinated by the corners of his mouth. The first hint of a beard shadowed his skin, giving his face a hungry look in the last glowing embers of the fire. Without thinking, she reached up to touch the left corner of his mouth. Her finger traced the upward curve of his lip, which increased at the lightness of her touch.

His hand touched her chin and drew her toward him. The first touch of their lips was tender, tentative. Sarah felt the sweep of flames that burned away all hesitations and doubts. There might never be another time so right. This one night, she would risk her heart, and her body, to Daniel.

She leaned into the kiss, opening her mouth. Her tongue teased and dared his, pushing them both past the point where they could draw back from each other. As his tongue danced along her lips, igniting a star burst of sensations, Sarah wound her fingers in his hair.

Daniel felt himself slipping into a swift stream of sensations. Hunger and need rode above a deep joy that made every touch, every tiny second, a wonder to him.

He eased to his knees and drew Sarah up to hers so that their bodies touched as they continued to explore each other with hands and mouths. He shifted his attention from her lips to her neck, drawing a soft moan of pleasure from her.

Sarah felt her body melting and gave herself to Daniel's strong arms as he gently eased her onto the floor. He followed, his lips trailing down her neck to her breasts. The thin silk of her shirt was no defense for his persistent kisses. Her pleasure increased, and so did her need.

The excitement Sarah demonstrated only aroused Daniel more. He drew back from her, touching her cheek with the lightest of touches until she opened her eyes. For a moment they were unfocused, but then he saw them clear.

"What?" she asked, breathless.

"Nothing," he answered, because he'd already seen what he was looking for in her eyes. He bent his head so that his

lips sought hers, and this time their hunger bound them together in a sublime, sweet feast that finally left both completely satisfied.

*Ah, the excesses of youth. It's a good thing there's one
levelheaded creature in this house. Maybe I'm just old and
cantankerous, but I keep hearing something outside. The
wind is kicking some butt out there, and the shutters are
bumping the house. But there's something else. Someone
else.*

*I think I'd know it if it was Jean-Claude. He didn't strike
me as the kind who would lurk around in the cold, dark, wet
night while everyone else was warm and cozy inside. There's
an edge to him, though. He's the kind of man who would
hurt a woman in a fit of jealousy. Fragile ego, or some such
psychobabble. I'm just glad Dolly and Bureau Boy made
their way to each other. It's clear to me there's a lot of
mixed-up feelings there.*

Listen!

*There's footsteps on the porch. It sounds as if someone
sat down in the swing! A prowler who wants to swing and
watch a storm? This is strange. I'd better take a look. But
there's nothing from this window, either.*

*It's time to get Daniel up and dressed. I don't think this
is a situation where he really wants to be caught with his
pants down, or off, as the case may be.*

"Hey, Danny Boy! Bureau Boy! Hey!"

*Let me put my little paw on his mouth to keep him quiet.
Yes, now he hears it, and he's not going to disturb Dolly.
Good, she needs her sleep—and we boys can probably work
better without her tagging along.*

*Now he's dressed and it's into the night for us. Thank
goodness he found another gun! There are nights like this
when gun control seems to be an issue without a real answer. I'll bet the guy outside has some kind of weapon.*

Take it easy with the door. That's it. I'm out and walking along the porch. There's someone in the swing, someone tall. He—or it could be a she—is wearing a hat. They're sitting so very still, and the wind is cutting across that water like icicles thrown from the North Pole.

"WHAT DO YOU THINK you're doing?" Daniel kept the gun at his side as he stepped in front of the seated stranger.

The blast of red pepper spray to his eyes was so unexpected that Daniel thought for a second he'd been blinded. "Hey!" He cried loudly enough to wake the dead, hoping Sarah would hear him and take precautions.

The tall figure darted past Daniel. Though he hesitated for a second at the door, he didn't see the cat. Familiar launched himself from the railing and struck the man's head. The cap flew off, and along with it went Familiar. His hold on the material was all he'd been able to grab.

Snatching up the hat, the man darted down the stairs and disappeared into the woods.

"Daniel?" Sarah's concerned voice came from a crack in the door. "What's going on?"

"Get some water and some towels." Daniel knew better than to rub his eyes, but he couldn't control the tears that streamed down his face. "I've been sprayed with pepper."

"What?" Sarah hurried outside, her nearly nude body shivering in the icy blast. She grabbed Daniel's shoulders and helped him back inside. He was blinded by the pepper and in intense pain.

"A man, I'm certain, but I didn't get a good look at him. He was sitting in the swing. When I went up to him, he blasted me with the pepper."

"Sitting in the swing?" Sarah mused over that fact as she eased Daniel into a chair and then went to get warm water and towels to blot his eyes. "Should we go to a hospital?"

Daniel shook his head. "No. This will wear off, but if I ever catch that guy, I'm going to mop the floor with him."

Sarah allowed a smile because she knew Daniel couldn't see her. She used the warm towels to remove as much of the pepper as she could, then used a mild soap all over Daniel's face.

"Better?" she asked.

"Yes." At least his eyes had stopped tearing. "He was a tall man. Have any ideas?"

Sarah heard the undertone in his voice. "What are you getting at?"

"Your friend was tall. The man who visited earlier."

Jean-Claude Minton was tall, but Sarah didn't say his name. Jean-Claude had gone back to New York, first of all, and second, even though he'd been a spoiled brat, he certainly knew better than to attack a federal agent with pepper spray for no good reason. There was no reason on earth he'd sit out on his own porch in a storm and then attack one of Sarah's friends.

Except that he'd always been a brat.

"Sarah, do you know who that might have been?"

"No," she answered honestly.

She looked up and met Familiar's questioning gaze. While she held a towel to Daniel's eyes, the cat went straight to the photo album on the coffee table. With deliberate care he placed a paw on the cover. Sarah shook her head. Familiar had identified the culprit, but this was one instance where Daniel would be better kept in the dark. This was personal, a matter of petty jealousy, and ridiculous to boot.

"Sarah, are you keeping something from me?" Daniel knew he sounded peevish, but it was infuriating not being able to see, and he could sense something going on around him that he couldn't understand.

"It's Familiar. He wants to go out."

"Let him. He's one heck of a watchcat."

Sarah put Daniel's hand on the towel he held to his eyes, then got up and went to the door. She eased the black cat out into the night with a little shove. She didn't want Dan-

iel to see the cat with the photo album. If it was Jean-
Claude, it was a stupid thing for him to do. Stupid and juvenile.

"Sarah?" Daniel's voice was uncertain. Sarah went to
him and touched his face. "It's okay. It's just the two of us
in this together. But we'll figure it out."

Chapter Eleven

Sarah woke cradled in Daniel's arms. Easing out of bed so as not to disturb him, she stood before the window and stretched in the golden morning light. The storm had battered the bay house for several hours before breaking up, leaving the sunshine fresh-washed and beautiful.

As she dressed, Sarah studied Daniel's face. His eyes were still red and puffy, but he'd slept well for the remainder of the night. The pepper attack had been painful, but not damaging. Once the burning and irritation abated, he'd drifted into a sound sleep.

The temptation to touch his cheek was almost irresistible, but she managed to check the impulse. He was tired, and she wouldn't risk awakening him. As hard as the last few days had been on her, they'd been much worse on Daniel. He'd lost a friend, possibly his career, his self-respect and his home.

Yet he'd had so much to give her. Daniel Dubonet was a generous man when it came to love-making. A very generous man.

Sarah slipped from the room without disturbing him. There were several things she wanted to attend to before he awoke. One was a call to her mother.

Downstairs in the kitchen she put on a pot of coffee and dialed the Biloxi number. When she lifted the receiver to her ear, there was no sound. Toggling the switch hook up and down, she tried to clear the line, all to no avail. The phone was dead.

"The storm," she said to Familiar, who was pacing back and forth in front of the refrigerator. He'd disdained the cat food she'd brought and only sampled the pizza, but she knew he was hungry.

She poured him a saucer of milk and could clearly read the contempt on his face.

"What is it you want, pâté?"

"Meow!" He puckered his whiskers.

"Perhaps, la chat would prefer some grilled swordfish?" She adopted a haughty French accent.

"Meow!" Familiar sat down and nodded.

Sarah looked at him. He was actually telling her what he wanted. Grilled swordfish. She opened the freezer and began poking around. The darn cat would probably prefer it fresh, but that was out of the question. Maybe she could find something suitable in the freezer since Uncle Vince loved seafood.

After scrounging around for several minutes she held up a package of fish. "Will tuna suffice?"

Familiar nodded again.

"Good, then your menu is planned, so drink your milk." Sarah nudged it over to the cat with her toe. "Now I have to figure out how to make the telephone work. Either that or we're going to have to drive into town and report it. Lucky we know that the phone company keeps crews working night and day. They should be able to get out here and get this fixed."

Sarah realized she was talking a blue streak to the cat. She shut her mouth with a firm clamp and poured a cup of coffee. She was getting as dotty as a bat in the blazing sun.

"How about a cup of that?"

She turned to find Daniel standing in the doorway, his face still sleepy and a question in his eyes. "I need some caffeine."

"Coming right up." She poured another cup and handed it to him, letting her fingers brush his, a whisper of affection and desire. She was taken aback by the rush of emotions she felt for Daniel, and the flush of confusion. No man had ever affected her in such a way, and it was almost as disconcerting as it was exciting. She sought something to say that wouldn't reveal her turbulent emotions. "The phone is dead."

Daniel's expression froze. He picked up the receiver and held it to his ear. "Deader than a doornail, as we used to say as kids." He kept his face bland, but his voice registered his concern.

"What?"

"I don't believe in coincidences. The storm might have knocked the phone out, but it's strange that we also had a visitor."

"I see." Sarah hadn't connected the two events. Maybe it was more than wind that had knocked out the phone.

"I'll check." Daniel took his coffee and went to find his boots. "Be back in a minute," he called as he slammed the front door.

Tempted to follow him, Sarah went through the refrigerator for breakfast food instead. She had to steady herself, to give Daniel a chance to show what he was feeling for her.

She forced her thoughts back in line with breakfast. Uncle Vince kept the place stocked like a palace. Sighing as she counted up the fat grams, she pulled out bacon, eggs, a cloth sack of hand-ground grits, butter, and the makings for biscuits. It was only on rare occasions that she indulged in a traditional Southern breakfast, but the hours of the night she'd spent in Daniel's arms counted as a very special occasion indeed.

Daniel had to work his way around to his own feelings on the matter, but she felt wonderful. It was almost as if some stranglehold on her emotions had been broken. She'd protected herself against feeling anything for so long, but now she was free. Free to experience all of the pleasure Daniel gave so readily. And, perhaps, the pain that came with it. There were no guarantees in relationships; she knew that. She'd been afraid of losing someone for so long that now the sudden freedom was...exhilarating.

Daniel made his way around the house, stopping at the window that looked in on the kitchen. The black cat was sitting on the floor, watching every move that Sarah made. And Sarah...He smiled at the sight of her. She was luminous this morning. When he'd first awakened, he'd had a stab of concern that she might wish the night had never happened. But one look and he knew that she had no regrets. The question he confronted now was, what were her expectations? And what were his? He'd never met a woman quite like her. She was independent, responsible, mature, fun, giving—and very vulnerable when it came to her past.

That was tricky ground with Sarah. He had to walk there with her, to know it and understand it, but he had to let her pick the path. Until then, he had to figure out what was wrong with the telephone.

He saw the line, torn from the connecting box. A large limb was across the line, pinning it firmly to the ground. He was turning to go back into the house when he saw the big blue-and-white truck bumping through the trees. The telephone crewman got out and waved.

"Bad storm passed through. We've got line damage reported."

"The lines are down." Daniel spoke the obvious. "You're out and about pretty early." How was it that the crew truck had showed up so conveniently? He was instantly suspicious.

"That wind whipped through here like a buzz saw. Never seen this kind of damage before." The repairman pushed his hat up on his forehead. "We'll be busy for the next three days. Folks around here like their privacy, and they like their telephones to work."

"I'll bet." Daniel watched the man as he started to unpack ladders and gear. "You must have been working all night."

"Nope. Just came on, but this is a neighborhood with a lot of pull. Folks report phones are out, and we send a truck." He inspected the wire. "I'll ask you to check the phone in a minute," he said.

Daniel watched the repairman. It did seem strange, but the tree limb was on the line, there had been a storm, and it was a wealthy neighborhood. He started back around the house when he heard Familiar's deep meow. He couldn't place the cat immediately, but as he listened to his cry, he moved around the house to where the woods grew dense and thick. He saw the cat's tail moving among some brush and shrubs.

"Meow!" Familiar demanded.

Daniel's training reminded him to look around before he stepped into the shadows of the trees. The telephone man was at the side of the house, but his attention was focused on his work. Daniel disappeared into the woods.

"What is it?" He felt like a fool talking to the cat. Now if it had been a dog...

He felt the prick of sharp claws in his shins. "Meow!" Familiar demanded as he moved away.

"Okay," Daniel said with a sigh. So he was sleeping with a chef and following a cat through the woods. He'd been kidnapped, knocked unconscious and robbed, and he had lost his job. So his life was taking some unexpected turns.

"Meow!" Familiar stood beside a dark object that was nearly hidden by the shadows of the woods and leaves.

"What?" Daniel used a stick to dislodge the item from the leaves. It was a hat. A dark hat. He lifted it on a stick so that he could examine it better.

"Well, well. It looks like the hat our intruder was wearing." And it did, but Daniel could not make a positive identification. Still holding it on the stick, he started back toward the house with Familiar in the lead. At the edge of the woods, the cat stopped. Daniel paused, wondering what was on Familiar's mind.

The telephone man was climbing into his truck, and Sarah was on the porch, waving at him as he pulled away. The work had gone quickly.

Once the repair truck was gone, Familiar ran across the yard, calling to Sarah.

"Well, it's about time for breakfast, you guys," she said, leaning on the porch railing as she watched Daniel and Familiar come out of the woods. Her eyes went to the object Daniel carried, and a frown touched her face. "What is that?"

"Familiar found it. A hat."

Sarah started down the steps, her heart sinking with each step. That darn cat had managed to dig up evidence, even without the photo album that she'd hidden in the top shelf on the closet.

"Is something wrong, Sarah?"

There was no point trying to lie to protect Jean-Claude. "My cousin, or my adopted cousin, Jean-Claude, used to wear a boating hat sort of like that." She stopped at the foot of the stairs as Daniel came toward her. A flash of gold on the cap caught her attention. "It was very much like that hat," she said grimly.

"Jean-Claude?" Daniel nodded. "So you thought it was him all along?"

"He's very spoiled. Or at least, he was." She shrugged. "He has some kind of idea that he's interested in me. It's foolish, certainly, but..." She felt the stain of embarrassment heating her cheeks.

Daniel understood it all. Jean-Claude had come to pay court to Sarah and discovered that she had other male company. He'd waited, on the porch, and then sprayed Daniel with pepper. It was a mean and petty thing to do.

"Jean-Claude was always spoiled, and when he didn't have things exactly his way, he acted like a brat. Even things he really didn't want, he didn't let other children touch." She felt the heat in her cheeks.

"You're not responsible for his actions, Sarah," Daniel reminded her.

"He told me that he was changed, mature, different. But I have no proof of that. None." She pointed to the hat. "If this is his idea of the right way to behave—"

"We're both jumping to conclusions." Daniel gave her that out.

"Could the hat have been in the woods for some time?"

"No. It was covered in leaves, but there is no decay of the material. I'd say the hat has been stored someplace, but not on the ground. Someplace like a cabinet."

"The boat house. Maybe we should go take a look."

Daniel carefully placed the hat on the edge of the driveway. He had no access to labs or anything else now, but it might prove to be a valuable clue at some later date. He would preserve it, just in case. For now, though, he had Sarah to consider.

He put his hands on her shoulders, rubbing gently and drawing her toward him so that she soon rested in his embrace. "I can see clearly why a man would desire you and risk any behavior to have you." He kissed her forehead.

Sarah's laugh was shaky, but there. "I know, I'm a good cook. Never underestimate that. My mother always told me that the way to a man's heart was through his stomach."

"That, and..."

"I have a charming personality?" There was real humor in her voice again.

"Yes, there's that. And I hear you make your own clothes."

They laughed together, and Sarah took his hand. "Breakfast is ready, and I'm starving." Daniel had not overreacted. He wasn't pointing the finger at Jean-Claude or anyone else.

"Meow!" Familiar said, bounding up the stairs ahead of them both.

"That settles that," Daniel said, eyeing the cat with renewed respect. "Familiar says it's time to eat, and I think we should all pay more attention to that cat. Let's eat, put on some warm clothes and go take a look at that boat house."

After bacon and cheddar cheese scrambled eggs, Familiar curled up on the sofa beside Sarah as she placed the call to Biloxi. Tactfully, Daniel had decided to inspect the boat house while she talked with her mother.

When the line proved busy, Sarah put the phone down and stroked Familiar's shimmering hide. Something wasn't right. Mora had call-waiting. There shouldn't be a busy signal. She dialed the number again. This time the phone rang ten times before she replaced the receiver. Worry pulled her brows together as she sat in front of the renewed fire. One hand stroked the cat while the other tugged at a strand of her straight blond hair. She finally picked up the receiver and dialed again.

Still no answer.

"She has a machine," she told the cat.

Of course, the machine could be off, or her mother could be on the other line, so caught up in conversation that she didn't want to answer the incoming call. That was a possibility. But not a strong one. Mora was the kind of person who was afraid to let a phone ring for fear it was someone needing her. In that respect, Sarah was just like her.

She dialed her uncle's home, remembering on the sixth ring that he was in New York, and if anyone answered it would be Jean-Claude. That prompted her to replace the receiver with a quick slam. Of all the people on earth, Jean-Claude was the last one she wanted to talk to.

Familiar stood and stretched, then walked to the door.

"Good idea," she said, grabbing her coat. "Let's give Daniel a hand down at the dock."

The wind bit into her face as she stepped away from the protection of the house. She'd failed to realize how much colder it was on the water than in the city.

With Familiar at her side, she found Daniel in the boat house. He was looking but not touching.

"Be careful," he advised her. "Someone jimmied the lock off." There was disappointment in his words.

Sarah knew without asking that Jean-Claude had just receded as a viable candidate for the attack. Anyone could have broken into the boat house and taken Jean-Claude's hat. Anyone. Instead of disappointment, she felt a keen relief. More than anything she didn't want to involve her uncle in anything ugly. There had been enough of that in the past.

"That doesn't mean it wasn't Jean-Claude," Daniel said as he watched the play of emotions across her face.

"I know." She smiled at him. "It just means that maybe it wasn't. Or that probably it wasn't. It could have been a kid, someone who's been hanging out in the boat house for weeks."

Daniel nodded. "The dust has been disturbed. Someone has been coming and going here." He nodded toward the candles and beer cans in one corner. "From what you've told me about your uncle and his friends, they don't seem the type to come down here in the dark, drink beer and burn candles."

"Kids," Sarah agreed. "And the pepper, that seems like a kid thing to do. Like on a dare." Maybe her suspicions about Jean-Claude were wrong.

Daniel nodded in agreement. "But I tell you, if I could get my hands on whoever that was, I'd give them a little taste of red pepper in the eyes. It isn't a pleasant experience."

Sarah walked across the room and into his arms. The way he grasped her, his eagerness showing in the feel of his hands along her back and the quickening of his breath, made her bold. "I could show you a cure for all of that. Or at least take your mind right off it."

"Yes, ma'am," he said, mimicking her Southern accent. "I'll bet you could." His lips found and held hers. In that instant, passion flamed between them. Sarah forgot everything except the taste of his kiss, the sensation of liquid heat that coursed through her at his touch.

"Daniel," she whispered his name against his ear as she kissed the lobe and moved along his neck. She wanted to give him the pleasure that she felt, to show him that she needed his touch, and needed to feel his response to hers. As her lips touched the base of his neck, she felt him grow still. Instinctively she pulled away, wondering at the sudden change of his mood.

"Excuse me." The male voice came from outside the boat house.

Sarah heard the slightly accented voice and turned to find Jean-Claude standing in the doorway.

"Jean-Claude." Her voice was breathless, and she cursed the flush that she could feel crawling over her body.

"My timing is not good," he said, his composure perfect. "I had thought to be of assistance. I can see I'm not needed here. I am sorry for the interruption." He turned on his heel and started back to the house and to the dark sedan that was parked near the stairs.

Sarah threw one confused look at Daniel, who stood, his own composure still askew, but with a dark anger beginning to burn in his eyes.

"Jean-Claude!" Sarah called after him. "Wait a minute." When he failed to stop, she called again, this time angrily. "Wait a minute, damn it. Why are you—?"

He turned back. "I could not get an answer on the telephone. The company said the phones were down. I was worried about you." His look shifted to Daniel. "I can see that my concerns were ... misplaced, *chérie*. There is nothing that I can do for you." A haunted look touched his face. "Perhaps there was nothing I could have done. We are all victims of our past, Sarah. You have made a terrible mistake."

"Jean-Claude." Sarah reached out and touched his arm. She'd never imagined she would see Jean-Claude so upset. She heard Daniel step close behind her and stop. She hesitated, remembering Jean-Claude's warning about Daniel. "This is Daniel Dubonet. He was worried about me, too."

Jean-Claude's smile was sarcastic as he turned to the FBI agent. "Perhaps I should have expressed my concerns last night. Perhaps I would be the man in the boat house today. At least I can protect her."

Sarah felt as if he'd slapped her. She stepped backward, aware too late of the angry flush that touched Daniel's cheeks. This was the Jean-Claude she remembered. Had she imagined that sadness only a moment ago?

"I don't think timing was your problem," Daniel said softly. "If Sarah had wanted your concern, or your comfort, she would have let you know." There was a growl in his voice.

"I'm not so certain she would feel safe with you, Mr. Dubonet, if she knew all the facts about you." Jean-Claude was a study in anger. His dark eyes burned and he cast Sarah a searching glance. "Has he told you that he was fired? That he is considered a renegade, a possible thief and a murderer?''

There was a moment of silence when Sarah thought Daniel was going to throw the first punch. She held out both hands, but the men ignored her. "This isn't necessary. Please—"

"Sarah knows about me. She knows a lot more than you'll ever know." Daniel bit the words as he spoke. "It wasn't me who she thought was here last night, acting like a spoiled brat."

Sarah wanted to punch them both. They were acting like gladiators, fighting over the spoils.

"Both of you," she spoke with cold authority. "Out! Now!"

At last she had their attention. "I'm not some bone that two dogs can fight over. And that's exactly the way you're behaving. Now get out." She stalked past them and went up to the house. Without looking back, she climbed the stairs and went inside, slamming the door for good measure.

In a moment she heard the roar of the car Jean-Claude had driven to the house. Then silence. Looking around the room, she realized that Daniel couldn't leave. His keys were on the counter beside the cold coffeepot. Well, he could walk.

"Men!" She said the word with venom as she looked out the window.

"Meow." Familiar sat on the rail watching her.

She opened the window. "Be warned, Familiar. If you're up to any male tricks, this isn't a safe place to be."

"Meow," he answered as he gracefully jumped inside.

JEEZ, I don't blame Dolly a bit, but she isn't using her head. There's something about that Jean-Claude fellow that doesn't add up. I'm not certain what it is, but it's definitely there. And Daniel wasn't much better, I'm sorry to say. Old Bureau Boy could win the Cro-Magnon award. I mean, re-

ally. If he'd come across with that caveman act any more intensely, he would have knocked Sarah over the head and dragged her home with him.

And the real pain is that so far we've discovered nothing to help solve this mystery. So what if Jean-Claude peppered Daniel in a jealous fit over Sarah? That doesn't resolve anything. It only adds another twist to the puzzle. Why? Why is he suddenly so concerned about Sarah? Why does he care so much now? The answer could prove to be interesting—and very dangerous.

Chapter Twelve

Sarah threw another log on the fire and tried to keep her attention from straying out the window to where Daniel and Familiar scouted the premises. She was caught between the devil and the deep blue sea, as her mother would say. She'd gone to the telephone five times—and each time she'd resisted the urge to call her mother. Instead she'd called the airlines and checked flights to Biloxi out of Washington. There were several direct to New Orleans, and that knowledge made her feel better. Still, she lifted the receiver with trepidation. What if Mora didn't answer?

But she did, and her breathless voice came over the line.

"Mom!" Sarah felt a surge of relief and joy.

"Sarah, my goodness. Is something wrong?" The question all mothers ask slipped from Mora's mouth.

"Nothing now that you've answered the phone." Sarah smiled.

"And why wouldn't I answer the phone? I don't work. I go to the grocery store on Thursday, and do my hair on Friday morning. Other than that, I'm home."

Mora wasn't exaggerating. Her life was bounded by routine, and that was the way she liked it.

"I called about an hour ago. When you didn't answer, I was worried."

There was a hesitation. "I was on the other line."

Sarah almost didn't believe her ears. Mora always answered the phone. Always. Unless it was an emergency on the other line. Or unless... Cal Covington had been dead nearly twenty years. Was it possible Mora had someone else in her life?

"So what's going on in Biloxi?" Sarah made her voice deliberately chatty.

"Is something wrong up there?" Mora asked, maternal concern evident.

Sarah sighed, unable to lie to her mother. "Nothing for you to worry about. Just some strange occurrences."

"Not that FBI man? Vincent said he would take care of it."

"No, no, Mom, that's okay." Sarah felt a flush touch her cheeks. If her mother only knew about her involvement with Daniel. She'd either be relieved to know Sarah cared for someone or horrified that it was an FBI agent. Or maybe both.

"Sarah, you sound pulled tighter than a barbed-wire fence. What is going on? That's the third time I've asked."

The thousand miles of distance hummed between them, and Sarah realized how much farther apart they were emotionally. If Mora had found companionship, Sarah was glad, but she couldn't tell her mother that. The subject could not be raised between them. They'd lived their lives trying to avoid painful subjects with each other—and now Sarah had to ask about her father.

"Mom, it's about Daddy." She swallowed and could almost hear the echo of disapproval on the telephone line.

"There's no point talking about any of that." Mora's voice was suddenly prim. "I thought you'd put that behind you, Sarah. It's over and done. Nothing you think or do will bring your father back. You've got your entire life ahead of you and you can't get bogged down in the past."

"I know." Sarah spoke softly, willing her mother just to listen. "Things are happening up here, though, Mom. I think someone believes Dad had some money hidden somewhere."

"Are you in danger?" Fear shot through Mora's voice.

"No, no. I'm fine." She cleared her throat. "You're going to have to trust me on this. Trust my judgment. I'm not a little girl anymore and I need to know the truth."

"It's best to leave the past dead and buried, Sarah."

"You can't protect me from the truth. You'd do that even if it cost you your life. And you'd protect Dad, too."

A long silence fell between them.

"Someone up here is telling stories that Daddy took money to set up a gambling business. A lot of money. That he sold out as sheriff."

"That's a lie." Mora's voice was still but deadly. "That's the same lie Joshua Jenkins told. He stood at Cal's grave and before he left the cemetery he was lying, saying Cal had hidden the money and that he wouldn't give up until he had it. Cal never took a dime!"

Sarah felt tears spring to her eyes. She remembered the funeral, the anger her mother had displayed. Now she finally understood. "Who would say that Daddy took money? There was an informant to the FBI. Someone who knew Dad and knew enough about his business to say it and make it look like it might be true."

"An informant?" Mora sounded as if all the air had been sucked from her.

"Listen, Mom." Sarah tried to word everything carefully. "Daniel Dubonet, the FBI agent, he's helping me. And he found out that Joshua Jenkins was told by an informant that Dad had taken a payoff."

"That's a damn lie." Mora's fury was red hot. "That man claimed there was half a million dollars that Cal took. He kept on and kept on, until he nearly drove Cal crazy. And me, too. He'd show up sitting outside the house while Cal was at work. I almost had a breakdown."

Sarah swallowed her tears. She simply could not give in to the sorrow she felt. Not now. "He's an old man now, Mom. Daniel—"

"Stay away from that man. For ten years I've tried to get you to date and meet nice men and you take up with an FBI agent." Mora almost spat the last words. "Think of your father, Sarah. Think of what they did to this family."

"Daniel's different, Mom." She tried to think of the best way to express it, but there weren't any words. Not yet. "He's going to help me. Maybe we can prove Dad was innocent of all that."

"Ha! More than likely he's using you. That's what they're trained to do."

Sarah knew she couldn't fight her mother's bitterness. There was too much time and history, too much distance. Maybe in the near future she could arrange for Daniel to meet her mother. If Mora gave him half a chance . . .

"Mom, who was close enough to Dad that might have given information to the FBI?"

"No one."

Sarah ignored the stony coldness of the answer. "Just give me a chance. I don't want to scare you, but people have been following me. There's been some trouble with some of my food. It isn't that I want to pry into the past, I have to do this. And I need your help."

"Come home, Sarah."

"I can't." Sarah's smile was sad. "It isn't in my blood to run. And I'm going to solve this thing. It would sure be a lot easier if you'd tell me a little about what happened."

Mora's sigh spoke of her capitulation. "No one was closer to your father than Graham Estis."

"The deputy?"

"Cal's right-hand man. I haven't seen him in ten years, but he's living down in Ocean Springs. He's working as a deputy in the Jackson County sheriff's office." There was a pause. "Graham loved your father. He would never have done anything to hurt him."

"Maybe not intentionally."

"Well, if you're going to poke around in this, Graham is a good place to start. He can at least put you on the right track."

"Thanks, Mom." Sarah gripped the phone tighter. "I love you, you know."

"I love you, too, Sarah. You just be careful. And bring that man down here for me to inspect. If you say he's helping you, I have to try and take it on faith. But I'd like a good look at him."

"We'll be down, maybe before you know it."

"'Bye, honey."

Sarah replaced the receiver and wiped the tears from her cheeks. How had so much time and distance gotten between her and her mother? It had always been the past, there between them, pushing them apart. And today, they'd taken a big step in moving a lot closer together.

"Sarah?" Daniel stood in the doorway. "Sarah, I'm sorry about that scene with . . . Is something wrong?"

Her anger had been washed away by her tears. The scene at the boat house was forgotten as she looked at Daniel and remembered how supportive he'd been. How much he'd risked on her behalf. She gave him a tentative smile. "I'll talk to Jean-Claude later. He's as much to blame as you. Maybe more."

"He made it sound like you just—"

"I can defend my own honor, but thanks. It's odd to me that Jean-Claude would be so upset." She motioned him to sit beside her. "But I'll deal with him later. I spoke with Mom. She told me something that may help us."

He smiled back, catching the hint of excitement from her. "What?"

"Graham Estis, my father's deputy. He was always up at the sheriff's office and helping Dad with things. They were close, and if there was anything to tell, Dad might have told him."

"Maybe we should take a little trip down South."

"I checked the flights. We can book one out of Washington tonight."

"Let's pack up and head that way."

THANK GOODNESS *we're getting out of here. There's something about this place that gives me a bad feeling. And a few questions that need solid answers. Like, who would break into a boat house, leave all kinds of expensive tools and equipment, and steal an old hat?*

It looked like Jean-Claude out on the porch, but I couldn't be certain. Why would Jean-Claude come out here to sit on the porch and then attack Daniel? That's no way to win a lady's heart. This entire case doesn't add up.

I keep going back to Socks and his reasons for hiring me. He wanted to prove that Sarah was not involved in anything. Correct me if I'm wrong, but national security is the province of the Secret Service. So Socks calls me in, and the Secret Service calls in Daniel Dubonet.

I've never worked with the feds before, but I know how jealous they are of their turf. Why would the Secret Service call in an agent from the FBI to watch a chef?

I've begun to believe that maybe it's Daniel who's being set up, and that Sarah is a pawn in the game. To be completely honest, I'm stumped on this case. Maybe when we get back to D.C. I can sneak over to the White House and see what the First Cat has gleaned. I also need to make an appearance at home. Magdelene has probably called the kitty pound looking for me. She'll be frantic and completely unreasonable. Oh, well, it's a small price to pay to be so loved.

IT WAS ONLY two o'clock, but Sarah felt as if each minute that ticked by was an opportunity lost. They were almost home, with Daniel following right behind them in his car. Familiar sat beside her on the front seat, and even he was tense. Disdaining any attempts Sarah made to comfort him, Familiar sat with his paws on either the seatback or the window and perused the traffic. He acted as if he were looking for something, or someone.

"You're not making this any easier, cat," she offered.

"Meow." Familiar continued to stare out the windshield, head moving slowly as he took in all oncoming traffic as they made the turn onto the street that led to Sarah's.

"Good grief." Sarah slapped her forehead. "I've got Lucinda's big party to cater. I can't go to Mississippi!"

Familiar turned his green gaze on her as if to say that he knew that already. His intense eyes watched her a moment before he returned to his vigil.

Pulling into the alley, Sarah silently cursed her forgetfulness and her stupidity. Daniel would be determined to go to Biloxi alone. And that was the worst thing he could do. Mora would be terrified of another agent—even a fired one—prying into the past. She had to convince him to stay in Washington. Until she was free to travel with him. She could cancel the party, but that would be a real slap in Uncle Vince's face. No, she had to cater the event, and she had to convince Daniel to wait for her.

Inside the shop she put on a pot of coffee and pulled out her cookbooks. She was about to broach the subject of Lucinda's party when the telephone rang. Picking it up on the second ring, she was surprised by the deep voice that asked for Daniel Dubonet. With eyebrows raised, she passed the telephone to Daniel.

"What do you want?"

Sarah was surprised by the anger in Daniel's voice, and the way he half turned from her to hide his scowl.

"I'm not exactly feeling that I owe the Bureau anything," Daniel said carefully, "but I'll think about it. Maybe we could trade. The information you want for some facts about Cody's murder." A tight smile touched his features. "Think about it, Gottard. I'll be in touch." He replaced the receiver and turned back to Sarah.

She saw the anger burning in his eyes, and she knew him well enough now to let him take his time. Opening one of the cookbooks, she blindly scanned the page.

"That was Paul Gottard, my superior in the Bureau. He wanted me to come in and talk with him."

"About what?" Sarah knew, but she wanted to give Daniel a chance to talk about it.

"He wants to know about you. What I've discovered about you. Who your friends are. How you snagged such high-profile political contracts with your business. Those kinds of things."

"Things he could easily obtain by asking me," Sarah noted.

"Don't think I haven't thought of that."

"What are you going to do?"

Daniel sat down at the table, his hand going automatically to his thick hair and tugging gently. "This is something we should talk about."

Sarah got two cups and poured the coffee before she took a seat beside him. She reached out and touched his arm, stroking the skin with a gentle pressure. "The fact that you want to talk about it with me tells me a lot I needed to know."

"You said it last night. We're in this together. Now everyone else is a suspect. We have only ourselves to rely on." He looked around the room. "And that blasted cat, wherever he got off to. At any rate, we have to decide what to do."

"Talk to him. I have nothing to hide. Every job I've ever gotten has been one I've worked for. There's nothing in my past I'm ashamed of. So talk to him. See what he *believes* is the truth."

Daniel lifted her hand to his lips and kissed the palm. "You trust me enough to let me do that?"

"I do." She curled her fingers inside the strength of his. "And I have something I need to do." She quickly explained about Lucinda's party.

"I think it's imperative that you cater it," he agreed. "And I intend to be there, too."

She looked into his eyes, knowing that she could never dissuade him—and that she didn't want to.

"This may be the best plan. We can travel to Biloxi in a couple of days. That will actually give me some time to call a few people. Even though I don't have a badge, I still have friends. Since Graham Estis is in law enforcement, I can pull a few strings and get some information on him. And I can keep an eye on things at Lucinda's party. If someone is trying to ruin you, that's going to be the place to do it."

Sarah felt a chill run through her, and she couldn't help the fact that her hand clenched in his. "I don't want to be ruined. I don't want anyone to be hurt."

"Neither do I." He opened her fingers, then linked them with his. "I'll go down to the Bureau this afternoon."

"To tell your boss what you know about me?" She was half teasing.

"To tell him everything I know about you—that you're more than decent. That someone is framing you for something. And that Joshua Jenkins might have been on the wrong track."

Sarah couldn't stop herself from leaning across the table to kiss him. It was a vice, like tasting the chocolate filling for an éclair. One tiny little taste was never enough, but it was all she could have right now.

Daniel felt her pull back from the kiss. It would be so much easier to scoop her into his arms and carry her up the stairs to her apartment. So easy and so right. But that wasn't how they were going to play this hand.

"I want to make some calls, then I'm out of here," he said.

"Go ahead. I have to run some errands. If I'm going to prepare these dishes, I have to get some ingredients."

Daniel stood and pulled her to him. His hands moved up and down her slender back, caressing each muscle and curve. "When I get back, will you put on that sexy chef uniform for me?" he asked. His eyes danced with mischief.

"Only if your weapon is loaded and you let me pull the trigger," she answered, biting his lower lip gently.

"And I thought you were a modest Southern girl."

"I am." She laughed. "But I also know how to talk dirty."

"I see that you do." He kissed her again, this time taking her breath away with the intensity. When he finally released her, they were both breathing in short and shallow gasps.

"I'll be back in three hours," he said, picking up his keys.

"I'll be here," she promised. "I'll be covered in food, but I'll be here."

DANIEL WAITED outside Paul Gottard's office, feeling as if every pair of eyes around were watching. His pride suffered at the idea of being fired, and his sense of fair play was outraged.

"Mr. Gottard will see you now."

Daniel smiled at Cindy, the secretary he'd known for the past year. She gave him a look brimming with sympathy. "I've only been accused, Cindy, I haven't been convicted," he said softly as he passed by her. When he looked back, he could see she was blushing.

"Daniel." Paul waved him into a chair. "I was beginning to wonder if we'd ever see you again."

"I didn't know if it was safe to come here," Daniel countered, glad to see the surprise that passed briefly over Gottard's stony features.

"Are you implying that someone from this agency has tried to harm you?"

"Save the bluster. I'm saying outright that someone, very possibly with Bureau connections, injured me, stole my weapon and badge and abducted me. Can I make it any plainer than that?"

"I'm sorry you feel that way."

Daniel could see that Gottard was furious, but he wasn't a smidgen madder than Daniel felt.

"You wanted to know about Sarah Covington. Well, from everything I can detect, she's an excellent chef."

"And how did you come to that brilliant conclusion?" Gottard's eyes were hard.

"I think it was the potato salad."

Gottard leaned forward in his chair. A tiny muscle ticked for several beats beneath his right eye. "This isn't a game, Daniel. I didn't call you here to give you an opportunity to exercise your wit or vent your spleen. You're in trouble. Very serious trouble. The only reason murder charges haven't been filed against you is because of me. So let's stop this damn silliness and talk."

Daniel had often admired Paul Gottard's strategies, and his ability to hide his emotions. Now he saw how ruthlessly the man could cut to the bone of an issue. And he admired that. "Okay." He dropped the smug tone of voice. "I checked Sarah Covington thoroughly. She is exactly what she appears to be. Nothing more, nothing less."

"What about her past? Has she spoken of it?"

Daniel nodded. "Extensively. She was only a child when her father died, but she believes he was falsely accused—and pursued. Hounded is the word she used, I believe."

"We've checked her finances. Except for some small amounts of unexplained cash, she's made her own way. There were no windfalls."

Daniel's smile was humorless. "It was a false trail."

"It would seem so." Gottard leaned back in his chair and let his vision drift to a watercolor on the wall. It showed a front porch with a magnolia tree in bloom and a view of water. "That's the Biloxi beachfront," he said. "Before the casinos went in. It was a lovely, simple community."

"All things change." Daniel had no idea where Gottard was heading. His boss seldom made it a habit to reminisce in front of agents, or if he did, Daniel had never known about it.

"Cody was a loss to us."

"And to me." Daniel tried to see behind the faraway look, but he could tell nothing. He felt his hands clench the arms of the chair. Gottard was a tricky man.

"You know he was shot."

"I know." Daniel had seen the wound and knew that there was nothing he could do to help his friend.

"With your weapon, Daniel."

At first Daniel couldn't believe what he was hearing. Gottard's gaze was like a magnifying glass, inspecting him for any clue. "I told you my gun and my badge were taken when I was abducted from the Bingingtons'."

"We have no proof of that." Gottard's assessment was brutal.

"I called and reported it."

"That doesn't make it true."

Daniel felt the inclination to slug Gottard. Only years of practice checked his temper.

"Daniel, I'm giving you the facts. As many people would interpret them."

"And what do you believe?"

Gottard sighed. "I don't know. Joshua Jenkins said you paid him a visit. He was extremely interested in your 'career.'"

Daniel waited silently. He'd learned years ago that the best information sometimes came in a void.

"Jenkins said he gave you some information on Sarah's background."

"He did."

"And did she confirm any of it?"

"She denied it all, unequivocally. In fact, she feels Jenkins was operating under a personal vendetta against her father. And I'm not so certain she isn't correct. Jenkins said there was an informant, someone who was feeding him information about Cal Covington."

"And did you discover who that informant is?"

Daniel hesitated. "Jenkins didn't give me any names."

The first smile crossed Gottard's face. "Which isn't any answer at all, Agent Dubonet."

"Agent?" Daniel waited, wondering what game Gottard played now.

"That's as ambiguous as your answer. And possibly as dangerous. It's a dance, Dubonet. The gathering of this type of information is a dance. It's your turn to lead."

Chapter Thirteen

Blast those photographers! How can I get near Socks if they're going to go into a motor-drive frenzy every time the First Cat tries to peep out the window? I can see now why Socks had to hire me to do his investigating. The poor cat can hardly do his business without making the national news. If I ever wanted fame, I know now that it isn't in the political arena. 'Tis far, far better to suffer amongst the masses, unknown and unfettered.

No time for poetic philosophizing. I have to get inside the White House. There's something troubling me, and it involves Chef André. The man who peppered Bureau Boy last night was tall. And there was something familiar, no pun intended, about him. A peculiar odor. Not toothpaste, after-shave, soap or powder, or any of the other perfumed substances that humans use to hide their natural scent. I'm not particularly fond of the seasoning, but I do believe it was garlic. A man who either cooks a lot or had recently eaten a lot of garlic!

Possibly a chef, would you think? I would. A jealous chef?

There's my break. A delivery man is hauling fresh seafood into the kitchen entrance. With a spurt of speed and a little luck— Yes! Now to find Chef André and then Socks.

There's the kitchen headquarters, and Chef André is in the middle of what appears to be a staff meeting. Guys and gals in white suits, listening very closely to André run over the daily schedule. He's tall, slender, and he has that very slight accent. More New Orleans than French, but just enough to sound foreign. Hmm. When he spies me, all hell is going to break loose, and I can't get close enough to him. Not that it matters. Every single one of these chefs smells of onions and garlic and seasonings. Drat! Better take a look at the calendar. To satisfy a point of personal curiosity.

Here it is, and yes, Lucinda's party is marked down for tomorrow. Even though no one from the White House staff is working it, it's on the calendar. Backtracking, I see the Bingington soiree is here, as well as junior's birthday party for the Georgia senator. Odd that outside jobs are kept on the main calendar. Very odd. Why would André care? How would he even know?

Now it's time to vacate and find my boss. Outside the hustle of the kitchen, this place is something else. Security people everywhere. All very official. All very professional. All very absorbed in their own work, thank goodness. I'm just strolling along acting as if I belong. Now I can make a dash for the personal quarters—the domain of the First Cat.

Socks, I hope you have some answers for 009. This feline is in need of some procedural advice.

SARAH ROTATED her tired and throbbing shoulders. She'd shopped, loaded, unloaded, mixed, seared, sautéed, battered, braised, puréed, pitted and pared until she couldn't think straight. The menu was under way for the party of the year. She would turn out a table that would make Lucinda Watts feel down-South at home and uptown elegant. The pecan-fudge flambé would be the crowning touch, just a little razzle-dazzle for a woman who knew the fine art of show business. Sarah smiled. It wasn't that she was a better cook than many of the fine chefs working in D.C. It was that she had an intuitive sense of her clients and what they liked. With a flaming dessert, Lucinda would feel that she'd gotten her money's worth. And every dish was in progress.

She tried not to check the clock. The hour hand was creeping along, and still there was no word from Daniel. Had they arrested him? That was a distinct possibility. Would he call? Would they allow him to?

Sarah knew the Miranda law as well as any television cop, but she also knew that once a man disappeared into the bowels of the federal intelligence community, rights weren't always honored. After all, did the FBI have the right to hound her father, literally, to his grave? Did they have a right to decide that he was guilty of some crime without even a scrap of evidence?

The answer to both questions was no. But they'd done it, anyway. Her fingers fumbled in a drawer and picked up a pencil. Trying to keep her eyes off the clock, she started making a list of the serving pieces she needed to gather.

Minutes passed before she glanced at the clock and realized she was chewing the pencil. There was only one item on her list.

She got up and paced the kitchen. She had garlic baking in the oven and a half dozen dishes in various stages of production. She couldn't go hunt for Daniel. Mumbling dire curses under her breath, she looked up the FBI number and placed the call.

Paul Gottard was Daniel's boss, and she asked for him. A young woman explained that he could not come to the telephone.

"I'm looking for Daniel Dubonet," Sarah explained. "Has he been in?"

There was a slight hesitation. "I couldn't say," the woman answered.

Sarah thanked her and replaced the phone, knowing that the secretary was lying. Daniel had been there, but they were not acknowledging the visit. Did they have him somewhere in the basement of the building? It was a ludicrous—and terrifying—thought.

She called his apartment and let the phone ring. As a last step, she dialed Uncle Vince. There was no answer there.

Another five minutes passed and Sarah felt the tension knot tighter. Where was Daniel, and what was he doing? When he did finally call—and he *had* to call or show up—she was going to give him something to worry about.

And Familiar, too. That rascally cat had abandoned ship as soon as they'd arrived back in the city. One day Sarah was going to follow him around and see exactly where he went.

She was so deep into her interior tirade that the sound of the front bell ringing didn't register until she heard Sandra Fowler's sharp voice.

"I will not have any more of this, Sarah Covington. Not another minute, do you hear me?"

Sarah wiped her hands on her apron and pushed through the door into the shop.

"What—?"

"No excuses. I know you're behind this. Those telephone men climbing all over the poles. My phone—my *business* phone—was down for two hours yesterday afternoon, and this morning it sounds like a tin can! My clients depend on me to have a working telephone."

"What—?"

"You young folks have to have all the latest gadgets and doodads. It's ridiculous. You don't care who you inconvenience, just as long as you have everything your own way."

"Hold on a—"

"Well, I've taken this matter into my own hands. I've called the phone company myself, and they're looking into you. If you don't watch it, missy, they're going to cut your telephone out completely. It's a privilege to own a phone, not a right. A privilege. And when you abuse it, you lose it."

"Wait!" Sarah slammed a hand down on the counter. The loud noise seemed to short-circuit Sandra, and for the first time since she had entered the building, she paused.

"I haven't ordered any new telephone equipment. I haven't even been in town."

"You ordered that cable thing. That new..." Sandra stopped at the look on Sarah's face. "I'm sure they said it was your phone. I'm positive."

"Why would I want cable through my phone when I never have time to watch television?" Sarah felt like she was talking to a hardheaded child.

"But they said—"

"I can't help what they said. I haven't ordered any new phone equipment or changes. In fact, they were working on the lines a few days ago. There had been some problem." As she talked, a nagging worry grew at the back of her mind. Two telephone men, two separate phone incidents. It wasn't just coincidence. What was it Daniel told her—there was no such thing as coincidence in a law officer's mind.

"Sarah?" Sandra looked with some concern at the chef.

"It's okay. I'm just worried about the phone."

"Well, is it working?"

Sarah nodded. It had been working all afternoon, but there was an odd, hollow sound to it.

"Check it, and if anything is wrong, I'll report it."

Sarah ducked into the kitchen and lifted the receiver. The dial tone was there, just a little tinny sounding.

"It's fine," she said, walking back into the shop. "I wouldn't worry about any of it."

"I'm going to report this. I—"

"Leave it alone, Mrs. Fowler." Sarah smiled to make it sound less like a direct order. "I have some friends at the phone company. I'll get them to take care of it."

"Okay." She nodded. "That would be easier, just to get someone you know to handle it. Better service." She started toward the door and had pushed it halfway open when she stopped. "By the way, I saw that cat again this morning. He was hustling down the sidewalk like he had business at the White House." She frowned.

"You never know with Familiar. He might be advising the president at this very moment." Sarah grinned.

"I don't care who he advises as long as he stays away from my shop and my customers." With that, she made her exit.

"That woman would die if she couldn't get the last word." Sarah spoke aloud, and there was more than a hint of amusement in her voice. As soon as she went back into the kitchen and saw the phone, all amusement ended. Someone had been tampering with her telephone. Had they really tapped it? If so, who? Why? What had they heard?

It was another niggling concern that nibbled and ate at her as she continued to prepare her food. And wait for Daniel.

She was almost sick with worry when she finally heard his knock at the back door. Darkness had fallen over the city and the streets outside were empty of parked cars. Sarah knew because she'd checked every three minutes.

"Where have you . . . ?" The question died on her lips as she looked at him. "What happened? I was afraid they'd arrested you and were holding you prisoner in some dark reaches of a federal building." She tried to smile, but she couldn't. She'd really been afraid for him.

"Have you talked to anyone today?"

Daniel's question caught her by surprise. "About a hundred stores. Lucinda. The FBI." At Daniel's startled expression, she found a smile. "I called to check on you. They wouldn't even tell me you'd been there."

"That's interesting." He paced into the room, then lifted the cover of a pot on the stove.

Sarah took the hint and began to put together a plate. "Funny you should ask about the telephone. Sandra Fowler was over here this afternoon ready to string me up by my heels because she thought I'd ordered some new phone equipment and created an inconvenience for her."

"Your lines have been tapped. Very professionally. And I suspect you've been under surveillance by a 'team' of phony phone men."

Sarah wasn't nearly as shocked as she'd thought she would be. Instead, there was a distant vibration of anger and a feeling of helplessness. Her parents had had this conversation years ago. Cal had been convinced the phones to his home and office were tapped. But he'd never been able to find an official of the phone company who would verify his suspicions.

"How did you find out?" She put a bowl of gumbo in front of him.

"There are no records, but I had some friends who worked in electronic surveillance. They did a little hunting around and found the work order for a crew to go out in a telephone company truck." He picked up the corn bread she put beside his bowl and bit into it.

"The FBI ordered a tap of my phone?"

"Yes."

"Does this happen often?"

"More than the average citizen would ever think, but not as often as the movies would have you believe."

Sarah sat down and played with a piece of corn bread. Her appetite was gone. "How long?"

"Since the day you saw the man in the alley. He wasn't a phone company man. He was with the Bureau."

"Great." She felt a sudden fury. Someone had invaded her privacy, had tapped into private conversations when she had no idea they were listening. The very idea made her mad enough to spit nails.

"Makes you feel violated, doesn't it?" Daniel was watching her with a spoon raised halfway to his lips.

"It does. In fact, it's bringing back memories of what I went through as a child."

He wanted to say something to comfort her, but there were no words, and he knew it. "I can't undo what's happened, Sarah, but I can try to make whoever is responsible for all of this pay."

"All afternoon I've been worried sick about you. I've been trying to figure out why this is happening. What's triggered this? Do you have any ideas?"

Daniel shook his head. "It is odd. You've been in Washington three years. You've had this business now for almost a year. Nothing has changed. You haven't applied for a loan or opened a new checking account—"

"How do you know all this?" Sarah was amazed.

"The FBI can access all of your financial records. And they did. Gottard gave me a rundown today while I was visiting him."

The sense of outrage was even greater. Sarah sent a venomous glance at Daniel, but she knew he wasn't to blame. "This country is going to hell in a handbasket when the government can find out everything about a citizen without his even knowing he's being examined."

Daniel put his spoon down and reached across the table for her hand. "It's a tough call. National security over personal rights. That's one that will be argued again and again. Right now, the Bureau has the power to pull any financial records. It's how we find money laundering, all types of white-collar crime, as well as drug conspiracies and God knows what else."

"You sound like you approve of it." She was shocked.

"Sometimes I do. But when it comes to you, because I know you, and I know what a decent person you are, I find it wrong."

He let that sink in awhile as he picked up the spoon and ate some of the spicy gumbo. As he ate, he carefully watched the play of Sarah's emotions. He could see she was offended, and angry, but she also understood. It wasn't an issue with an easy answer.

"Since my finances are clear, why does the FBI still think I'm hiding money, or doing whatever they think I'm doing?"

"It could be the casinos down on the coastline. There could be something funny going on there." Daniel had racked his brain trying to think of what might have triggered the interest in Sarah and her past. There wasn't a single thing, or at least, he didn't see it. Paul Gottard had originally given him the assignment to check Sarah out, but the director had not given Daniel all of the necessary information.

"What should we do?" Sarah saw the fatigue in the skin around Daniel's eyes. He was tired. Worn down and dog tired.

"Let's book some flights for Biloxi for day after tomorrow. But we'll have to go to a pay phone and use assumed names."

"Why?" Sarah didn't object. She just didn't understand.

"They can trace our moves if we use credit cards or our real names. I'd just as soon not have a tail while we're working along the coast. If there's a problem with those casinos, I'd like to try to figure it out and live to tell about it."

"Great." Sarah felt worse, if possible. Now she couldn't even go home using her own name. "Should I buy a trench coat and a hat?"

Daniel's fingers circled her wrist. "I prefer that chef suit. The material has a way of clinging to just the right places."

Flattered and embarrassed, Sarah bent to kiss him. "I don't know why I was lucky enough to drag you into my life, but I'm glad you're here."

"Me, too." He looked around the kitchen. "Is everything secure down here or do we need to stir and whip before Lucinda's party tomorrow?"

Sarah walked to the stove and flicked the switches off. "Everything's fine. For the moment. I think I'd like to... interrogate you upstairs."

"And I thought all along I was coming here for the cooking." He took her hand and pulled her against him. He gave her one swift, passionate kiss before leading her out of the kitchen and up the stairs.

SARAH GAVE Daniel a wink as he helped her carry her supplies and dishes into the enormous kitchen of Lucinda Watts's beautiful estate. Sarah stopped, almost causing Daniel to collide with her, as she saw the dimensions of the kitchen, the spotless black-and-white floors and what appeared to be miles of white counter space.

"I could cook a feast fit for a king here," Sarah said.

"I think that's exactly what you've done," Daniel said, edging past her with a heavy load and putting it on a countertop. "Lucinda must have an excellent money manager. She's had a few rich boyfriends, but I know they never supported her in this style."

"How do you know?" Sarah regretted the question. The more she was learning about the FBI, the less she liked it.

"Lucinda had the ear and, uh, other anatomical parts, of some very powerful men. We kept a close eye on her, and I'm not a bit ashamed of that fact."

"I wouldn't put it past you guys to have videotapes."

Daniel laughed softly. "I never got invited to a screening, if they did."

"That's not funny." But Sarah couldn't help but smile. Daniel was wearing a wig, a fake mustache, a chef's hat and apron. He was going to be her assistant. And he was going to learn the true meaning of kitchen labor.

"Is that a smile of appreciation for my handsome appearance?"

"A smile of delight at your outrageous mustache." She tweaked the end of it gently. "I'd kiss you but I'm afraid I'll end up wearing it."

"I'm an expert at disguise."

"And a few other things I could list."

"If you're going to talk like that..."

Sarah raised both hands in surrender. "You're right. We have work to do. Get that big box out of the car, please."

"Yes, Madame Chef."

Daniel disappeared out the door and came back in groaning under the weight of a box. He'd no sooner put it down than the lid flew open and a black blur leapt to Sarah's feet.

"Familiar?" She was astounded. "That cat is amazing. He has more tricks than Houdini."

"And he weighs a ton." Daniel bent down to pick Familiar up. He stroked his head while he held him in his arms. "I'm glad to see this guy. He was a big help at Idlewild. He might have saved your life, you know."

Sarah eyed the cat. "He's an amazing creature." There were a million questions she wanted to ask about the cat, but she knew there were no answers, at least none that Daniel could give, and Familiar wasn't talking. "All I can say is that he'd better skulk around here and lie low. I'm not sure Lucinda is an animal lover."

"Meow." Familiar leapt to the floor, turned a flip and then rubbed lovingly against her legs.

"He's telling you that he can win the hardest heart." Daniel was laughing as he bent to pick up the cat. "This guy is a rogue and a charmer. I'm going to take him over to this chair here and take some lessons from him."

"Excellent. I'm going to cook."

Eight hours later, Sarah was sitting on a stool and drinking a glass of iced tea. The hors d'oeuvres were prepared, the bar was set up and ready, the meal was in the last stages of preparation. Daniel was sitting across from her, his shoulders sagging and his head resting on his arms.

"This is hard work, Sarah. I'm beat."

"Me, too."

"Meow." Familiar sat on the table, his yellow-green eyes almost shut.

"I can't wait until this dinner is over. I think the first of the guests are arriving."

"Then I'd better hoist myself up and change uniforms."

Sarah gave him a quizzical look.

"I managed to wrangle—well, produce a near-perfect copy of—an invitation for both of us. I brought a tux for me and a little red dress for you."

"I can't—"

"Think of it, Sarah. A chance to mingle with the elite, to see your government at work in the places where it functions the best—secret deals made at cocktail parties and dinners."

She chuckled softly. It was tempting, but there was no way she could be in the kitchen and in the dining room.

"Just for cocktails? This isn't just a joke, you know. There's a chance you might spot someone among the guests that strikes a chord with you. Someone you've seen before, someone who doesn't really belong."

"Like us," she observed. "Okay." She felt impulsive and foolish, but everything was under control in the kitchen. What would it hurt to flit among the socially prominent for half an hour? There was little chance anyone would recognize her, except maybe Vincent Minton. The chances of her recognizing some evil-doer were slim, but it was better than doing nothing to help Daniel.

"I'll get our clothes."

Sarah went to check all of her pots one more time and give instructions to the serving staff as they shifted from kitchen to party with laden trays. She'd worked more than one party with them before, and she knew they could be trusted to do their jobs properly.

"What about you?" she asked the cat.

"Meow." Familiar closed his eyes and feigned sleep.

"Right. I'll believe that when this party is over." Familiar was not a cat to lie around and take it easy. The minute her back was turned, he'd be into something.

Daniel returned with the clothes. Sarah felt a shiver of anticipation when she saw the low-cut back of the beaded red dress. The chiffon skirt was full and sheer. It was one of the most feminine dresses she'd ever seen.

"You borrowed this from central casting down at the Bureau?"

"Actually, I bought it when I was running errands for you today."

"Daniel!"

"Well, I was hoping we'd have more than this one occasion for you to wear it. Maybe even down in Mississippi. I hear those magnolia-laden nights can be very romantic."

Sarah kissed his cheek as she took the dress. "You continue to surprise me. And delight me."

He picked up a strand of her blond hair and tugged it gently. "I try. Now, let's change and sashay out there to check out the crowd. I want to get an idea of who we're dealing with. Since I don't have access to the computer, I couldn't get the guest list, but I'll bet there are two dozen senators, maybe the vice president, a few members of the cabinet and some very influential business people. I hear there's been a plan afoot to locate some heavy-duty military business down in the Southern states. This could be the party where those plans are finalized."

"What if someone tries to...do something here?"

Daniel kissed her forehead and then her nose. "That's a possibility, and that's one reason I want to mingle with the crowd. If there are any strangers there, maybe we can tag them before anything happens. And Familiar will guard the kitchen."

"Thanks." Sarah kissed him gently, with a tenderness that made her eyes suddenly brim with emotion. Before she embarrassed herself, she took the dress into the bathroom and changed while Daniel did so in another bathroom. In ten minutes, with her hair pulled into a sophisticated chignon, she was ready to mingle.

"My, my, you sure do clean up nicely."

She laughed at the look on Daniel's face. "I thought you preferred that chef uniform."

"I did, but you know what they say. Variety is the spice of life. That red dress is pretty spicy."

Sarah took his arm and headed for the door. She turned back to give Familiar a warning look. "Stay in the kitchen."

He only blinked his eyes at her and pretended to sleep.

Daniel tugged her through the door and toward the sounds of laughter and a hot jazz band.

Neither Sarah nor Daniel saw the shadow that fell against the large kitchen window and then abruptly disappeared.

Chapter Fourteen

Sarah gave herself to the feel of Daniel's strong arms as the band riffed to the end of a song.

"I'd better get back to the kitchen," she whispered to him. She'd had one-half glass of champagne and a wonderful dance. No one had stopped them or questioned them, and there had been no sign yet of Uncle Vince.

"I hate to let you go." Daniel gently pressed his hand into the exposed flesh of her back, his fingers caressing the skin and promising much, much more.

"I'd feel better if I was doing my job." Sarah watched the seventy or so laughing people as they sipped their drinks and sampled the goodies she'd created. It was gratifying.

"I'm going to mingle some more, make sure all is in order, eavesdrop on a few conversations and see if I can determine who is here from the FBI."

"You don't recognize them?"

"It isn't exactly a small club." Daniel laughed. "I know, we all wear the same shoes and underwear."

"And drive those dark sedans."

"Right." He couldn't take his eyes off her. She was the most beautiful woman in the room. Almost too beautiful. Several men had been watching her with obvious interest. It would be smart for her to return to the kitchen before she was approached.

"See you later." She forced her body to leave his side. She had work to do, and so did he. Only three feet from him, she balked. "Is that Jean-Claude?" She'd only caught a glimpse of a tall, elegantly dressed man disappearing from the room.

"I haven't seen him." Daniel studied the crowd. "I'll keep my eyes open."

"Thanks." Sarah ignored the unreasonable concern that touched her. It wouldn't be unusual for Jean-Claude to be at a party at Lucinda Watts's. "Back to the ovens for me."

The only change in the kitchen when she returned were the empty trays that had been returned for more delicacies. The party tidbits were being well received. Sarah took three minutes to change clothes, tying her apron as she reentered the kitchen only a little breathless. She stopped in the middle of the room. Lucinda Watts, in a dazzling gown of blue sequins and jet, was hovering over the opened oven.

"This smells delicious." Lucinda put down the spoon she'd been using and shut the oven door. "Everything is wonderful, so far."

"Thanks." Sarah had a genuine smile for her employer of the evening. The party was loaded with plenty of people who would give parties in the coming weeks. Sarah's reputation had received a big boost. "Thanks for giving me this chance."

Lucinda's blue eyes were shrewd. "I knew your father. He gave me more than one or two chances." Her smile was tight. "And I always repay my debts. One way or the other."

Surprised at the hint of unpleasantness in the words, Sarah kept the smile glued to her face. "That's an excellent policy."

"Cal was a straight arrow." Lucinda's eyebrows drew together. "He was a good man, as far as I knew. But that's all a dead issue now. The fact is, you're a good cook." Her face brightened. "Pork chops with corn bread stuffing, right?"

"That's what you requested, with all the trimmings, and gumbo as an appetizer."

"Just like the good old days when folks knew how to eat and didn't worry about calories or fat grams or any of that other foolishness. It might sound strange to a non-Southerner, but that's exactly what these men will love. There's more truth to the old saying that a man's stomach rules his heart—and his wallet."

Lucinda Watts was a wise woman who'd learned her lessons in the school of hard knocks. Sarah liked her frankness, but there was an edge to her. With her blue eye shadow, very subtly applied but there nonetheless, and her sequined dress that showed off her firm figure and long legs, Lucinda was what she'd once been *and* what she wanted to be. It was a combination of a woman who was earthy and yet socially skilled, someone who'd suffered but who had survived. Someone who went after what she wanted and didn't count the casualties that got in the way.

Lucinda's gaze swept over the room and settled on Familiar as he pushed open a closet door and came out. "I see you brought your own good-luck charm."

"I didn't realize he was in the car," Sarah admitted. "But he hasn't made any trouble." The cat was wobbly, as if he'd been sound asleep. And in the closet? Sarah felt a chill of concern.

"Well, I grew up with cats and dogs running around the house. Some of these fancy folks would have a fit if they thought there was a cat in the kitchen, but what they don't know won't hurt them. Just keep him out of sight. I'm working a deal in there that could mean my ultimate retirement to a life-style I admire—and desire." She laughed. "I don't want any deals queered by a black cat. This could be the most important dinner of my life."

"He'll stay with me," Sarah assured her.

Lucinda paused at the door. "By the way, you're a pretty good dancer." She walked out, letting the door close softly behind her.

Sarah felt a flush of guilt, but her overriding concern was for Familiar. As soon as she was certain Lucinda had departed for good, she hurried over to the cat. "What happened?" She stroked his head and was relieved to hear a purr. She gently ran her hands over his body. He gave no sign of discomfort or injury. As she inspected him, his vision seemed to clear and he meowed. Loudly. She was in the middle of trying to silence him with soft words and strokes when the door opened.

"Sarah, they'll be ready for the appetizer in ten minutes."

She looked up to find the headwaiter watching her. He was staring at Familiar. She stood. "Coming right up."

One eye on Familiar, she bent to the oven and started putting the finishing touches on the main dishes. A serving staff would take heaping platters to the seated diners. Sarah had everything ready for the first course when the waiters appeared.

"Working with you is like clockwork," one of the waiters said. "Always professional. And believe me, from the comments I'm hearing, this is going to pay off. You'll be busy for the rest of the holiday season."

"Thanks." Sarah nodded.

Thirty minutes later she was putting the main course on trays. Daniel had popped in twice to report that all was well at the party, and Familiar was pacing the kitchen, almost tripping her every time she took something from the oven. It wasn't like the black cat to be so aggravating. He was actually clawing up her pant leg and trying to get to the pork chops. Yet when she offered him a sample, he didn't want to eat any of it. Maybe he was coming down with some kitty illness. She'd have to find a really good vet in town.

"Okay." She nodded as the trays of pork chops were lifted and taken in to the dining room. She turned back to the stove, failing to notice that Familiar had followed right on the heels of the second waiter.

She'd drawn in her breath to give a sigh of relief—only dessert remained—when she heard the sound of breaking dishes and a low murmur of surprise that turned to...fear?

What in the world had happened? She went to the door to listen. If the waiters had dropped the dishes...but that was impossible. Those guys had never bungled a meal in their lives.

"Sarah Covington!" Lucinda Watts's voice was wild with anger. "Get in here and get this damn cat!"

"Familiar." Sarah's quick look around the kitchen told her the awful truth. Familiar was nowhere to be seen. She hurried into the dining room, her eyes unwilling to register the mayhem that appeared. Two platters of pork chops were on the floor, and Familiar stood beside them, hissing at anyone who tried to get near. Several women were clutching their throats in near hysteria while a couple of men had risen, ready for whatever action was necessary. There was a lull in the conversation, then a rush of noise.

"Get that damn cat out of my house before I kill him." Lucinda stood at her place at the table, hands braced on the beautiful linen cloth. She was trembling with fury.

"Familiar." Sarah spoke softly to the cat. "He must be sick," she said, realizing too late that such a statement would only make matters worse.

"Get that diseased cat out of here." Lucinda's voice rose to just below a shriek. "Take him to a veterinarian and have him confined. If he has some disease, I want to know. We may all have to have vaccinations or something." At the murmur of concern that flew around the table, Lucinda snapped her mouth shut.

"Maybe we should just shoot him." The man who sat at Lucinda's right stood. He signaled to two men who stood at parade rest near the dining room door. At his motion, they reached into their jackets and started forward.

"Don't you dare touch him." Sarah's concern for the cat finally overrode her horror at the scene. "I'll take care of him." She scooped Familiar into her arms and hurried back to the kitchen with him. She had to get him to her car before some other bozo got the bright idea of killing him.

"Give him to me." Daniel appeared at her side and she passed the cat off to him. "I was standing outside the dining room, pretending to be Senator Beaumont's aide. Familiar literally flew across the room and tackled the waiter. When he'd knocked one down, he went after the other."

Sarah felt tears building. It was so stupid, but she was furious, therefore she was ready to cry. "They were going to kill him."

"Let's get out of here."

Sarah nodded. "First, let me clean up some of that mess. I can't just leave my food all over the floor like that. It's humiliating." In the kitchen she found several large plastic bags. Dreading every step, she returned to the dining room where the guests were still seated at the table in shock.

"I hope you're satisfied." Lucinda almost hissed at her. "All of my plans, ruined. My very future put in jeopardy. You'll pay for this, young woman."

Sarah was so startled by the expression of pure hatred on Lucinda's face that she stopped, plastic bag in hand, frozen beside the two unfortunate heaps of pork chops. The two waiters, chagrin evident in their faces, had backed up against the wall.

"Lucinda, there's no need to upset yourself further." Vincent Minton appeared at her side and gently put an arm around her, pulling her against him. The look he gave Sarah was filled with understanding and disappointment. Guiding Lucinda, he turned her away and led her from the room.

"Let me give you a hand." The headwaiter appeared beside Sarah and bent to assist her in cleaning up the pork chops.

"Don't touch them," she said woodenly. She couldn't believe what had happened. Familiar had never behaved in such a fashion. Something was wrong with him. But what?

What would make him attack two waiters and ruin an elegant party? She didn't even question that he had done it deliberately. As the waiter reached toward the food, Sarah blocked him. "Really, don't touch them."

"What?" He backed off several inches, giving her a look that showed his concern for her mental stability.

"There might be something wrong with the pork chops." She spoke without analyzing her thoughts. "There had to be a reason he attacked like that. Maybe…" She eyed the food, remembering the way Familiar had attempted to get her attention in the kitchen. And failed. "Let me do this," she said. "Serve some wine or do something to distract the guests." She could feel every eye in the room on her. She was finished, that much she knew. She'd never get another job catering in D.C. As shocked as everyone was now, as soon as they got home they'd be buzzing with the gossip that Lucinda Watts's big dinner had been destroyed by some stupid caterer who'd brought her cat with her. The real facts didn't matter. By breakfast tomorrow, the story would be blown completely out of proportion. The only thing they wouldn't get wrong would be her name, and Lucinda's. Unfortunately, Lucinda would suffer as much public humiliation as Sarah would herself. In the D.C. scheme of things, Lucinda was responsible for hiring incompetent help, a sin almost as deadly as being incompetent.

Sarah bagged the food and hurried from the room. There was nothing to do but pack up her stuff and get out of there as fast as possible.

Daniel met her in the kitchen, and in less than fifteen minutes they'd almost packed the car. "What about dessert?" he asked.

"Leave it. Better yet, put it down the garbage disposal." Sarah had considered serving the remainder of the meal, but she was certain Lucinda wanted her out of the house as rapidly as possible. Besides, she was uncertain about the food, about what might have been done to it. She started shoving the delicate pecan tortes down the disposal. "How's Familiar?"

"Trying like hell to get out of the car," Daniel said. He shook his head. "I have no idea what got into him. He was vicious. So aggressive, I thought he was going to take that waiter down by the throat. And when the poor guy tried to save the platter of food and hand it to one of the guests, Familiar launched himself at the platter."

"Is there any way you could get something analyzed at the lab?"

Daniel thought for a moment he'd misunderstood her question. "You mean, the FBI lab?"

"Right." She stared directly at him. "I don't think anything's wrong with Familiar. I think something is terribly wrong with that food."

Comprehension touched Daniel's face. "He deliberately knocked the food to the floor so that no one would eat it."

"He tried to stop me in the kitchen, but I guess he didn't want to get rough with me." She found, even among the disastrous events, that she could still smile. "He didn't mind getting rough with the waiters."

"They're guys," Daniel said, smiling, also. "They can take it."

"Can you get access to the lab?"

Daniel had wondered how he was going to tell her he wasn't exactly fired. Not exactly, if he understood Paul Gottard's message. He wasn't fired and he wasn't an agent. He was in limbo, tucked away somewhere without any protection, and without any legal privileges. But he might be able to get something through the lab, even though the very thought of Cody Pruett made him feel guilty.

"Maybe. I'm not exactly certain what my status with the Bureau is right now. I'm under suspicion for murder and misuse of my authority. They don't believe I lost my badge and gun, but they aren't willing to arrest me. In fact, I'm still assigned to your case, if you can assign someone who may or may not work for you.''

She bit back the harsh criticism that formed on her lips. It wouldn't do Daniel any good now to hear her low opinion of the FBI. Instead she shifted the focus to the immediate problem. "I know there's something wrong with the chops. The question is, how did it happen? The only time I left the kitchen was when I was with you, mingling among the guests.''

"And Familiar was there in the kitchen. He would have warned us if anything was amiss.''

Sarah's eyes opened wider. "But he was in a closet. He came out acting like he'd been asleep! Lucinda saw him and commented on his presence at her party.''

"I'll bet someone pushed him into that closet, maybe even knocked him out.''

"And when I came out of the bathroom from changing clothes, Lucinda was at the oven. She'd been stirring something in the pan.''

"The pork chop pan?''

Sarah nodded.

"Familiar may have not only saved your career, he could have saved someone's life. Several someones. Grab your coat and let's get out of here. I have a meeting with Paul Gottard I have to make, and I want you with me. It's time he met you for himself.''

Sarah swallowed back her instant protest. The idea of meeting the FBI director made her mouth go dry. Gottard had not been in the agency when her father was a sheriff, but that didn't change her opinion of the way the FBI worked. After all, look at what they were doing with Daniel. He didn't have to go into great detail to let her know he'd been left hanging out on a limb, just swinging in whatever breeze happened to blow. She could see the bitter hurt in his eyes. He wasn't fired, but if anything went wrong, the FBI would deny that he worked for them. Great!

"Sarah." Lucinda's voice was like a whip cracking.

Both Sarah and Daniel turned to face her. She stood at the kitchen door with a very anxious Vincent Minton just behind her.

"Lucinda," Vincent said softly, "it was an accident. I was poor judgment to bring the cat, but Sarah would never deliberately create such a mess."

Lucinda shook off his hand. "Where is that animal? I've called my doctor, and he says the cat must be quarantined They may need brain tissue to determine if he's mad." Her smile was ugly.

"Bad news, Mrs. Watts." Daniel stepped forward. "He escaped from my arms when I was trying to put him in the car. He was so upset. He's around the house somewhere. tried to catch him, but he's terrified."

"Liar." Lucinda's blue eyes glittered. "I want that animal impounded."

"He's gone." Daniel held his ground. "We'll look for him, and if we do find him, we'll take him to a vet of our choice to make certain he's not ill."

"He was perfectly fine before we got here," Sarah tried to assure her. "I'm positive he isn't sick."

"Get out." Lucinda's voice was icy.

"Now, that's one order we'll very gladly obey," Daniel said. He started to pick up the pans and the plastic bags o pork chops.

"You misunderstood me. I said get out, and I mean now."

Sarah couldn't believe the fury in the woman's voice. She saw Uncle Vince shake his head at her, urging her to comply with Lucinda's order.

"Daniel, leave it," she said. She knew she'd get her gea back later. At the moment she wanted to escape with Fa miliar before they thought to go out and check the car.

"Right." Daniel eased the pots back onto the stove. With a deft gesture he maneuvered the pork chops into the fold of his coat. "We're out of here." He took Sarah's arm and hustled her out the door. "Don't look back," he warned.

"The pork chops," she moaned.

He patted the coat. "We always get our chop," he said. He pushed her toward the car and the outline of a small black cat who was sitting in the back window watching for them.

"Duck, Familiar," Daniel said as he put Sarah in the passenger seat and ran around to get in the driver's side. He didn't waste a backward glance as he started the motor and zoomed away from the beautiful house.

"CINDY, WOULD YOU just ask him to speak with me a moment?" Daniel felt the frustration level building to a steamy head. He looked at the door behind which Paul Gottard hid, and considered breaking it down.

"He won't see you," Cindy said. Her stony-faced secretarial training was about to break, though. "Daniel, he really can't see you now." She glanced at Sarah. "Not now."

"Let me speak to him."

"No. I can't. It would mean my job."

"Then he's in there, and I mean to see him."

"Don't do it," she warned. "I'll have to call security, and they'll arrest you. What good would that do? Assault charges won't look very good on your record."

"I don't give a damn about my record!" Daniel couldn't help shouting. "I've had a great record, up until now, and it obviously doesn't count. Why should I get concerned over a bad record? I need to talk with Gottard."

"He has someone else in there." Cindy whispered the words. "He really can't see you."

"Who?" Daniel demanded.

The stony face dropped back over her features. "Get out of here now, before I have to call someone, Daniel. You're in enough trouble without deliberately starting more." She gave Sarah, who was standing silently at the far corner of the room, a withering look. "Take my advice, Daniel, get her and get out of here before someone sees you."

Daniel knew instantly what Cindy meant. She was a smart cookie. She'd heard enough conversations and typed enough letters. Sarah Covington was a hot topic at the Bureau. She was being discussed from the top officers down and anyone caught defending her was suspicious.

"Tell Gottard I quit. Tell him to take his job and his badge and his gun and—"

Sarah's hand fell across his arm and the gentle pressure of her fingers stopped him. "Let's go," she whispered. "Now."

His gaze met hers and he saw her anger, and her pain for him. "Right. Before I do something I might really regret." He turned back to Cindy one last time. "I know you're only doing your job, and I'm leaving, if you'll tell me one thing. Who's in that room with him? Tell me or I'm going to break down the door, whether it causes trouble for me or not."

"You'll leave? Quietly?"

"You have my word."

Cindy looked at the door, then up at Daniel. "I think you're getting the shaft, Dubonet. It's none of my affair, but you're being railroaded. Joshua Jenkins is in there."

"Jenkins." Sarah said the word like a curse. She felt a surge of anger, and the swelling of tears in her eyes. Damn! She wasn't going to cry. She might break the door down herself and wring the truth out of that old man. How was it possible that he continued to live and thrive and prosper while her father was dead? And he was still besmirching the name of Cal Covington, and her own. She knew that as surely as she drew breath.

"Sarah." It was Daniel's turn to draw her back from the brink of fury. He bent to her ear and whispered, "Let's go. I have another bright idea."

"What is it?"

"Private lab. We can get the same tests run. It's expensive, but it's all we've got."

"I'm sorry," Cindy said. "I really am. Now get out of here before I get fired." She glanced anxiously at Gottard's office door. "Hurry up and get out of here."

"Thanks," Daniel said as he and Sarah started for the door.

To their surprise, Cindy got up from behind her desk and walked to the door. Stepping into the hallway, she signaled them to follow her.

"What is it?" Daniel asked.

She shook her head and hurried them toward the front entrance. When they were out in the dusk she looked around again. "Listen to me, and listen good. Don't trust anyone. Not anyone at all. Don't tell anyone your plans, and if I were you, I'd consider moving out of the Washington area for a while. Maybe forever."

"What is it?" Daniel asked. He could see the tension in the woman. She was risking a lot to talk to him.

"Stay off the phones. The ones at the catering shop are bugged, that much I know for sure."

"We found that," he assured her. "Why are you telling me this?"

Her face drew together in consternation. "I'm not really sure. Except that Cody and I were friends. Good friends. And he spoke a lot about you. He thought you were really great. And I know you didn't kill him."

"They honestly think I killed Cody?" Daniel found it hard to believe.

"Whether they believe it or not, it sounds to me like they're getting ready to stick the blame on you. And Ms. Covington, too. The worst thing that ever happened to you was getting involved with her. Cody might be alive . . ." She shook her head. "No, that's not right. Just get out of town and disappear. You know how to do it. Now, I've got to go. Don't call me and don't come back here again.'' She entered the building and slammed the door behind her.

Chapter Fifteen

"I never thought I'd be traveling back to Mississippi with a cat hidden in my carryon." Sarah leaned over the crowded airplane seat and stroked Familiar's head. The black cat gently nibbled at her fingers. "Lucky you knew the security guard at the gate or we'd never have gotten him through."

"We couldn't leave him. Lucinda is a woman with a good deal of power and a lot of anger toward you and Familiar. She isn't above having someone break into your place and take him."

"And if she got her clutches on him, nothing good would happen to my fine furry friend."

Familiar clamped a little harder on her hand, indicating that since he couldn't speak, he'd participate in the conversation the best way he could.

"Ouch!" Sarah shook her hand free of his mouth. "Even when he's silent he's an uppity critter."

"Wait until the tests come back on that meat before you totally condemn him."

"I'm waiting, and I'm certain he's right." She wanted to lift him into her lap, but she didn't want to alert the airline to his presence. He was a stowaway. Sarah couldn't stand the idea of putting him in the luggage compartment, and they also didn't want a record of the cat traveling, even though they themselves were using assumed names. The less trails they left, the more certain they were that they weren't being followed.

"I wish we'd been able to call Mom." Sarah was still concerned. With the turn everything had taken, Mora might be in danger.

"It'll be better if we contact her once we're there. And after we've talked with Estis."

"You're right." Sarah knew it, but the facts were still difficult to accept. She cast a sideways glance at Daniel. Since the aborted meeting with Paul Gottard, he'd been as hard as steel. She knew he felt betrayed, and used. Those were probably the two worst feelings a person could deal with. Except guilt. And judging by Daniel's expression every time Cody Pruett's name was mentioned, he had a plentiful helping of that emotion, too. The toughest part was that there was nothing she could do to comfort him.

Reaching over, she captured his hand and squeezed it. "We're going to figure all of this out."

"Knowing the answers won't change things."

How many times had she thought that very same thing? How many years had passed with her trying to believe that? "It won't change things, not for either of us. But it will put things to rest. At least for me. And I think for you, too. Someone was responsible for what happened to Cody, and for what happened to my dad."

"Do you think revenge will make either of us feel better?"

She lifted his hand to her lips and kissed it softly. "No, I don't believe anything could make the pain and loss go away. Nothing can bring Cody back. Knowing the truth may or may not affect what you're feeling toward the FBI now. It could certainly change my feelings. And it will positively put an end to the tragic things that are happening all around us. That's what we have to think about. If we don't find out what's going on, more innocent people will suffer and possibly die."

Daniel strained against his seat belt as he turned to envelop her in his arms. "You sure know how to drain the self-pity out of a guy." He squeezed her tight. "Thanks. I was almost six feet under with feeling sorry for myself."

"I've been there." She kissed his cheek. "Now, how are we going to convince Graham to talk with us?"

"Do you remember him?"

"Brief moments. I haven't thought of him in years. He was always at the house with Dad. You know, he'd stop by for breakfast and a late supper. He wasn't married then. I guess he was really just a kid. But Dad thought he was very sharp."

"FBI trained, according to Jenkins."

"You say that as if you don't really believe it."

Daniel made a derisive sound. "I don't believe anything I've been told by them. And Jenkins is one of them. That's what I'm trying to figure out, if he was using me the entire time. How big an idiot was I?"

"You were only trying to do your job the best way you knew how. By the book. That doesn't make you stupid or dumb, Daniel. You know that." She nudged his shoulder. "Now, back to Graham. I was eleven, so he was at least twenty. Maybe twenty-two."

"He still has a long career ahead of him."

"Retirement for a sheriff's deputy isn't exactly plush." Sarah was trying to imagine the young, shy officer as a mature man. He had been smart. Cal's right hand, as it seemed. And he had known a lot about fingerprints and chemical analysis. It was very possible he'd been trained by the FBI. "I wish there was some way we could check out his past."

"So do I, but under the current circumstances, I don't think there's a snowball's chance in hell. Even the people at the agency who would like to help me will be afraid of any contact. Their careers could be ruined.''

''I know.''

The captain's voice alerting that landing was in ten minutes came over the air, and Sarah bent to check on Familiar. She could tell the cat was growing weary of his confinement in the carryon, but there was nothing she could do. ''Another fifteen minutes,'' she whispered to him. ''Then we'll spring you.''

Less than half an hour later, with Familiar asleep on the seat between them, they were crossing the five-mile bridge across Lake Ponchatrain and on the way to the Mississippi Gulf Coast. The lights of New Orleans glittered behind them as they rose higher and higher on the bridge. Ahead, the distant shoreline was only a faint sprinkling of lights.

''We'll get a room in Biloxi,'' Daniel said. ''Then tomorrow, bright and early, we'll have a talk with Estis.''

''And contact Mom.'' Sarah tried not to worry. Surely Mora would be fine. No one in their right mind would think she knew anything.

''I know you're worried.'' Daniel brushed her cheek with his right hand as he drove.

''Meow.'' Familiar stretched and moved to curl up in Sarah's lap. She stroked his head and scratched under his chin, eliciting a purr. ''When will those tests be back?''

''Possibly tomorrow. I didn't leave a number. I just said I'd call and check.''

''What if there's nothing there?''

''I don't know.'' Daniel glanced at Familiar. ''He seems fine now, and I don't believe he took such a dislike to Lucinda that he'd destroy her Washington future on a mere whim.'' He grinned. ''Though it was a spectacular scene.''

Sarah, tired to the bone, couldn't help grinning, too. ''I've had nightmares about something like that happening. But she was so damn mean to me, I don't even care. My career is probably ruined, and I can't get awfully shaken up about it. Mom's right. If push comes to shove, I can move back to the coast and work at one of the new casinos."

"And what about me?" Daniel's question was put in half jest, but there was an undertone of sincerity in it.

"Last time I heard, you were unemployed, too." She was teasing, but she wanted him to know she sympathized. "It would seem we're both in the same boat, and neither of us did anything to deserve it. We can both try our luck at the casinos. You'd make a distinguished blackjack dealer."

"I'm trying to learn to savor the feel of being unemployed." His grin was rueful. "But it does give a certain amount of freedom. I suppose I could work as a valet at one of the casinos. Maybe even practice up my singing act. I used to be pretty fair at ballads."

Sarah laughed out loud. "What a pair we'd make."

"Maybe if we practiced, we could become the new Fred and Ginger of the gambling world. You were pretty good on your feet."

"Thanks, but no thanks. I know my talents are in cooking, not dancing, but I'll support you in your efforts."

His hand caught hers and held it tightly. "Thanks for that, Sarah. And thanks for making me laugh. It's the best medicine now."

"Except for sleep. Let's hit the strip and park this chariot. I'm about to fade away."

"Tell me where we should stay and how to get there, and then you go to sleep," Daniel offered.

"I think the Cabana Royale in Biloxi would be a good choice. Stay on I-10 until I-110, then take a right on the beach. It's about two miles. That'll put us close to Jackson County, and close to Mom."

Daniel nodded. Lights in the rearview mirror caught his attention. For the past twenty miles, the same vehicle had been behind them. He really didn't believe they were being followed, but, the way things had gone, anything was possible. Instead of telling Sarah, he kept it to himself. She had enough to worry about with her mother.

"I'll drive us there while you rest," he said.

"Meow." Familiar stretched up, looking over the center console into the rear window.

"Go for it," Daniel told him as the cat made a dash for the rear window. "Just bob your head like one of those little dogs folks put up in the window." He drew a sigh of relief as the car behind him put on a burst of speed and passed in a long streak of black paint and darkened windows.

Still staring at the road disappearing behind them, Familiar perched in the window and seemed to sleep.

THE MISSISSIPPI SOUND glittered in the bright sunlight and Daniel slipped out of his jacket. "They're wearing shorts. It's November!" He pointed to the tourists romping on the white sand beaches. It was too cold to swim, but not too cold to enjoy the day.

"There were plenty of Christmases I wore shorts." Sarah made a face. "I hated that. Christmas is best when it's cold."

They drove along Highway 90 and Sarah pointed out the sights, many of them connected to personal memories. "This place has changed," she said with a note of wistfulness in her voice. "The casinos have really sprung from the sand. It's so... different."

"Growth and progress." Daniel's tone was tinged with a bitter acceptance of economics. "More jobs, more money. Growth."

"But why does everything from the past have to be swept away in the tide?"

"It's cheaper and easier to build new." They passed several of the homes that made the stretch of beach from Bay St. Louis to Pascagoula famous. "Now that's what I imagine when I think of the Old South."

Sarah sighed. There was still plenty of the past left, at least for a while. Besides, it did no good to bemoan change. "Graham is working the night shift, so he should be home now."

"And probably asleep."

"We could wait until after lunch." Sarah didn't want to wait. She didn't think she could stand to wait.

"What about it, Familiar?" Daniel noticed that the cat was watching the cars as if he expected to see someone he knew.

"Meow."

"Familiar says do it now," Sarah said. In fact, there *had* been a sense of urgency in the cat's tone. She wasn't imagining it.

They crossed Biloxi Bay and entered the small town of Ocean Springs. Daniel had obtained Estis's home address by calling the Jackson County sheriff's office in the guise of a floral delivery man looking for Graham Estis. He'd also learned that the deputy worked nights, had recently separated from his wife and was living alone in the family home at 211 Jefferson Street.

Daniel found the well-kept lawn and parked beneath an enormous live oak. The old Victorian house sported a fresh coat of pale yellow paint and a new tin roof. It was picture-perfect, right down to the pansies blooming in the flower beds and the bare pecan limbs of a small orchard in the backyard.

"Looks like he had a solid family life," Daniel said. "Wonder what went wrong."

Sarah tried to imagine. It was impossible for her to get beyond the young man who'd been so polite and so easy-going. Was he really the one who'd lied about her father? "It's tough to be married to a cop," she said. "I heard my mother say it often enough."

"Erratic hours," Daniel admitted.

"And more. Let's talk with him and see what he says." She could feel her heart pounding. Now that she was on the scene, she didn't want to be there. She was stepping through a door to the past that could change her forever.

"Sarah?" Daniel stood at her car door, waiting.

"I'm ready." She gave Familiar a pat, but he jumped out before she could stop him. "Familiar." She hurried across the lawn after him with Daniel one step behind her. "Familiar!" The cat was up the steps and nudging the front door open.

Damn! He was inside the house.

"Familiar." Sarah hesitated on the steps. She didn't want to go bursting into someone's house, but she darn sure didn't want Graham Estis to discover a stray cat had invaded his home. He might think Familiar was dangerous and hurt him.

"Sarah!" Daniel's hand on her shoulder stopped her in her tracks. "Wait a minute. Let's knock."

"He might hurt the cat."

"He might hurt you if you go bursting into his house." Daniel's fingers tightened. "Use that pretty head of yours."

She knew he was right and quit trying to pull away from him. She knocked briskly against the wood of the already open door and called his name. "Graham Estis, it's an old friend of yours. Graham?"

The old house was neatly kept. She could see the polished wood of the hall and the mahogany table beneath an antique mirror. A beautiful arrangement of silk flowers graced the table, adding the sense of a woman's touch to the room.

"Graham?" Sarah felt her anxiety notch even higher. Where was he? And where was that cat?

"I'm going in," Sarah said suddenly. She pushed the door open wide. Daniel grabbed for her but missed.

He was almost inside the house when he heard the sound of tires screaming as a black sedan whipped around the corner and headed out of the dead-end street. Sarah, only two feet inside the door, turned back to see what the commotion was about.

"That's the car from in front of the beauty shop." Sarah knew it wasn't possible, yet she recognized the car.

"Are you sure?" Daniel dashed out to the street to see if he could get a tag number.

"I'm positive." Sarah walked to the edge of the porch and waited for him. "I'm absolutely positive."

"There are a million black and dark blue cars." His voice was cautious.

"But that car was the same one. There was that red dirt on it, and a Mississippi tag. It's that strange blue tag. I noticed it several times in front of the beauty parlor."

"I didn't get the number."

"But it was Mississippi, right?"

"I didn't make it positively, but if it wasn't Mississippi, it was close." Daniel didn't want to admit any of this. If that car had followed them from Washington... But that was impossible. They'd flown. And without telling anyone. They'd even used assumed names. And since they knew Sarah's telephone was tapped, they'd carefully avoided using it for any important calls. Daniel's mind hadn't fully turned the events inside and out when a tragic thought struck him.

"Damn!" He ran up the steps and inside the house, not even bothering to pretend to wait for permission from the owner.

"Daniel, what is it?" Sarah's heart lurched. She recognized that look on his face. It meant trouble.

"The phone at Idlewild." He slammed his fist into the wall of the hallway. "Estis, are you here?" His voice was angry, worried.

"What about the phone?" Sarah followed him into the house.

"That telephone man. I should have trusted my instincts. He wasn't real." His fist hit the wall again. "Damn! I should have seen it. I should have known." He turned to Sarah. "You spoke with your mother about Graham Estis that day as soon as the phone was repaired."

A chill as cold as the bitterest winter ran through Sarah. She knew then what they would find in the neat Victorian house with the tin roof.

"Graham? Familiar?"

The black cat appeared at the end of the hallway. He sat down as if he waited for them. When Sarah tried to enter the room, he grabbed her foot with his claws.

"Wait here," Daniel said. Before she could protest, he pushed into the room and closed the door behind him. Graham Estis was in bed. The bullet wound was small, a professional job, and completely effective. Just to be on the safe side, Daniel went to him. A chill had already settled over the body. With great care, Daniel carefully removed any trace of his touch.

"I'm sorry," he whispered as he turned from the bed.

"Is he...?" Sarah stood in the doorway. She'd pushed the door open, but the sight of the body in the bed had stopped her cold.

"Dead." Daniel pulled her against his chest and held her as the first wave of anger and sorrow ran through her.

"It's my fault," she said. "I said his name. I gave it away."

Daniel held her tightly. "Sarah, they wouldn't have killed him unless he knew something. Something important." He shook her lightly to stop her angry tears. "You didn't kill him. He did that to himself years ago, when he became a part of whatever it was that destroyed your father."

Sarah forced herself to calm down. She had to think. Daniel was admitting that he believed there had been some conspiracy in years past, a plan to ruin her father. And he believed Graham Estis had been part of it.

"A good agent never believes in coincidence," Daniel said as he moved her toward the front door. "Familiar?" He looked back to find the cat was right behind him. "We have to get out of here, erasing every trace that we were at this house." As he spoke, he took a handkerchief from his pocket and wiped the bedroom and front doorknobs. "We didn't touch anything else."

He guided her down the steps, glancing at the neighboring houses to see if anyone had noticed them. "Don't cry," he said softly to her. "We can't make any kind of scene. Don't cry." He put her in the passenger seat, and Familiar hopped in with her.

Walking around the car, Daniel looked up and down the street. No one was about, for the moment. There had been no need to put a tail on them. Someone who knew every move they intended to make was already in Mississippi. Waiting to see if they'd come. Watching to see if Daniel and Sarah were on the right path.

Beyond a shadow of a doubt, Sarah, and possibly her mother, were in serious danger.

Daniel got behind the wheel. He said nothing to Sarah until they were coasting over the Biloxi Bay bridge and reentering the town of Biloxi. "Where does your mother live?" he asked, trying to keep his tone casual.

Sarah heard the fear that lay beneath his question. She gave the address only a block from the beach. "Hurry, Daniel," she whispered. "Please hurry."

THINGS HAVE GONE from bad to worse here. I don't know who snared me from behind and threw me in the closet at Lucinda Watts's estate. Even though I'd been knocked on the head—a most insulting attack against an agent of the First Cat—I heard them rattling around in the oven. Since Dolly wouldn't let me near the pork chops for a sniff, I had to take matters into my own hands on a hunch. I know someone tampered with those chops. As it was, I bet my lovely black hide on my intuition.

But I don't have a clue as to who it was!

Another troubling thing is Lucinda. Her attack on Sarah was vicious, but very calculated. It was almost as if she'd planned this entire debacle. Except she didn't count on me to make such a fiasco of the meal. I had the distinct impression that maybe she wanted someone to eat that bad meat.

I know, I could be prejudiced by the fact that she wanted to have me shot, or failing that, to have slices of my brain tissue probed under a microscope. That tends to make even the most docile feline a little aggressive.

I've had this feeling since we started this trip that someone was watching us. I could never put my paw on it exactly. There was a car behind us coming out of the airport. I'm positive. But they passed us. Headed right over here to murder Graham Estis, I'll bet.

I know we need to beat it from here before the cops arrive and charge Dolly and Bureau Boy with murder, but I sure would like a little more time to look around this place.

There are some awfully handsome antiques here. These things cost big bucks. Eleanor has a few of those posh magazines for interior decorating lying around the house. There's been a significant number of the pages turned to miniature beds and miniature furniture. I get the impression that there may be an addition to the Curry family in the future, but they aren't telling me—yet. And I'm keeping my kitty claws crossed that this interest in baby things is a passing trend. Nonetheless, I've noticed a few of the prices for those pieces, and it's enough to make a cat's hair stand straight on end. Yikes! Ten grand for a baby bed. Right! That would outfit an orphanage.

But there were several pieces in the Estis house that looked to be expensive. I'm wondering how a cop made that kind of purchase. Family inheritance, possibly. Not from the wife's side, though, or she wouldn't have driven off and left them.

There's plenty here to look into. Plenty. But Mora is the key concern right now. I can see by Dolly's pretty face that she's terrified. Bureau Boy isn't exactly light of heart, either. This traffic isn't helping matters. It just goes to show that just because people have two hands and two legs, they aren't qualified to drive. I know dogs who could do a better job of operating a vehicle than some of the people on this road, and I don't believe dogs have a lot of brain power.

Here we are, pulling into the yard. The place looks okay. No signs of a struggle. But there wasn't a struggle at Graham Estis's house, either.

Wait! What's that out by that azalea bush? Oh, holy gizzards, it's a woman lying out in the yard. Judging by Dolly's face, it must be her mother.

Chapter Sixteen

"Mom!" Sarah was out of the car before Daniel could even stop it. Leaves crunched beneath her feet as she ran the fifty yards to the still form that was sprawled across the grass. "Mom!" Sarah heard her voice break.

As she reached the body, she felt strong hands pull her back. "Let me," Daniel insisted. Pushing Sarah aside, he knelt beside Mora Covington's pale form. Practiced hands felt for a pulse at her neck, and he gave a grim sound of encouragement. "She's alive."

"Let's get her in the house!"

"Not so fast," Daniel said, examining Mora for injuries and broken bones. "Get a blanket. Get several blankets," he ordered Sarah. Very gently, he pulled at the bottom of Mora Covington's eye. The pale color of the tissue indicated shock. "Call an ambulance!" he called after Sarah.

Mora was cold, too cold, and he chafed her hands and legs as he waited for Sarah to return. When he heard the door slam, he looked up to see her running toward him, her face obscured by at least five blankets.

"What happened?" Sarah dropped down on the opposite side of Mora and began to help Daniel pile on the blankets.

"Shock, at least that much I can tell. Why, I don't know." Daniel's voice was terse with concern.

Sarah looked down at her mother and felt the tears threaten to destroy her self-control. Bitterly she fought them back. Mimicking Daniel's gestures, she took her mother's hand and began to warm it with brisk movements.

"She doesn't seem to be hurt," Daniel said. He was trying to find anything—anything with a shred of truth in it—to give Sarah to cling to. He could see the anguish in her face. If only they'd come to Mora's house the night before. If only they'd somehow warned her. If only... the two worst words in the English language.

"Listen." Sarah cocked her head to the distant sound of a siren. "It's the rescue unit." She spoke with a strange surety. "In small towns, you can tell the different sirens," she said, grasping at any bit of trivia to keep talking, to keep from breaking down. "That's the rescue squad, and it's coming this way. That's who I called. They'll be here in just a moment." She blinked rapidly. "In just a moment, Mom. Just hang on."

"She's stable," Daniel assured her, knowing that his words would be of little comfort. "She's going to be fine, Sarah, just fine. Really."

"What happened?" Sarah's terrible grief made the question sound even angrier than she was.

"We don't know." Daniel was gentle. "She could have been walking to the neighbor's to borrow a cup of sugar."

"Right." The one word cut across Daniel's gentle voice. "So where's her cup? Where's the sugar? Don't you think it's more likely that someone came up here, tried to get into her house, and she was running for help before she was frightened nearly to death?"

That was exactly what Daniel suspected, but he had no proof and he didn't needlessly want to scare Sarah. Whoever had killed Graham Estis had more than likely come straight over to Mora Covington's house with the intention of either killing her or frightening her into total submission. But what did Mora have to be frightened about? Cal was already dead, his reputation ruined.

"Daniel, you think someone was trying to hurt Mom, don't you?"

Daniel looked up into Sarah's eyes. She was angry, and she was afraid, but she was also thinking. Her intelligence and spirit made him want to reach out to her, to tell her that everything was going to be okay, that the bad guys were going to suffer for what they'd done. Trouble was, he wasn't certain who the bad guys were anymore.

"I think she was frightened."

"By the men who killed Graham?"

"Probably."

"You think they were trying to kill her?"

Daniel swallowed. "No." He waited, hoping he had some other choice than what he was about to say. "I think they were trying to kill you."

Sarah blanched but she never stopped rubbing her mother's hand and arm. She looked away from Daniel only when the emergency truck pulled into the front yard and two men rushed over and gently moved her away. Still stunned from Daniel's statement, she stumbled over to a tallow tree and leaned against the trunk. She could remember that tree from when she was a child, climbing its tender young branches and earning a scolding from her father.

"How is she?" Daniel asked the paramedics who gave a quick examination of Mrs. Covington as they loaded her onto a stretcher.

"Heartbeat is regular." The paramedic shrugged. "We'll know more when we run some tests. Jerry's going to try to bring her around."

As he spoke, one of the paramedics broke a small vial under Mora's nose. She struggled on the stretcher, lifting her hands as if to ward off a blow.

"Cal!" The one word was a cry of complete anguish. "Oh, Cal, I didn't mean to hurt you. Don't!"

"Easy, Mrs. Covington," the paramedic said as he eased her back to the stretcher. He wore a grin of satisfaction. "That ammonia brought her around," he said to his companion. Neither of the men saw Sarah, still standing at the tree. Every bit of color drained from her face. Daniel told the rescue squad that they would follow the ambulance to the hospital and waved them on their way before he went to Sarah.

"She was running from my father's ghost." Sarah's voice was dull.

"You're jumping to conclusions." Daniel knew he would have assumed the same thing, but it wasn't the only possibility.

"When Dad died, something broke in my mother. She became paranoid, unsure of herself, afraid of everything. The FBI questioned her over and over again. She almost had a breakdown. And I never understood why. She changed from a beautiful woman who laughed and played and planned jokes and parties to a rabbity woman who was afraid of her own shadow."

"Sarah, some people—"

"Why would she be afraid of my father's ghost? Why would anyone be afraid of Dad?"

He took her arms and gently rubbed them. She was cold, too. The morning was brisk even though the sun was shining. "She could have been having a nightmare, some twisted vision of the past. It doesn't mean anything, Sarah, and you're jumping to some conclusions you might well regret."

"There's something here," Sarah insisted.

"I agree, but I'm not certain it's what you think it is. Now take the car to the hospital. That blasted cat is around here somewhere and I'll find him." He lifted her chin so that she had to look at him. "And I'll check the house for some clues. You haven't even considered that maybe someone broke into the house and terrified your mother."

The relief showed in Sarah's eyes first, and then the corners of her mouth. "I love you, Daniel," she whispered before she kissed him tenderly. "I never thought I'd allow myself to care this much for anyone else I could lose, but I love you."

"I'm pretty fond of you, too, kid," Daniel said. He found the flood of emotions difficult to manage. He wanted to scoop her into his arms and take her away—anywhere where she could laugh and smile and not have to face the pain that surrounded her. The past and her father's death were everywhere she turned, and he knew that they would have to be probed and cleaned, like an old wound, before she could ever heal. But, God, how he wished it was over and done.

Sarah kissed him softly once more. "I'm going to the hospital. If Mom's awake, maybe she can tell us what happened to frighten her."

"Now that's an interesting approach to the mystery, Sherlock," he said, hugging her close. "Ask some questions, look for clues. Who would have thought of such a method?"

"Oh, you." She punched him lightly. But his teasing had done wonders for her. The nightmare images that had washed over her were gone, at least for the moment.

"Hurry on to the hospital." Daniel gave her the keys. "When Mora really comes to, she's going to be frightened and confused. She's going to need you, Sarah."

"I know." Sarah smiled. "And it's perfectly okay." She climbed into the driver's seat and waved as she pulled into traffic.

Daniel's thoughts were still with Sarah and the strange tangle of her family as he glanced around the yard for Familiar.

"Kitty, kitty." He felt a rush of concern. Familiar wasn't the kind of cat to make trouble at a time like this. Where had he gone? He'd been in the car when they'd arrived at the Covington house. "Familiar?" He walked to the front door.

Deep inside the house he heard a drawn-out meow.

"Familiar!" He sighed with a sudden weariness that went deeper than his bones. All he needed was for the cat to decide to play games. Before he entered the open house, he checked the door. There was no sign of a forced entry.

"Kitty, kitty." He called the feline as he'd heard Sarah do it. When there was no response, he walked into the foyer and on into the den to find the black cat.

Familiar was sitting on a sofa in the dimly lighted den. It took Daniel several moments to see him. When he finally discerned the cat's shape, he flipped on a light switch and flooded the room with illumination. Unperturbed, Familiar settled onto a red silk cushion in a room that looked as though it was part of a television stage set from a past era.

"Come on," Daniel said. "We've got to look for clues. If we don't, Sarah's going to lose her mind worrying about her family."

Familiar didn't budge.

"Come on, cat." Daniel moved toward him with capture in mind. Familiar stood and darted from the room toward the kitchen.

"No time for chow," Daniel said, keeping all of the frustration he felt out of his voice. Familiar was a very sensitive animal, but when it came to food, all other issues seemed to grind to a halt.

Daniel heard the cat bounce around the room and scamper down a darkened hallway.

A sense of danger washed over Daniel. He was in Sarah's mother's home, trying to catch Familiar, but he also couldn't help taking in every minute detail of the Covington home. And it was one eerie place. It was as if the world had ended in the 1960's. The furnishings, the decorations, the books on the coffee table, all reflected a past long gone. There wasn't one new piece of furniture in the place.

Hurrying into the kitchen, Daniel unsuccessfully tried not to draw any conclusions. Was Sarah's mother disturbed?

Sarah hadn't mentioned the possibility. Maybe it was something that had happened to her after Cal's death. There was plenty about the Covington family he wasn't clear on yet. But the more he saw, the more he wanted to be with Sarah at the hospital.

"Meow!" Familiar's playful voice came from a room down the hallway.

"Damn it, cat, get back in here." Daniel felt his control slipping. His need to be with Sarah increased with each passing moment.

"Meow!" Familiar's silky voice came from the end of the hallway.

"You'd better not be playing a game," Daniel warned him. He hurried toward the room from where Familiar was calling.

He pushed open the last door on the hallway and knew immediately he was in Mora Covington's bedroom. The sense of being an intruder was almost too strong for him to ignore as he hit the switch for the overhead light and finally located Familiar on the dressing table. The cat was pawing at a mirror as if he was playing with his own reflection.

"Great. Sarah's at the hospital and you've gone bonkers on me." Daniel scooped the cat into his arms, unprepared for the writhing mass of claws and teeth. Familiar had never, never behaved like such a wild thing! He dropped the slashing fur ball to the dresser and was amazed to see Familiar completely calm as he pawed at the mirror again.

Daniel noticed the pictures tucked into the edge of the silvered glass. Tugging carefully, he pulled out the one Familiar was pawing. In it were two men and two women. One man was Cal Covington and one woman, Mora. She was incredibly beautiful, and the way Cal looked at her would make an innocent girl blush. There was love and hunger in that look, and Mora basked in it. The third man, looking on with an indulgent smile, struck a chord with Daniel. He recognized him almost immediately as Sarah's beloved Uncle Vince, with his arm around a pouting Lucinda Watts.

In a flash, Daniel knew what Sarah had never realized—that Vincent Minton had been drawn to Mora Covington. He might have been a longtime friend of the family, but it was Mora who held him, not Cal, as Sarah had always supposed.

Daniel carefully replaced the picture. "That's a triangle where two sides don't know the third side exists," Daniel said. Mora's words came back to him. She'd said she hadn't meant to hurt Cal. Maybe Mora *had* been aware of Vincent Minton's feelings for her. Maybe she'd acted on them. Maybe that was why Vincent was always looking out for Sarah. And just maybe that was why Mora was living in a time warp and suffering from a guilty conscience. The pieces clicked into place.

"Meow." Familiar watched the expressions pass over Daniel's face.

"I don't want to be the one to bring this up to Sarah," Daniel said. He saw the ripple effect of what his discovery might mean. If Cal had been aware that Mora was unfaithful to him, he might have become depressed and carelessly lost his life.

An unfaithful wife on top of an FBI investigation would do even the stoutest man in.

"But we don't know that she was unfaithful," Daniel reminded himself and the cat. "We're getting as bad as Sarah, jumping to conclusions all over the place."

He scooped up the cat and held him as he took in the room again. The bed was slightly rumpled, as if Mora had gone to sleep at some point in the night. He noticed the chenille bedspread and the glazed lamp beside the bed. The past. Perhaps a time when Mora and Cal had been happy. They would have been newlyweds with only a dream of Sarah in mind. Sadness touched him and he left the bedroom, taking care to close the door.

Maybe it would be easier for Sarah not to go back. Digging into the past could sometimes turn up things that no one wanted to know about. Skeletons in the closet. Relatives who'd been hung as horse thieves. He sighed and felt Familiar break into a purr against his chest.

"I gave Sarah the keys, big boy. Looks like we'll have to wait here."

"Meow." Familiar wriggled to get free and Daniel put him on the floor. He went straight to the telephone and stared at it.

"I could call and see if the test results are in," Daniel said. He checked his watch. Sarah had been gone for less than an hour.

He withdrew the number to the private lab from his pocket and dialed. Familiar hopped into his lap as he sat at the table and counted the rings. When he finally got an answer, he was already champing at the bit.

Three minutes later he replaced the receiver and automatically began to tug at his hair. All of the pork chops had been sprinkled with a dusting of arsenic. It would have been enough to make everyone who touched them sick as dogs. Possibly even deathly ill. Daniel had expected another poisoning, but something more in line with the ipecac—not a potentially deadly poison. Certainly not one as easily traceable as arsenic.

It wasn't that hard to obtain, but who would do such a thing? He thought back over what little he knew about the poison. In one big dose, it could be fatal, but in small quantities, it often took a long time to have a deadly effect. In the early 1900's, arsenic had been used by society ladies to maintain a pallor that was thought to enhance the porcelain qualities of their skin.

But whoever was at work at Lucinda's party hadn't intended to produce cosmetic results. There was enough to create sickness, and in certain cases, death.

Who and why were the immediate questions.

Suspects immediately popped into his mind. Lucinda Watts had been in the kitchen, as had the serving staff. And Sarah. And... He couldn't think of anyone else, but there had been times when the kitchen was empty. He wanted to kick himself. It had been a good idea to get Sarah to check out the guests, but in doing so, they'd left the kitchen vulnerable.

And someone had taken advantage of that.

Why was a harder question. Why would Lucinda sabotage her own party? That could be answered a million ways, especially in light of the photograph he'd just seen in Mora's bedroom. And the fact that Lucinda might have a motive certainly didn't rule out the possibility that any one of the guests or servants might have done it. He shook his head with the futility of trying to reason it out. And the case was compounded by the murder of Graham Estis. Somehow it all tied together, and Sarah was at the heart of it. That was all he knew for sure.

"While we're waiting for Sarah, let's check out the rest of the house," Daniel said to Familiar. As he slowly got to his feet, Familiar sprang down beside him and gave his shin a playful nip.

BUREAU BOY is finally beginning to see the complexity of this picture. It's like a giant coil, with everything spiraling out from the core of the past. I haven't gotten everything worked out, not completely, but I think this trip to Mississippi was a good move. I won't get into a discussion about my traveling accommodations—stuffed into an overnight bag like a pair of dirty socks. But at least I got here, and I didn't have to travel with the luggage.

There's something that's been troubling me since we left that deputy's house. I'm sure Bureau Boy noticed it, but he hasn't commented. Probably his inferior brain hasn't linked it all up yet. But Graham Estis was either shot while he was asleep, or he knew the person who shot him. How do I know this? Because there was no sign of a struggle. And I believe he knew the killer. Why? Because the bedside light was still on, as if he'd been up talking with someone. Which is what I think happened.

Like Bureau Boy, I believe Graham's killer came straight over here to Mama Covington's house and scared her half to death. The question is, how? Mama Covington was in a housedress, but her hair was combed, as if she'd been awake. My best guess is that she wasn't in the yard more than an hour. Maybe daybreak. Strange that none of the neighbors noticed her. Why didn't someone see Mora? Or at least hear her if she screamed? That's a very good question, and I know Agent Dubonet will address it, as soon as it occurs to him. Or as soon as I figure out a way to make him think of it.

He's poking around the house now. Careful not to touch anything. All of the doors look good. If someone entered the house without permission, they came through an unlocked door. Nothing is disturbed. Jeez, maybe these lamps are glued to the table. Like a television set. I keep thinking Lucy and Ricky are going to enter, stage left, and do a skit. They'd be right at home here. Maybe we should check next door and see if the Mertzes are around.

Or maybe we should just check next door. Ask a few pertinent questions, like, did you see or hear anything unusual? I'll try a claw at the portal. Ah, that got Daniel's attention. Remarkable how the sound of shredding wood can make a human snap to attention. That and claws sharpening in the sofa. Better than any alarm clock ever invented. And so much more fun on those dull and rainy afternoons when a cat has to be confined inside.

Well, holy Toledo, here comes Dolly herself, pulling into the yard in a blast of gravel. Who's in the front seat with her? Damn! There's the phone.

"WAIT!" Sarah rushed across the yard, leaving her passenger in the car. "Let me answer it." She gave Daniel's shoulder a squeeze as she ran by to the ringing phone. Taking just a second to catch her breath, she said hello in a voice that sounded very timid, very afraid.

"Mora?" The voice carried a slightly French accent.

She held the receiver away from her ear so that Daniel could hear.

"Mora. We have to talk."

Very carefully she replaced the receiver.

"Did you recognize the voice?" Daniel asked. He couldn't be certain. He'd heard it before, but he couldn't be sure where.

"Yes." Sarah swallowed. Never in a million years had she expected to hear that voice. "It was Chef André."

Chapter Seventeen

"I'm fine now," Mora assured Sarah and Daniel as they settled her onto the sofa. Sarah pushed an ottoman under her feet and got the afghan from the back of the sofa to warm her up. "I wasn't hurt and I couldn't stay in that hospital. I told them I had to be home."

"How about some tea?" Sarah asked. The hospital had released Mora after determining that she'd stumbled and fallen, more than likely striking her head on the ground. The tests she'd grudgingly allowed them to run had shown she was in good health.

"Tea would be fine." Mora watched her daughter with more than a little anxiety. "Then we have to talk."

"Yes," Sarah agreed, "we do, Mom."

Daniel, with Familiar at his side, had taken a stand a few feet behind the women. Conflicting emotions pulled at him. He liked Mora Covington, or at least the little he'd seen of her. She was a retiring woman with a very easy manner. But the evidence he'd uncovered in the house led him to believe that she knew far more than she'd ever revealed. He could easily suppose that, over the years, her silence had cost her plenty. She was so diminished from the beautiful young woman he'd seen in the photographs. Sarah was right. It was as if someone, or something, had pulled the life out of her.

Sarah returned with a tray of teacups, cookies, and a steaming pot. In a matter of minutes she had everyone served.

"Tell me what's going on with you two," Mora said without preamble. "I heard the gossip in the hospital emergency room. Graham Estis was murdered. It isn't just a coincidence that you were asking about him, is it?"

"No." Daniel answered when Sarah hesitated. "We came down here to see Mr. Estis. We were hoping he could clear up some matters of the past for us."

"Something involving Cal?" Mora's voice grew thin and strained.

"Yes." Sarah answered this time. She took a big measure of support from the look Daniel gave her. "All of these years, we've never talked about what happened. Now—"

"Why now?" Mora was suddenly angry. She put her teacup down on the side table. "Why, after all these years of protecting you from the truth, should I talk about it now?"

"Because someone may be trying to kill her." Daniel's stark words took all of the anger from Mora. She sank back into her chair, growing even more frail than she had looked before.

"They think you have the money, don't they?"

Mora's question made Sarah gasp. "You knew about the money?"

The laugh Mora gave was flat and mirthless. "Yes, I knew all about the money. I heard about it for months after your father died, how he'd taken a payoff and then tried to cheat the organization."

"Mother." The word was a sorrowful condemnation.

"Oh, Cal never took any money. He never took anything in his life. That was the shame of it." Mora took a deep breath. "And the irony is that I got to spend exactly twenty dollars of it."

Daniel moved forward and placed his hands on Sarah's shoulders before she could move. He gave her support and also restraint. Beneath his hands he felt her trembling.

"You took the money?" Sarah didn't believe it. Her mother wasn't the type to play games with organized crime. Not Mora Covington. Mora was afraid of a shutter creaking in the wind or the sudden rattle of a tree branch against a screen. She was afraid to buy new furniture or even to sit out on her front porch and read a book.

"Yes, it was me. I took some of the money. Not anything at all like they said I did. I took it with the promise that I would convince your father to look the other way when some of those fancy yachts pulled into the harbor along the coast. I took the money and told them that I could make him ignore the limos and the drinking and the fancy women. It was none of anyone's business. Those rich people wanted to game and play on the coast, and why shouldn't they be left alone?" A small fire had begun to burn in Mora's eyes. She sat up straighter, held her head a bit higher.

"This wasn't some Puritan community. Gambling and whoring and drinking and dancing were always here, just like they're in every town, but especially coastal towns. The joints were here and as long as it was local girls and local gamblers, no one cared. It was the big money that finally turned everyone's head. Too much money. Those fools were flashing it around, dropping hundred-dollar tips on young girls who had worked in backbay fish houses for two dollars an hour." Mora's eyes glazed as if she'd slipped into the past. "They were pretty girls, but tough. That kind of money made them even tougher."

"Your husband saw trouble coming, didn't he?" Daniel prodded gently when she fell silent.

"That he did. Cal saw it with those girls, and even if he'd wanted to ignore the gaming, he couldn't ignore the disappearance of that girl. Betty Jean Corley.'' She shook her head. ''She was Lucinda Watts's baby sister.''

''My God.'' Sarah sank into a chair.

''Betty Jean was mighty grown for the age of fifteen. She fooled most everybody. And she could dance. She made Lucinda look like she had a steel rod up her spine, and Lucinda could move.'' Mora laughed. ''Your father used to sneak me into some of those clubs when we first came down here. There were a couple of joints on the state line down by Louisiana that made those along the Biloxi strip seem like kindergarten. Cal had no problem letting folks be folks. Until Betty Jean was found stabbed to death. Then it was a different matter, and even though I begged him to stay out of it, he started poking around.''

''And so they decided to frame him.'' Sarah spoke softly. Somehow it all seemed old and familiar, as if she'd known most of it all along. All except that her mother had taken a payoff. ''What happened to the money?''

''Oh, it's here. Right here in this house. Been here all along.'' Mora waved a hand around the room. ''Tens and twenties. No big bills. I thought I knew something about how to do business with that kind. I was a fool.''

''Dad never knew anything about the money, did he?'' Sarah wasn't certain she wanted to hear the answer to this question.

''No, he never did. I never told him because he didn't deserve to know.'' Mora lifted her chin as she stared directly at her daughter. ''He didn't deserve to know he'd married a woman who'd sold her husband's honor. I might have been foolish and vain, but I wasn't a complete coward, Sarah. I didn't tell your father because he wasn't the kind of man who could forgive me for something like that.''

Sarah started to leave the room but Daniel's firm grip held her in place. She felt Familiar's claws dig into the hem of her jeans, also holding her in her seat. She knew what they were trying to do, but it was killing her to listen to her mother.

Whether Mora knew it or not, she was responsible for Cal's death.

"I made a mistake, Sarah." Mora's voice was firm. "I've paid for it every day of my life. But your father never suffered because of what I did. I tried to give the money back when I realized he was going to do his duty. I told those men that he wouldn't listen to me, that I had lied to them about how much influence I had with him. I begged them to take back the money." A bitter smile touched her lips. "But I'd made a pact with the devil. They owned me as surely as they owned the cars they drove. Only they didn't own Cal, and I never, never gave them a chance to get him through me."

"And how did you prevent that?" Sarah gave her mother a scornful look. She saw the hurt pass over Mora's face, but she hardened herself against it.

"I told them to tell Cal what I'd done, that it wouldn't stop him. And then I did nothing. I waited for them to do it. And I loved you and your father and I kept on making supper each night and helping you with your homework and pretending that I hadn't lost my soul." She finished on a note so soft, Daniel thought he might have misunderstood her.

One thing for certain, he did understand about the house. Mora had kept it just as it was when her life had been happier, when it had been a real home.

"You lied to me." Sarah's voice shook with anger. "All of these years, you've *pretended* to be one thing, when all along you've been nothing but a liar." She flinched as Daniel exerted pressure on her shoulders. "No, I won't stop." She shook free of him only to feel Familiar's sharp claws digging into her thigh. The sudden, fierce pain made her gasp.

"Oh, I lied to you, Sarah. I did that, and I don't regret it. I gave you a living, breathing parent, someone who took care of you and loved you because your father was dead. You couldn't have both, so I gave you the only one left."

She took a deep breath. "Don't you think it would have been easier to tell you the truth? How many days, while you were at school, did I plan out what I was going to say? How I was going to tell you the truth and relieve myself of the horrible guilt I felt. Oh, I wanted to tell you. I wanted to scream it from the rooftop and tell everyone else, too.

"What I did was wrong, but not the reasons. Cal was under pressure, financial pressure. His job that he loved didn't pay him enough to give you the things he wanted for you. Like college and dental work. He talked about getting a second job, but then we'd never have seen him. He could have taken the kickbacks that a lot of other lawmen took, but he wouldn't do it. So I did. I did it for him and you, Sarah. For my family. And that's the same reason I never told anyone the truth. For my family."

In the silence that followed, Daniel clearly heard the ticking of the old clock on the mantel. It seemed that everyone in the room was frozen by emotion. He tried to speak, only to find that his throat was dry. Taking a sip of the now cold tea, he cleared his throat.

"You did a very brave thing, Mora." He saw Sarah's shoulders square in anger. "It might not have been the right thing, but you did what you thought was best for Sarah. I understand that."

"I can only hope that one day, when Sarah has a daughter of her own, she'll understand how a mother will do anything to protect her child. Anything."

Before anyone could stop her, Sarah broke from the room and ran. She pounded down the hall and into a back bedroom. The sound of a slamming door echoed through the old house.

"She only did that twice before in her entire life," Mora said. She was too sad even to wipe the tears that ran down her face. "Once was in high school when I made her wear a dress to a school event, and the other time was in grammar school. One of the kids said her father was a crook and she hit him in the face with her book. I told her she had to take the punishment the school set out for her. It didn't sit well."

Daniel was torn between his need to check on Sarah and the need of the older woman for some shred of compassion. He took a seat in a chair beside her and reached over to press her hand. "The past is over and done. We all have things we'd undo if we could. Right now, though, I'm worried about the future."

"Is someone really trying to hurt Sarah?"

"I believe they are. But we don't have any idea why. Can you help us?"

"It may be the very last thing she'll allow me to do for her," Mora said, defeat flattening her voice. "I never wanted her to go to Washington. All those politicians. Deals here and there. It's the same thing no matter what you call it. The very same thing as went on along the coast back then."

"Mora." Daniel gently led her back to their subject. "What happened to you last night?"

Even to her doctor she'd refused to say anything about what had driven her out of her house and into her yard. Now she didn't even pretend to hesitate. "I got a call last night."

"From who?"

"I recognized his voice. Funny, after all these years I knew his voice as if I'd heard it only the day before."

"Who, Mora?" Daniel felt as if he were sinking deeper and deeper in molasses.

"I never knew his name. Never saw his face, but he was the one who called and offered me the money."

"What did he say last night?"

"He said they were coming for me. That I'd reneged and that now it was time to pay. He sounded so evil. He said I knew one day there would be an accounting, and now it was time. As if I haven't paid every day, every hour, since I took that money."

"So you were going over to the neighbor's house?"

"Mr. Clement has a gun. I was going to borrow it, and I was going to shoot whoever came up on the porch. But that bastard was waiting for me out in the yard. He jumped out of the bushes and chased me, but I dodged under the clothesline and it caught him right in the throat. Sounded like it choked him good." She gave a tight grin. "Then someone jumped out from the other side and hit me on the head. That's the last thing I remember."

"You never saw them?"

"It was too dark. They could have killed me, but they think I still have all that money. I have some, but not what they said I took." She patted the sofa. "And it's right here, under the upholstery. All ten thousand dollars of it." She wiped away a fresh trickle of tears. "I sold my family for ten thousand dollars. I only spent twenty dollars on a new dress to wear for Cal's birthday dinner. I intended to save the rest for Sarah's education. Cal didn't make enough to send her to college, and he wanted it so desperately for her."

"Oh, Mora." Daniel felt a terrible tightness in his chest. What a tragedy. One small mistake, and how she'd paid for it. "Can you think who would want to hurt Sarah?"

Mora frowned. "There was talk, right at the first, that I'd taken a lot more money. Or rather, that Cal had taken a big payoff. A lot more than ten thousand. That man called me up and wanted to know what I'd done with the rest of the money. I told him I only had the ten thousand."

"And?"

"He said we'd pay. The entire family, including my little girl." She swallowed. "I never believed anyone would blame this on Sarah. Never in a million years."

"Who were these men, Mora?"

"I don't know."

"How did you get the money?"

"A friend of mine in New Orleans let them leave it at his place. Then I went there and got it."

"Your friend's name? Was it Vincent Minton?"

"No, no." She shook her head. "Vince was never involved. He was a friend. Nothing more, though there were times when I thought he might want more." She sighed.

Daniel knew he would pursue Vincent Minton at a later date. Now he had to have the name.

"The man in New Orleans who helped you. Who is he?"

"Croxier. André Croxier."

Daniel felt as if large chunks of information had physically shifted in his brain. "Chef André. The White House chef?"

"Yes." Mora looked up at the intensity in Daniel's voice. "Don't involve him in this. He was a friend to me, but this type of thing could ruin him in Washington. Unsavory connections. I know how a place like Washington works. André has worked hard to get where he is, and he's been a good friend to me. He helped Sarah in the very beginning."

"My God, Mora…" Daniel was astounded that she didn't see what he saw so clearly. She was worried about protecting the man who'd probably ruined her life. A man who very likely stole a large portion of the money, left her and her family to suffer the consequences, and now still called himself her friend.

"You won't involve André, will you?"

"I won't involve anyone unnecessarily." He could no longer hold back his need to check Sarah. He'd given Mora as much as he could. It wasn't forgiveness or anything close, but he'd listened to her, and in the process he'd learned a great deal. "I'm going to see about Sarah." He rose and, to his satisfaction, he watched as Familiar hopped into Mora's lap and gently nuzzled her hand.

"Sarah always wanted a cat," Mora said, her expression drifting back to the past. "When she was little, she begged to have one, but I never knew if we were going to have to move on a minute's notice. There was always the sense that they watched and waited, ready to harm her. It nearly drove me mad. And I could barely keep our life together without worrying about a pet.'' She stroked the cat. ''I'm glad she finally has Familiar. He's a big comfort.''

Daniel wanted more than anything to relieve Mora's suffering, but there was nothing he could do. He was a stranger, and this was a family matter.

He turned slowly away and went to the bedroom. He half expected the door to be locked, but the knob turned under his hand and he entered to find Sarah flung across a double bed still flounced in the ruffles of her teenage years. She was all cried out, but her face was still buried in the pillow.

''You look like a young girl,'' he said, taking a seat on the bed and gently rubbing her back.

''I feel like a fool.''

''Sarah, she did the best for you that she could. What she did wasn't so wrong. She realized the mistake and tried to give the money back, but—''

''How can you defend her?'' Sarah sat up, eyes red and angry.

''Because I understand.''

''Right. The FBI has taught you to bend the truth just like my mother does.''

He grasped both of her shoulders and held them firmly. ''She did it for you and your father. Not for herself.'' He gave her a tiny shake. ''If you stop feeling sorry for yourself for sixty seconds, you might see how much she loved both of you. And how she's suffered because of it,'' he finished on a softer note.

Sarah turned her face away but his hands held her body firm. ''Don't you think I can see that? She did it for me. She took the money to give me the things Daddy couldn't afford to give me. I know that. She never took anything for herself. And that makes me as guilty as she is!''

She tried to struggle free, but Daniel pinned her back on the bed, holding her against the mattress as she fought against him.

"Sarah!"

"Let me go, damn you. I don't need you to sympathize with her. She's buried me in guilt."

"Sarah!" He shook her against the bed, making the old springs creak.

She tried to butt him with her head to no avail.

"Okay, you made me do this." He lowered his head to hers and pressed her back into the bed. When she couldn't jerk or thrash, he kissed her. He drew back quickly, then looked into her eyes. "I love you, Sarah."

"Let me up." She panted, but she no longer struggled.

"I love you." He kissed her again, gently this time.

"I'm not a child you can distract," she finally answered when she could talk.

"I hope you don't think this is a distraction. I've never been more serious about anything in my life. I love you."

As she watched the expression on his face, Sarah's anger began to slowly fade. She did love him. Whatever else she'd lost in the last few days, she'd found Daniel. The light from the bedroom window caught the clean, straight line of his nose and the generous bottom lip. She could see the faint stubble of a beard, but it only gave him a rugged look, heightening the deep blueness of his eyes. He was so handsome, and so good.

"I take you very seriously," she answered.

He slowly released the grip on her arms, rubbing where he'd held her tightly. "I'll let you go if you promise not to take a swing at me."

She couldn't help but grin. "It depends."

He tightened his grip slightly. "Then I'll say this fast. Your mother made a mistake."

"And my father died because of it," Sarah answered. She wasn't angry anymore.

"That may or may not be true. I don't think it is. I think your father died because some ruthless, evil men preyed upon your mother and then turned their energy toward destroying him. Your father was a scapegoat, and I think I'm beginning to figure out who betrayed him."

"Who?" The last remnants of Sarah's self-pity fled. "Who?"

Daniel pulled her up to a sitting position so they could face each other. "Chef André, for one."

"How?" Sarah didn't believe what he was saying.

Daniel quickly related what Mora had told him. "Don't you see? There was a lot more money. The gang thought they were really buying your father off. Not just Mora or her wifely influence—they thought they'd paid *him* to leave them alone. Then when he started investigating Betty Jean Corley's death, zealously investigating, they thought he'd double-crossed them. And—"

"They set him up."

"They paid off Graham Estis."

"And God knows who else."

"Right."

"Very possibly, Agent Jenkins."

Daniel took a breath. "That's a distinct possibility. Jenkins pursued your father relentlessly. He might have been paid to do it."

"And Gottard?"

"There is a chance that somehow they've gotten to him. This time, I was the sacrificial lamb." His face reflected chagrin, sorrow, and a bitter acceptance. "I was perfect. The renegade. The guy they could trust to break the rules to get to the truth. That's me. All they had to do was wind me up and set me in motion and I did all the rest, including put my friend in danger and then get framed for his murder."

"But they haven't charged you yet," Sarah noted.

"That's the beauty of it. If I'm charged, they'd have to take me into custody. But they need me to be here with you, to lead you into the trap they've set to snare you."

"Why?" Sarah asked again. That was the same old question that applied to everything that was happening to them. "Why? This was all years ago."

"That's what I don't know, but I'm beginning to know where to look to find an answer."

"And where is that?" Sarah could feel the excitement radiating from him. He was on the trail. She could feel it.

"Think about it. Every event you've catered recently was Southern."

"But that's not unusual," Sarah interrupted. "I cater Southern events almost exclusively. That's my hook, my forte."

"I know, but at every recent event, except that birthday party for the Georgia senator, there have been very powerful people. Businessmen, legislators, congressmen. Movers and shakers. And let me point out that the child's party was the first thing you've catered where no one was poisoned— or nearly poisoned." He told her about the lab reports on the pork chops.

"You're right." Sarah saw it all begin to make sense. "Maybe at first they only wanted to use me to make a few folks sick."

"I think it was more than that. I think they intended to frame you for murder. By poisoning people. That way, they'd get rid of the roadblocks and also put you behind bars. It would be the perfect revenge."

"Who are these people?" Sarah asked, her voice small and worried.

"Your mother doesn't know. She had only a telephone contact."

"How are we going to find out?"

"We're going back to Washington."

"And?"

"A lot depends on Paul Gottard."

Sarah leaned forward and grasped Daniel's knee. "You aren't going to trust that man, are you?"

Daniel's grin was tight. "Absolutely not. I'm going to use him exactly the way he's used me. Now, let's book a flight home before we're accused of killing Graham Estis. It wouldn't surprise me to see that happen, since you haven't obliged by killing someone at one of your dinner parties."

"No one has died, yet," Sarah said. "Thanks to Familiar."

Chapter Eighteen

Well, this is a little more my style. Sarah insisted on a seat for me, in a carrier, but at least I'm not stuffed into some bag with underwear and socks. And I'm relieved to be getting back to Washington. Magdelene is going to have a fit. I can only hope she hasn't reported my disappearance to Eleanor and Peter. They'll be worried sick.

All of these duties! How have I become so un-catlike that I'm worried about how humans feel? I must have caught this from Sarah. She's always worried about people. But thank goodness she and Mora made up. Now that was one heartwarming scene. It took ten years off Mora's age—she actually began to bloom. And then she ripped that upholstery off that old sofa and all that money flew around the room. Sarah told her to spend every dime of it and not to look back. An excellent suggestion. Now all we have to do on our end is resolve this mystery and make sure that everyone lives to see the money spent and justice done.

Chef André. That garlicky smell. It could easily be connected. Sarah scrubs her hands with lemon. But anyone who cooks or eats garlic a lot... I'm heading straight over to the White House as soon as we land. I want to speak to Socks. He can help with this, since I'm sure the great chef has prepared some specialties for the First Cat. Socks will be able to give me some pertinent details. Even if he isn't a Trained

Observer, he is a cat. By definition, he's astute and observant. Oh, yes, Socks will be my ace in the hole.

As for now, I'm going to charm the attendant into a sample of that first-class chow. It's not the best food I've ever tasted, but flying always gives me an appetite. And besides, that little brunette has a million-dollar smile. Even if the cuisine ain't caviar, she is choice.

SARAH PACED the length of her shop behind the tightly drawn shades. The call from Chef André had been so unexpected, so bizarre, that every nerve in her body jangled. It was almost telepathic. And he'd sounded so worried and concerned, asking about Mora and Jean-Claude. If Daniel weren't hiding upstairs, listening to everything that happened, Sarah knew she'd be scared to death.

The tap on the glass was gentle, but it made Sarah jump. Peeking through the blinds, she saw the tall chef standing hunched against the cold. Heart pounding, she opened the door to him.

"Sarah!" He examined her. "Thank goodness, you're okay."

"Why wouldn't I be?" She tried not to sound hostile, but she couldn't help it. This man might have ruined her family. "What did you want to talk to me about?"

André stared more closely. "This is a strange, strange night. First those cats. That Socks and a black friend of his. They almost drove me crazy in the kitchen. I was ready to call the president and demand that he retrieve that animal. But they left as abruptly as they came. Then Jean-Claude appeared." He rolled his eyes. "In such a state. That young man has not been right since he came back from the vineyards. He was asking many questions about the past, about his father's relationship with Lucinda. All water gone under the bridge. But he was also asking about you, little cabbage. The way he asked concerned me."

"Jean-Claude?" Sarah felt a pang.

"He said there was trouble at Lucinda's dinner party and no one had seen you since. Are you okay?"

"No." Sarah's hostility was wearing down. No matter how much she tried to believe that André had set up her mother, it didn't fit. She'd worked in his kitchen since she was a child. She knew for a fact that André had never benefited from a windfall sum of money. Like her, he'd earned everything. "I've been in Biloxi, André. Mora told me about the money."

"Ah, I tried to get her to tell you long ago. I'm glad she finally did." He looked around the room. "May we sit?"

"Sure." She motioned him back to the kitchen, knowing that Daniel would be ready to have a fit. He couldn't protect her as easily in the kitchen, but she didn't need protection from André. "I want you to tell me the whole story."

As soon as they were seated, André leaned forward. "Your mother's crime was in loving you and Cal too much. She was going to tell him that she'd inherited some cash. Take the pressure off him. I told her it was not a good idea. I warned her that men who paid for such things were not honorable." He shook his head. "She said it was nothing. Cal had no concerns with small games and parties, so the men were paying for nothing. And that was true. Cal never worried about the private games."

"What happened to the money, André?"

"Mora picked it up."

Sarah reached across the table and took his hand. "Someone is trying to kill me and maybe Mom. She got ten thousand. There was more. A lot more. Maybe five hundred thousand."

André's face registered scorn. "Or so they said. I saw your mother take it out of the bar well. There was ten thousand. No more."

"Could anyone else have taken the rest of it?"

André's expression shifted to shock. "All of these years, and I never considered it." He nodded. "Yes, the money was there for several hours while the restaurant was closed. Someone could have gotten to it before her.''

''Joshua Jenkins, maybe?''

André shook his head. ''No. He did not arrive on the coast until months later. After Betty Jean was killed and Cal started putting the pressure on the organized gamblers to pack up and leave. Sarah, I know you think Joshua Jenkins ruined your life, but I do not believe he was a crook.''

''I'm not so certain of that, André? Do you know who else might be involved?''

He shook his head. ''No. I have no idea. I keep in touch with Mora. She was always kind to me. She and your father both. I have been worried about her and I called…'' He smiled. ''Today, in fact. But the connection was bad. The phone was picked up, but no one answered. I wanted to tell her that Jean-Claude had been asking about her, too. I thought it was strange that he didn't ask his father, or you. That young man has been such a bitter disappointment to Vincent. It is sad.''

Sarah felt a chill trace down her spine. ''Yes, it is.''

''The past is a tangle, Sarah. Forgive the mistakes of those who love you. Mora was young and foolish, but she was not bad.'' André's smile was even sadder. ''I was in love with her. Maybe Vincent was, too. She was so much in love with your father that she never even suspected my feelings for her. Even now, she doesn't understand the reason I call and talk to her each week is because I care for her. She thinks it is because I am so fond of you.''

''Tell her, André.'' Sarah squeezed his arm. ''Tell her before any more time is lost.''

''WE'RE IN A TON of trouble now,'' Sarah said as she peered behind her bedroom curtain to check the street below the shop. After André's visit, she and Daniel had talked for two hours. They had no suspects and no plan for resolving the mess they were in. The only good news of the evening was

Familiar's return from one of his unexplained jaunts. As glad as she was to see the cat, she was ready to throttle him. He constantly circled her legs, meowing and biting her shins. Then he'd run to the steps as if he wanted her to follow him down the stairs. To the kitchen, no doubt. For some food. No matter how bad things were, Familiar always had a healthy appetite.

"Let's go, buddy." Daniel scooped the cat into his arms when he saw Sarah give him a murderous look. "Sarah's not in the mood to play kitty games."

"Meow!" Familiar leapt from his arms and ran down the stairs, stopping only long enough to make certain Daniel was following.

"Give him some milk and some of the broiled snapper," Sarah called after them, feeling a little guilty that she had ignored Familiar's appetite. The cat wasn't starving, though, and she was watching the street for the first signs that the FBI or the bad guys might show up and begin blasting at them.

Daniel didn't have time to give Familiar anything. As soon as he snapped the kitchen light on, Familiar had jumped on the pedal that opened the refrigerator door. He was rummaging around in the interior, his black tail whipping back and forth as he inspected foil-covered dishes and plastic bags.

"Your adopted mom is not going to like that sight," Daniel said. "If her career as a caterer weren't already ruined, the sight of you in her refrigerator would put her out of business."

"Meow!" Familiar tossed a plastic bag of chicken out onto the floor.

"Hey." Daniel started to make a grab for the cat, but a bowl of something very heavy hit his toe.

"Hey, cat!"

"What is it?" Sarah heard the commotion and started down the stairs to check it out. She arrived just in time to see

Familiar throwing two bags of flour out onto the floor with complete abandon. He was like a child having a terrible temper tantrum.

"Familiar!" She hurried toward him with the intention of pulling him out of the refrigerator. Daniel was too busy trying to catch the numerous bags and containers Familiar was tossing out.

"Hey, you!" She grabbed him just as he sank his claws into a bag of meat. When she tugged him out, the cat dragged the meat with him.

"Pork chops?" Sarah tried to grab the bag, but Familiar darted away, hauling the two-pound plastic sack with him. "Instead of snapper, you want raw pork chops?" She couldn't believe it.

Daniel put the last container back in the refrigerator and turned to watch Familiar scamper across the room with his booty.

"Looks like he wants pork chops," he said. Something about the situation did seem odd.

When he saw that neither Sarah nor Daniel was going to take the meat away, Familiar dropped it on the floor, made a few growling noises at it, and then lay on his side.

"What in the hell?" Daniel watched him with amazement.

Opening his eyes, Familiar stared at them. After a full minute, he returned to the sack of meat, made growling noises and then rolled onto his back, his legs straight in the air.

"Roll over and play dead," Daniel said. He looked at Sarah.

Understanding dawned on them simultaneously. "Pork chops!" They spoke in unison and Familiar sat up and began the dignified process of licking his fur.

"Lucinda Watts!" Sarah was beside herself. "We forgot all about her, and it was her baby sister who was killed. She would have a motive for all of this. She was at every party, too. And that dinner party, in her own home!''

"She had a reason to want to destroy your father, and she was making her contacts with organized crime even then." Daniel paced the kitchen.

"She told me that dinner party I catered was very important to her. Very important. She said it could mean that she'd retire in style." Sarah searched her memory but drew a blank until it struck her. "How did a striptease artist get enough money to set herself up in Washington?"

"Her marriages—"

"Or five hundred thousand dollars. That would do it."

Daniel slapped his forehead. "I can't believe it. Right under our noses."

"How can we find out?"

Daniel opened the phone book, dialed a number, then thought better and replaced the receiver. "I can't do this over the phone. I have to go in person." He drew his car keys out of his pocket.

"Who?" Sarah couldn't think of a soul, except her mother, who would voluntarily help them.

"Joshua Jenkins. It's the perfect opportunity to see if he's in this, too. We can set him up with what we know, see his reaction."

"Right now?" Sarah thought of the black night and the many people who might be watching her and Daniel. She didn't want him to leave. Mora was hiding with some old friends in Arkansas, and she wanted to make certain that Daniel was safe, too.

"It's perfect. He won't be expecting me."

"Familiar and I are coming, too. He might try to kill you if he feels threatened."

"No." Daniel shook his head. "Mora is supposed to call in half an hour, and if you don't answer, she'll die of worry. Stay here, but remember the phone lines aren't secure. I'll be back."

"Okay." Sarah didn't like it, but there was nothing she could do. "Go on before it gets any later, and hurry back." She swallowed the sudden spurt of fear that threatened to choke her. To hide her distress, she rushed into his arms and kissed him.

"Don't let anyone inside," Daniel cautioned her. "No one. Not even Santa Claus."

She nodded, unable to talk. When he furtively hurried out the front door, she locked every lock after him. Picking a wary Familiar up in her arms, she ran up the stairs and into her bedroom, locking that door, too. It wouldn't take Daniel all that long to run the errand. Everything was going to be fine, now that they knew where to look.

She'd just settled onto the bed with a book in one hand and the remote control for the television in another when she heard someone at the front door.

Fear tightened every muscle to the point that she felt paralyzed. Then she heard the familiar rap on the door. Two longs, two shorts, three shorts. She ran down the stairs in her socks, her face bursting with a smile.

"Uncle Vince!" She threw the door open and he captured her in his arms.

"I've been so worried about you since Lucinda's event. I've spoken with her, and she's no longer angry with you, *chérie.*"

Sarah tugged him inside, cast a quick look up and down the street, and then locked the door.

"Hoarding gold here in the shop?" Vincent asked with a raised eyebrow.

"No. I wish it were that simple." Sarah grabbed Vincent's hand. "Come in. I have a lot of things to tell you."

"Excellent. We haven't had much chance to talk lately and I've been concerned about you. By the way, Jean-Claude said he spoke with you."

Sarah sensed something in Vincent's tone. "Is something wrong with Jean-Claude?"

Vincent smiled, but it was an expression of sadness. "He is a disappointment, *chérie*. The two of you..."

"I'm sorry, I just don't feel that way about Jean-Claude." Sarah felt a pang for her uncle's dreams.

"He thought he could save you by marriage. You know he went to Idlewild to protect you. He told me about sitting on the porch and spraying your...friend with pepper." Vincent laughed, but it was harsh. "He thought you were in danger. That you would be hurt in my home. He is a foolish boy who has grown to be a foolish man."

"He thought Daniel was going to hurt me." She shook her head. "I'm sorry that happened."

Vincent patted her shoulder. "I brought a bottle of the very finest French wine for us to share," Vincent said, producing it from the pocket of his coat.

"Wonderful." Sarah led the way into the kitchen and deftly uncorked the bottle, all the while talking about her trip to Biloxi.

"I thought I saw Daniel leaving. Where has he gone?"

"He's running an errand." Sarah handed her uncle a glass of wine and took a sip of her own. "Uncle Vince, do you know anything about Lucinda Watts and how she became so wealthy?" If anyone knew, Vincent Minton would. She should have thought of him before Daniel left for Joshua Jenkins's house.

"Over the years I've advised Lucinda on some real estate." He smiled. "She's made good investments. In fact, she'd hoped to become a limited partner in one of my businesses. I've always admired Lucinda for her business acumen." His smile was brittle. "She has more...sense than Jean-Claude will ever have."

Sensing her uncle's disappointment in his son, Sarah sipped her wine again. "Delicious." She licked her bottom lip. "Did you know Lucinda's baby sister was murdered years ago?"

"Betty Jean." Vincent swirled the wine in his glass. "That was a long time ago. Lucinda had changed her name by then. She and Betty Jean were...determined to make a new life for themselves. Lucinda made it, Betty Jean did not."

"You knew them both?"

"As did your father. It was hard to work the coast and not know those two. They were at every party, dancing, drinking, bringing good luck to the gamblers. Those were the days when there was money to be made."

"And Lucinda did whatever she had to do to get a start."

Vincent picked up the bottle and refilled Sarah's glass. "She was shrewd and she worked hard. I admire that."

"Is she still ruthless? Ruthless enough to...kill?" Sarah couldn't help the shiver that passed through her at the memory of Cody Pruett and Graham Estis. She drank the dark red wine that made her feel so warm. Two murders that she knew of in the last month. In the past, how many others were there? Was her own father's death a murder at Lucinda's hand?

"Why do you ask?"

"I think Lucinda may have stolen some money...."

Vincent smiled, but there was no warmth in it. "She did. Many times. From husbands, from politicians who were glad to exchange large sums of cash for photos and negatives. From anyone she could."

Sarah felt sure victory. She started to rise, but she found her legs unsteady. Surprised, she glanced at the wine. She'd only had a glass and a half. She'd downed it quite fast, but not fast enough to make her drunk.

"She suckered many men." His smile was cold. "But never me. Never."

She heard Vincent's words and stared at him, her errant legs forgotten as she saw his eyes. "You?" The word was slurred.

"Yes. Lucinda is rather disturbed with me at this moment, but the little scene that you so obligingly created at her dinner party gave me the perfect opportunity to cut her out of my partnership. In fact, your cooking has presented a number of opportunities for me to . . . eliminate would-be partners.''

''My . . . food . . .'' Sarah realized it was pointless for her to try to talk. She knocked the wineglass off the table in one awkward gesture. Futilely, she looked at the clock. It was only an hour since Daniel had left. He'd never get back in time.

She swept the condiments off the table in front of her, but her arms and legs refused to do what she commanded. In the midst of the crash, Familiar leapt from the floor and knocked the portable telephone off the base. He slapped it several times until it skittered under the table, where he followed it.

''I hate cats.'' Vincent eyed the feline with contempt. With a suddenness that belied his age, he reached down to capture Familiar and was rewarded with a savage bite that pierced his thumbnail.

''You black devil!'' Vincent threw a kick that missed the agile Familiar by at least eight inches, but his shin hit the edge of the table. Holding his hand and limping, he gave up on the cat. Instead, he grabbed Sarah's shoulder.

''Where is Mora? I've figured out how to get rid of you and that snooping FBI agent, but your mother is another difficulty. All these years, she's been too afraid to do or say anything. She was afraid someone would come after *you*. I had her thoroughly convinced that the evil men who ruined her life would kill her daughter. Now it's time I put the past to rest. Mora has started talking, and I don't think she'll ever stop.''

Sarah could clearly hear everything that Vincent Minton said to her, but she could not speak or move with any accuracy. Whatever drug he'd given her had left her helpless.

''I'm going to kill you and arrange it so that your friend, Mr. Dubonet, looks guilty. This drug will wear off without a trace. The FBI has done an excellent job of setting him up as the murderer of that research analyst. Although that fool Gottard never believed Dubonet was guilty, he's left his man in a perfect trap. One I intend to exploit.''

Vincent rose from the table and slowly poured his glass of wine into the sink. Unable to control her body, Sarah tried to lunge at him, but she only managed to fall across the table. Minton ignored her as he went to the wine rack and selected another bottle, quickly opened it and poured himself a glass. "Not as good as the vintage I brought, but also not drugged." He took a long sip.

"All of this was completely unnecessary, you understand. I did use you, or at least, your cooking, to facilitate a few business deals. But when you called and told me the FBI was investigating you, I knew I had inadvertently reopened the door to the past. You weren't your mother. I couldn't frighten you into silence."

"Mo...m!" Sarah floundered against the table. The worst fear she'd ever known made her feel as if her heart would burst.

"Your mother could have had anything in the world she wanted. I would have given it to her. But she wanted only your father. She was a fool to scorn me for your father. But it made me realize she would not have been an asset to me, after all. And that damn Jean-Claude is so much like her. Weak. Foolish. He despises me and everything I've worked to build.

"Five years ago I started to bring him into the business, my real business. I'd kept it from him because I recognized his weakness. When he saw how things worked, he ran away to Paris. And then he discovered last month that I'd stolen the money from André's restaurant and left Mora in a noose. He found out that I had arranged for his 'uncle' Cal to walk into a bullet and put an end to that bastard Jenkins and his probing. So he dashes home to marry you, to make sure that I never hurt you again. He would protect you with my name. Such a noble boy." He laughed.

Sarah tried to make a sound, but her throat was frozen.

"Believe me, Sarah, I don't relish the idea of killing you. You've actually forced me into this position. Just as Betty Jean did when she tried to blackmail me."

"Bett . . . y . . . Jean."

"She eavesdropped on a conversation I had with my associates in New Orleans. We wanted a permanent structure, a place where we could spend weekends without interruption. I was the man who could put the deal together. Betty Jean heard my plans, and she tried to sell that information to Cal. Of course, we thought Cal was in our pocket, so we weren't worried, but Betty Jean had to be punished nonetheless."

Even through the paralysis of the drug Sarah felt a burning rage. This man who stood at her kitchen sink, sipping wine from her glass, was an imposter. She'd grown up believing he was the one man she could love and trust. The man who'd stepped in when her father died. The man who'd helped her with her education and her career. But it was all a lie. He'd done everything to control her, to keep her within his grasp. For his own purposes.

Though she could not run, or even walk, she felt Familiar beneath the table brushing against her leg. Fear for the cat darted through her. If Vincent saw him, he'd undoubtedly kill him. Unable to signal Familiar, she could only pray that he would remain beneath the table, out of sight.

"Where is that agent of yours?" Vincent downed the last of the wine and put the glass on the table. "Timing is all in a crime, you know." Vincent moved until he was directly in front of Sarah. "I'm expected at a cocktail party in fifteen minutes. I need to take care of you and Dubonet, then meet my social obligations. I was thinking of a shooting, here in your kitchen. Sort of as if you were trying to kill Dubonet, and he killed you instead."

He went to the cabinet and set out a plate and flatware. He carefully rinsed his glass, wiped it and then set it down on the table before filling it from the drugged bottle.

"See, you intended to poison him. He discovered it, shot you, and then got himself arrested for murder. Not very original, but it will work with Gottard and the FBI. Believe me, I led that Jenkins around by the nose for years. All I had to do was whisper in his ear that Cal was dirty. Just a whisper and a hint, a false lead and the promise of dire evildoing, and a payment to the easily bought Deputy Estis to lie to the good FBI agent. Jenkins never did catch on to how much I was using him. Never. The trouble was, though, that he'd never leave. He wouldn't give it up. Not until Cal was dead."

Sarah tried to swallow, but she could feel the muscles of her throat beginning to tighten. Panic struck when she wondered if the drug he'd given her would slowly paralyze her throat and then her lungs. She'd suffocate to death.

"Well, I was hoping to have Dubonet here when I finished this. As I said, timing is all. But let me get started. I think the body should be found in the bedroom." Removing a pistol from his coat pocket, he placed it on the table and moved so that he could pick Sarah up in his arms. She tried to fight him, but her arms and legs were like leaden weights. She could barely lift them, much less strike him.

Just as he bent to lift her, a black streak flew across the room, landed on the table and skidded. Gun, plate, wine and wineglass all toppled to the floor with a crash.

"I am going to kill that beast." Vincent stood. He looked around the floor for his gun. With a great dash, Familiar hit it again, pushing it up under the heavy commercial refrigerator.

Vincent aimed a hard kick at the cat but missed. "You black creature, you're going to pay." He got down on his knees and reached under the refrigerator, trying for the gun.

The back door burst open and Daniel rushed into the room. He didn't hesitate as he brought the toe of his shoe up into Vincent Minton's ribs, followed by an upward thrust of the knee into Minton's jaw and a hammer-handed blow to the base of his neck. Minton dropped to the floor in a heap.

There was the sound of the front door crashing in, and Paul Gottard and four FBI agents swarmed into the kitchen through the swinging door.

"Good work, Daniel," Gottard said, grinning. "Excellent. Now let's get Ms. Covington to a doctor."

"How?" Sarah forced the word out as she felt Daniel's arms encircle her. She was already beginning to feel stronger.

An agent stooped to pick up the telephone and return it to the base as Daniel talked. "When the phone was knocked off the hook, it automatically triggered the tap that the Bureau had put on your line. Gottard's men heard the call and reported it. One of the agents had followed me to Jenkins's house. Paul got the report, radioed his man... We came as quickly as we could." He tightened his hold on her. "The FBI not only heard everything Vincent Minton said to you, they got it on tape. He's going to prison for a long, long time."

It took tremendous willpower, but Sarah lifted her arms around Daniel's neck. "I love you," she whispered.

"You'd better get that young lady to the doctor," Gottard said, waiting for Daniel to get busy.

"Wait." Sarah felt her strength returning. She pressed against Daniel and felt his immediate response. "I think that Agent Dubonet has the exact medicine I need."

Gottard hesitated, then saw the look that Sarah and Daniel exchanged.

"Perhaps he does. I wouldn't ever want to underestimate Agent Dubonet again. Get Minton, and let's get out of here," he directed his men. In minutes, they were gone.

"Sarah?"

"Just hold me another minute, Daniel, and then I think need to be carried upstairs." She smiled, face hidden gainst his neck.

"If you can't walk, maybe we should go to the hospital."

"Oh, I think I can walk. I wanted to be carried." She ifted her head, revealing her widening smile. "You see, I'm aving myself for another form of physical exertion."

AGENT 009 *reported to the First Cat with a case solved and is favorite chef cleared of all suspicions. Socks wanted me o show up for the ceremony when Chef André names Sarah s his primary assistant at the White House. Imagine, André ad written down all of her catering engagements on his alendar to document her excellent work when he made his id to hire her! He is, indeed, a good friend.*

Too bad I had to decline the party, though. All of those hutterbugs are always following Socks around. With my uck, I'd get my mug in the newspaper and then Eleanor and Peter would cook my goose. They're still mad at me for rightening Magdelene with my "unexplained" disappearnce. Hey, I was working a case. Does Sam Spade have to heck in with his baby-sitter? Dashiell Hammett? How about ames Bond? You can bet Sean Connery doesn't call home very day at five.

At any rate, I'm home now, toasting my toes on a red silk illow in front of the fire with a bowl of my favorite sarlines on the floor beside me. Ah, a cat's life. And I should nention that my beautiful Clotilde was suitably impressed vith my courageous behavior and superior intelligence. I ust have to keep a low profile to be sure none of this gets come to the dame and Dr. Doolittle. I guess that's the price f being a "secret" agent to the First Cat.

It was rough saying goodbye to Dolly, and I have to ad-nit I'll miss that cocky attitude of Bureau Boy. We had some un. But they knew all along I was never really their cat.

Socks, Clotilde and I are arranging a little wedding surprise for the happy couple—an adoption of the cutest little black kitten from the humane shelter. That's going to be one lucky little kitty.

And now for a nap. Secret agenting is a wearying business. Once I've rested for a few hours I might have to saunter into the kitchen and make Eleanor prepare something special for me. It's not that I'm not satisfied by sardines, it's just that humans have this awful need to be needed. So I oblige whenever I possibly can.

That's the thing to remember. "A man may toil from sun to sun, but a cat's work is never done."

COMING NEXT MONTH

#297 EDGE OF ETERNITY by Jasmine Cresswell
Weddings, Inc.
Recluse David Powell got the unlikeliest guest at his isolated lighthouse
hideaway—his ex-wife, Eve. Hell-bent on a tell-all exposé, Eve probed
too deeply into David's hermitage, and now someone wanted her stopped.
Was it David, the man she'd never stopped loving?

#298 TALONS OF THE FALCON by Rebecca York
Peregrine Connection #1
She'd once been in his heart, now psychologist Eden Sommers
had to get into Lieutenant Colonel Mark Bradley's head. Helping
him recover his memory of a top secret mission might bring back
the lover she'd once known, but it might cost him his life....

#299 PRIVATE EYES by Madeline St. Claire
Woman of Mystery
P.I. Lauren Pierce was none too happy about having to hire a competing
P.I. as a lookout—especially when Bill Donelan seemed to watch more
than her back. But then Lauren's client turned up dead, and she became
the next target....

#300 GUILTY AS SIN by Cathy Gillen Thacker
Legal Thriller
All the evidence said that wealthy, powerful Jake Lockhart was guilty of
murder in the first degree. Only his attorney was convinced of his innocence.
Susan Kilpatrick was sure Jake had secret information
that could set him free. More than the trial was at stake if she was
wrong—so was her life.

AVAILABLE THIS MONTH:

HARLEQUIN®

I N T R I G U E®

Harlequin Intrigue
invites you to
celebrate

It's a year of celebration for Harlequin Intrigue, as we commemorate
ten years of bringing you the best in romantic suspense. And to help
celebrate, you can RETURN TO THE SCENE OF THE CRIME with a
limited hardcover collection of four of Harlequin Intrigue's most
popular earlier titles, written by four of your favorite authors:

REBECCA YORK	Shattered Vows (43 Light Street novel)
M.J. RODGERS	For Love or Money
PATRICIA ROSEMOOR	Crimson Holiday
LAURA PENDER	Déjà Vu

This unique collection will not be available in retail stores and is
only available through this exclusive offer.

Mail the certificate below, along with four (4) original proof-of-purchase coupons
from one Harlequin Intrigue Decade of Danger & Desire novel you received in July,
August, September and October 1994, plus $1.75 postage and handling (check or
money order—please do not send cash), payable to Harlequin Books, to:

In the U.S.	In Canada
Decade of Danger and Desire	Decade of Danger and Desire
Harlequin Books	Harlequin Books
P.O. Box 9048	P.O. Box 623
Buffalo, NY 14269-9048	Fort Erie, Ontario L2A 5X3

FREE GIFT CERTIFICATE

Name:_____

Address _____

City:_____ State/Province: _____ Zip/Postal: _____

Account # _____ 086 KCG-R

(Please allow 4-6 weeks for delivery. Hurry! Quantities are limited. Offer expires
January 31, 1995)

  HARLEQUIN INTRIGUE
DECADE OF DANGER AND DESIRE
ONE PROOF OF PURCHASE **086-KCG-R**

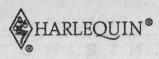

EDGE OF ETERNITY
Jasmine Cresswell

Two years after their divorce, David Powell
and Eve Graham met again in Eternity,
Massachusetts—and this time there was magic
between them. But David was tied up in a
murder that no amount of small-town gossip
could free him from. When Eve was pulled into
the frenzy, he knew he had to come up with
some answers—including how to convince her
they should marry again...this time for keeps.

EDGE OF ETERNITY, available in
November from Intrigue, is the sixth book in
Harlequin's exciting new cross-line series,
WEDDINGS, INC.

Be sure to look for the final book, **VOWS,** by
Margaret Moore (Harlequin Historical #248),
coming in December.

"HOORAY FOR HOLLYWOOD" SWEEPSTAKES

HERE'S HOW THE SWEEPSTAKES WORKS

OFFICIAL RULES — NO PURCHASE NECESSARY

To enter, complete an Official Entry Form or hand print on a 3" x 5" card the words "HOORAY FOR HOLLYWOOD", your name and address and mail your entry in the pre-addressed envelope (if provided) or to: "Hooray for Hollywood" Sweepstakes, P.O. Box 9076, Buffalo, NY 14269-9076 or "Hooray for Hollywood" Sweepstakes, P.O. Box 637, Fort Erie, Ontario L2A 5X3. Entries must be sent via First Class Mail and be received no later than 12/31/94. No liability is assumed for lost, late or misdirected mail.

Winners will be selected in random drawings to be conducted no later than January 31, 1995 from all eligible entries received.

Grand Prize: A 7-day/6-night trip for 2 to Los Angeles, CA including round trip air transportation from commercial airport nearest winner's residence, accommodations at the Regent Beverly Wilshire Hotel, free rental car, and $1,000 spending money. (Approximate prize value which will vary dependent upon winner's residence: $5,400.00 U.S.); 500 Second Prizes: A pair of "Hollywood Star" sunglasses (prize value: $9.95 U.S. each). Winner selection is under the supervision of D.L. Blair, Inc., an independent judging organization, whose decisions are final. Grand Prize travelers must sign and return a release of liability prior to traveling. Trip must be taken by 2/1/96 and is subject to airline schedules and accommodations availability.

Sweepstakes offer is open to residents of the U.S. (except Puerto Rico) and Canada who are 18 years of age or older, except employees and immediate family members of Harlequin Enterprises, Ltd., its affiliates, subsidiaries, and all agencies, entities or persons connected with the use, marketing or conduct of this sweepstakes. All federal, state, provincial, municipal and local laws apply. Offer void wherever prohibited by law. Taxes and/or duties are the sole responsibility of the winners. Any litigation within the province of Quebec respecting the conduct and awarding of prizes may be submitted to the Regie des loteries et courses du Quebec. All prizes will be awarded; winners will be notified by mail. No substitution of prizes are permitted. Odds of winning are dependent upon the number of eligible entries received.

Potential grand prize winner must sign and return an Affidavit of Eligibility within 30 days of notification. In the event of non-compliance within this time period, prize may be awarded to an alternate winner. Prize notification returned as undeliverable may result in the awarding of prize to an alternate winner. By acceptance of their prize, winners consent to use of their names, photographs, or likenesses for purpose of advertising, trade and promotion on behalf of Harlequin Enterprises, Ltd., without further compensation unless prohibited by law. A Canadian winner must correctly answer an arithmetical skill-testing question in order to be awarded the prize.

For a list of winners (available after 2/28/95), send a separate stamped, self-addressed envelope to: Hooray for Hollywood Sweepstakes 3252 Winners, P.O. Box 4200, Blair, NE 68009.

CBSRLS

OFFICIAL ENTRY COUPON

"Hooray for Hollywood"
SWEEPSTAKES!

Yes, I'd love to win the Grand Prize — a vacation in Hollywood — or one of 500 pairs of "sunglasses of the stars"! Please enter me in the sweepstakes!

This entry must be received by December 31, 1994.
Winners will be notified by January 31, 1995.

Name _____

Address _____ Apt. _____

City _____

State/Prov. _____ Zip/Postal Code _____

Daytime phone number _____
(area code)

Account # _____

Return entries with invoice in envelope provided. Each book in this shipment has two entry coupons — and the more coupons you enter, the better your chances of winning!

DIRCBS

OFFICIAL ENTRY COUPON

"Hooray for Hollywood"
SWEEPSTAKES!

Yes, I'd love to win the Grand Prize — a vacation in Hollywood — or one of 500 pairs of "sunglasses of the stars"! Please enter me in the sweepstakes!

This entry must be received by December 31, 1994.
Winners will be notified by January 31, 1995.

Name _____

Address _____ Apt. _____

City _____

State/Prov. _____ Zip/Postal Code _____

Daytime phone number _____
(area code)

Account # _____

Return entries with invoice in envelope provided. Each book in this shipment has two entry coupons — and the more coupons you enter, the better your chances of winning!

DIRCBS